Readers love the All for Love series by
NICKI BENNETT AND ARIEL TACHNA

Checkmate

"…a very engaging read, with dynamic characters that evolved through the book. I'm definitely looking forward to reading more in this series world."

—Two Chicks Obsessed

All for One

"The story is well written with an interesting, complex plot and unique, new characters as well as five others from the first book in the series."

—Rainbow Book Reviews

Stronghold

"In my opinion, *Stronghold* is by far the best love story in the All for Love series."

—The Novel Approach

"This is a wonderful series for people that enjoy historical romance."

—Alpha Book Club

By Nicki Bennett

Always a Bridesmaid
Evan's Heaven
Flight
Home for Christmas
New Traditions

DREAMSPUN DESIRES
#10 – The Cattle Baron's Bogus Boyfriend
#58 – Bad to the Bone

With Ariel Tachna
Under the Skin

ALL FOR LOVE
Checkmate
All for One
Stronghold

HOT CARGO STORIES
Hot Cargo
Something About Harry

THE EXPLORING LIMITS SERIES
Exploring Limits
Stretching Limits
Refining Limits
Breaking Limits
Transcending Limits
No Limits

OUT AND ABOUT
Out of Bounds

Published by Dreamspinner Press
www.dreamspinnerpress.com

By ARIEL TACHNA

Published by DREAMSPINNER PRESS
www.dreamspinnerpress.com

OUT
of
BOUNDS

NICKI BENNETT
AND
ARIEL TACHNA

Published by

DREAMSPINNER PRESS

5032 Capital Circle SW, Suite 2, PMB# 279, Tallahassee, FL 32305-7886 USA
www.dreamspinnerpress.com

This is a work of fiction. Names, characters, places, and incidents either are the product of author imagination or are used fictitiously, and any resemblance to actual persons, living or dead, business establishments, events, or locales is entirely coincidental.

Trade Paperback ISBN: 978-1-64080-802-7
Digital ISBN: 978-1-64080-801-0
Library of Congress Control Number: 2018940825
Trade Paperback published October 2018
v. 1.0

Printed in the United States of America
(∞)
This paper meets the requirements of
ANSI/NISO Z39.48-1992 (Permanence of Paper).

To Frances, who still shares our first loves.

ACKNOWLEDGMENTS

CONNIE, YOU always make our stories better.

Jane, Kelly, and Kristin, this story wouldn't be what it is today without all your help.

Prologue

"Erik, you can't be serious about applying for a transfer to Houston!" John Campbell ran a hand through his thinning gray hair and waved the other toward his computer screen. "Give me one reason why this is a good idea."

Erik Jansen closed the door to his manager's office before taking a seat in front of his desk. Not that everyone at the LA office of Bauer & Fitzroy Investments didn't already know the whole sordid story, but he didn't need to provide them with any more grist for their mill. "My effectiveness here has been compromised by everything that's happened over the past few weeks, John. Mark is already gone—" He swallowed down the rush of bile that rose to his throat even now, weeks after the events that made his staying in LA any longer impossible. "Things can get back to normal faster if I'm not around as a reminder of how we all screwed up."

"Really? That's what you're going with? After all the years we've known each other?" John shook his head and leaned back in his chair. "Take a vacation. You have plenty of time built up. Give things a chance to blow over and come back in a few weeks when you've had a chance to regain your perspective. You didn't do anything wrong. I don't know how to get that through your head."

"I'm not trying to assign blame to anyone. It's done, so now we just have to find the best way to move past it for everyone concerned." Erik was surprised how reasonable he sounded in light of everything he'd gone through and would be giving up. "We've already lost Barry Symons as a client. The whole situation needs to die down before the firm's reputation takes any more of a hit, and that will happen faster if I'm not around to keep it alive in everyone's minds."

"A vacation would serve the same purpose, without costing you nearly as much. The Houston office isn't nearly as big as this one, with far fewer opportunities for advancement. You'd be doing the same work, possibly even more, for a slightly smaller salary, and since we aren't transferring you, you'd be paying for the move yourself. That's a pretty big hit to take, not even counting having to start over in a new city. Is getting away from Mark worth that when he's already gone?" John asked.

"Gone but not forgotten," Erik said, shaking his head. "He might not have broken any regulations by having an affair with a client, but the impression of impropriety is still there. How can we regain that trust—" Erik broke off before his voice could betray how raw he still felt. Finding out that the man he'd dated for over a year, the man he'd thought he was building a permanent relationship with, had been cheating on him with one of Erik's own clients had shaken Erik to the core. He pulled in a deep breath and met his mentor's gaze. "It's like a divorce, John, with everyone feeling like they have to choose sides." Most of their coworkers and mutual friends—because really, how many friends did he have outside of B&F?—saw Erik as the wronged party, but Mark still had his defenders. "The last thing the firm needs is that kind of divisiveness. It won't be an issue once I'm gone." And he wouldn't have to face the daily reminders that everything he thought he'd had with Mark was nothing but a lie.

"I've been saying for years that a corporate culture of nonfraternization wasn't enough," John grumbled. "This just proves me right. It needs to be a stated policy. As your boss, it's your decision. I can't force you to stay. As your friend, I think you're making a mistake, but it's your mistake to make. You have so much potential to take on a bigger role in the firm, Erik. Hell, I'd have no hesitation recommending you to manage this office when I get my next promotion. Giving that up to manage a smaller office in a less desirable location could be seen by some as running away from a challenge instead of staying to face it."

"Houston is only less desirable if you love LA, and it has its own challenges, from what I can see. Rod Geller was coasting for years before he finally decided to make his retirement official. There's untapped potential for growth there for someone who's willing to put in the effort." A fresh start and a new challenge were just what Erik needed to put Mark's betrayal behind him.

John smiled, although it didn't quite reach his eyes. "At least wait until after the first of the year," he urged. "You don't need to spend Thanksgiving and Christmas looking for a new place to live and packing and unpacking."

"I'd like to make the new year a fresh start," Eric said. *And if I'm busy moving, maybe it won't hurt as much that I'm spending the holidays alone.*

"If that's your decision, then I wish you all the best." He rose and offered Erik his hand.

"It's been great working for you, John. I was a rookie when you took me under your wing fifteen years ago. But I've given this a lot of thought, and it's the best solution for everyone." And one where Erik wouldn't make the same mistakes again.

CHAPTER 1

LIAM GRUENE walked into the apartment he shared with his best friend, Kate Weaver, shortly after seven. It had been his night to close at the Karat Patch, the upscale jewelry store he managed in Houston, and he was ready to put his feet up and unwind. The store had been busy so close to Thanksgiving, and he didn't even want to think about what it would be like next week for Black Friday. He dropped his backpack on the table in the hall and toed off his shoes before heading into the living room to see if Kate had any preferences for dinner. They always ordered takeout on Fridays. He found her sitting on the couch, so lost in thought she didn't even look up when he walked in. That wasn't a good sign. She'd seemed to be doing better after she'd gotten home from her grandmother's funeral, but grief wasn't a linear process. "You okay, Katie?"

Kate's wide smile eased Liam's concerns on one hand and raised them on the other. That was the grin that had always led to them getting into trouble as children growing up together in Beaumont. "What's going on in that devious brain of yours?"

"I've been thinking…," Kate said, leaning forward and patting the couch cushion next to her. She'd let her long dark hair down from the upswept bun she usually wore at work, the less sophisticated look reminding Liam even more of the tomboy he'd run the streets with as a child.

"About what?" Liam asked.

"Our next great adventure. Nana said in her will that's how she wanted us to use the money she left me."

"What did you have in mind?" Liam knew the look on her face. He'd seen it at the start of every "adventure" that had landed them in Nana's living room. It had always been worth it.

"Starting our own company. How many times have we complained about not being able to meet LGBTQ singles who want more than just a hookup? We can go to clubs, or we can go on Grindr or PinkCupid or HER, but that's just sex."

"You want to set up a matchmaking business?" Liam asked incredulously. He couldn't count the number of times he'd complained to Kate, but it had gotten worse after his relationship with Todd ended. Todd's parting words—*Be glad you're good in bed*—still stung, even a couple of years later.

"No, I want to set up a business that organizes social events where LGBTQ singles can meet and mingle. Maybe they pay a subscription fee, or maybe they just pay by the event, but we host monthly activities where they know everyone there will be LGBTQ, single, and interested in meeting other people. And we advertise it as an alternative to anonymous hookups so we get people who are interested in more than that. It's not seedy. It's fun."

"What kind of events are you thinking about?" Liam had certainly bemoaned the inability to meet a man who was interested in *him* as opposed to his dick or his ass, but that didn't mean this was a good idea.

"The kind of things you'd do with friends. I'm thinking wine tastings, sporting events—both as fans and as participants—classes on cooking or dancing. A variety of offerings so if one event doesn't necessarily appeal, the next one might."

Liam considered that for a moment. The idea certainly had potential, and Kate had more than enough experience in her job as an events planner at the St. Regis Houston hotel to pull off whatever they decided to do in that regard. That left him with the business side of things. He ran scenarios in his head. "We'd have to start with something we could afford, whether we had ten attendees or a hundred. We don't want to start with something so big that we fail on the first attempt if we don't get enough interest."

"We could start with one event a month and grow from there," Kate agreed. "We'd need a bankroll to start with, for venue deposits and insurance and advertising, but Nana's bequest gives us that. Then as we start to bring in income from the events themselves, we can think about making them bigger or more frequent. Or both."

"Oh no you don't," Liam said. "You're not paying for this all by yourself. If we're doing this, we're doing it as equal partners, and that means financially too. We'll sit down and draw up an initial budget, and I'll put in half. I can cash in some of my stocks or take a loan against my 401(k), because you aren't going to be the only one taking a risk on your future with this."

"You don't need to do that. You heard what Nana said—she'd have left some of her money to you if she thought you'd accept it. Your portion is already in her bequest."

Liam flushed at the memory of his embarrassment during the reading of the will. He hadn't wanted to attend since Nana Weaver had been his surrogate grandmother, not his biological one, but Kate and her father had insisted. And as Kate had reminded him, she had written into her will that the bequest was for him as much as for Kate because she wasn't going to argue with Liam from beyond the grave about accepting anything she left him directly. Even so, that didn't change his position, but he'd had plenty of experience in the futility of arguing with Kate. He'd make an appointment with his financial advisor to discuss his options once they had an idea of how much they'd need. "We need more than money. We need a name and a business plan and goals and some ideas for what kind of events to start with. Did you have something in mind?"

"For which part of it?" Kate grinned, and Liam couldn't help but smile back at her. "I have some ideas, but I thought we could brainstorm together. I want this to be an equal partnership too, and besides, you always come up with the best plans. As far as a name, I was thinking something fun that lets people know our target audience is LGBTQ but also stresses that we're inclusive of the full spectrum."

"So something with rainbows or the transgender symbol or words like queer or out in it," Liam mused out loud. "We could do something that would play on out and outings, like going on an outing, although we'd have to be careful how we spun that, given how people might react to the idea of being outed before they're ready."

"I like that," Kate said thoughtfully. "We want people to know this will be a safe place to be themselves, with other people like them, whether they're looking for just friendship or something more… affectionate. 'Outings for All,' maybe? Though that might imply that we think everyone should be out, and while I might feel that way personally, I wouldn't want to make anyone feel uncomfortable if they only want to be out in our group."

"Yeah, the last thing we want is to keep people away instead of making them feel welcome," Liam agreed. He ran his hand through his hair, noticing idly that it was getting long again, and stood up to pace as he thought aloud. "Out… phrases with out…. Out there, out for the count, out of this world—that one has potential—out to lunch, out of the box. Do any of those do anything for you?"

"I think 'Out of This World' might be a bit out of our range, at least in the beginning." Kate laughed. "Hmmn, let me think. Out loud, out on a limb, out to lunch, out of the ordinary, out and about...."

"That's it! Out and About. We're offering them the chance to get out and about with other LGBTQ singles, a chance to meet people who share their orientation and their interests, and maybe have something come of it." Liam grinned broadly and spun Kate around by the hands. "Kate, darling, you're a genius. If you're really serious about this, I can put together some numbers and a business plan. It'll take some time, especially with the holidays coming up, but we can see what it would take to make it possible."

"We might look at the numbers and decide it's not worth it, but I think we owe it to Nana to try."

Liam couldn't argue with that.

LIAM LOOKED up from the calculations he'd been working on when Kate walked in the door from work. "There's wine open on the counter. Grab a glass if you want and come have a seat. I've been working on the business plan for Out and About now that the holidays are over and I have time to breathe."

"Is Nana's bequest enough to swing it?" Kate asked. She dropped her leather shoulder bag, kicked off her heels, and sighed before walking to the counter and pouring herself a glass of wine. "At least to get us started until the events start paying for themselves?" She took a seat next to Liam and wiggled her toes.

Liam pushed the papers in front of him across the kitchen table so she could look at them. "It depends on what we schedule and how we spend our money, but we should be able to make it with a matching contribution from my stocks and 401(k)."

Kate frowned. "I was hoping not to have to touch your investment money."

"And I told you I wasn't going to let you take all the financial risk," Liam reminded her. "Maybe we could do it without my contribution, but it will be easier—and much more likely to succeed—if we have a bigger startup budget. I've already made an appointment to meet with the company that manages my investments. Now take a look at these numbers and be sure you agree with them."

"You know I've always hated math." She studied the spreadsheet carefully and then nodded. "Looks good, even if it doesn't take off as quickly as we hope." Her smile made it clear how little she anticipated that happening. "What else have you worked out in all those notes?"

"Nothing definite, just some ideas for a logo and a tagline and some possibilities for the first few events, because we definitely want to have the second event announced before the first one takes place so people see we're here to stay and can plan for the second one if they enjoy the first. And best of all, Nana would have approved."

In so many ways, Nana had been a woman of her generation, keeping house and raising Kate's father rather than working outside the home, but in all the ways that mattered, she'd been far ahead of her time, and nowhere had that been more obvious than in her reaction when first Liam, then Kate, came out. If she'd been upset, she never let it show. She never tried to change them or convince them it was only a phase. She'd just gone right on loving them exactly as they were—gay and bi respectively.

"You're right. She'd love it." Kate's expression fell for a moment, but then it cleared and she nodded. "And somewhere she's looking down at us and smiling." She leaned back in her chair and flipped through Liam's notes. "I've been thinking about the first few events too. We want to plan a variety of outings that will appeal to different kinds of people. So I was thinking a Rockets game for sports fans, maybe something people can play, like a softball or volleyball game, though that might need to wait until it gets a bit warmer. A play or private museum tour for the less active. Something participatory, like a wine tasting or a cooking class, where we could partner with a shop that might get some sales out of it if people find something they like."

"I love you. I don't tell you that nearly often enough," Liam said with a laugh. "Are you sure you need me for this?"

"I just thought of the kind of activities I'd enjoy, though once we get people signed up, we can always ask them for ideas of what they'd like to do too. But I have no suggestions for a tagline, and we definitely don't want me designing a logo unless you want it to be stick figures. That's the limit of my artistic talent."

Liam wasn't the world's best artist, but he knew enough about graphic design to put together something basic like a logo. "The tagline I like best is 'No commitments, just fun.' What do you think?"

"I love it! It's short and catchy and just the message we want to send. So which idea do you like best for our first event?"

"I think we want something that really encourages mingling the first few times, so word gets around that we're a good way to actually meet people," Liam said. "I know a couple of wine shops we could approach, and the nice thing with that is, beyond whatever it costs to reserve the space for the event itself, it wouldn't matter if we have ten people or two hundred. The play would be fun, but it's not set up for a lot of interaction during the event itself, just before or after. We could save that idea for a few months down the road. But a cooking class or dance lessons would be good, and yes, we can do a sports event of some kind," he added when he saw the look on her face. She might have learned to put on the elegance and poise required of an event planner, but she was still a tomboy at heart.

"I'll leave the dancing to you, thanks. I'd much rather wear cleats than heels." She grinned and hugged Liam. "We're really going to do this, aren't we?"

"We're really going to do this." God help them, they were going to do this. "And it's going to be brilliant." And maybe they'd even get lucky and meet someone themselves.

CHAPTER 2

"HOW WAS your weekend?" Billy Pearson, Erik's administrative assistant, asked when Erik entered the offices of Bauer & Fitzroy Investments Monday morning. "Did you do anything exciting after the wedding? Rick and Darla were lucky with the weather. You never know what it's going to be like in January."

"It was a beautiful day for the ceremony." Erik gestured to the messenger bag he carried over his shoulder with a twisted smile. "I spent an exciting Sunday with John Roberts, Christine Stoddard, and Liam Gruene." When Billy frowned, he went on, "They're all clients I'm meeting for the first time. I need to be familiar with their backgrounds so they're confident I can serve their needs as well as Rod could." In fact he was sure he could serve them even better, but he wouldn't criticize the former office manager.

"Really, man? Due diligence is all well and good, but if that's your idea of an exciting weekend, you have got to get out more. You know what they say about all work and no play. You need to get a social life," Billy scolded. "And no, Rick's wedding doesn't count."

Erik, along with the rest of the staff of the financial services office he'd moved to Houston to manage, had been invited to the wedding of one of their top advisors. The ceremony had been lovely, all white lace and flowers and tuxedos, but it had left Erik feeling unusually lonely. He'd been in Houston for two months since shaking the dust of Southern California from his shoes, and the only people he could claim as more than nodding acquaintances in his apartment complex or at the grocery store were his coworkers. Now that Richard was married, Erik was the only unpartnered associate in the office—not that Erik had been attracted to Richard or would have acted on it if he had been. He'd learned his lesson about office romances, thank you very much. But listening to the happily married staffers chatting about planning date nights with their spouses or chauffeuring their children to their various activities only underscored how many nights he went home to an empty apartment.

"I haven't been here long enough to know all my clients yet," Erik countered, though it was a thin excuse. "It wouldn't be right to offer them less than the optimal advice for their individual situations." As much as he'd grown to like Billy, he wasn't about to tell him how he'd struggled to find a place for himself outside the office. Most of the professional associations he might have joined were composed of the same type of people he worked with. He wasn't especially religious, since in his experience most churches weren't very accepting of his orientation. And he was past the age when visiting a gay bar or, worse yet, trolling on Grindr held any appeal.

"Okay, I'll give you that... this time. But don't make a habit of it," Billy said with a wink. "You're good. Best boss I've had since I've been here. I don't want you to burn out and go running for the hills before I've even gotten you trained properly." His smile and dancing eyes invited a laugh at the shared joke, and Erik couldn't help but respond. Billy was the best admin Erik had worked with too. Laughter still ringing in the air, Billy waved Erik toward his office. "Mr. Gruene will be here in about thirty minutes, and there are a few things on your desk that need your attention this morning if you can get to them before he arrives. Oh, and Carrie wanted me to invite you to dinner next weekend. You can bring a date if you want."

Erik hadn't made an announcement of the fact that he was gay when he arrived at B&F's Houston office, though he wasn't trying to hide it either. He just believed in keeping personal life separate from business. But the first time Billy and his wife, Carrie, had asked him to dinner, a few weeks after they'd started working together, they'd also invited an attractive, single, female neighbor. Erik had made the best of the situation—Jessica owned a florist shop and was an interesting dinner companion—but the next day Erik let Billy know that while he appreciated the intention, his interests didn't lie in that direction. To his credit, Billy hadn't blinked at the revelation, but apparently he'd given up any matchmaking efforts. Erik wasn't sure whether or not to be grateful.

"I'll have to check my busy calendar to see if I can squeeze you in," he answered dryly. Billy's quickly cut off snort told him he knew how empty that threat was. He didn't bother telling Billy how slim the chances were of his meeting anyone he'd bring along to dinner. In his office, he extracted the file folders from his messenger bag and set them aside to address the items Billy had left for him. When that was done, he opened the file labeled *Liam Gruene*.

He scanned the information quickly to refresh his memory. Moderate investment portfolio for his age—early thirties—consisting of a small 401(k) rollover from a previous job and two larger investments in stocks made several years apart, plus regular deposits to a Roth IRA. He'd made some notes the night before, recommending a more aggressive blend of funds; at his age, Mr. Gruene could afford a bit more risk to increase his returns.

"Mr. Jansen?" Billy's voice came over the interoffice speaker. "Mr. Gruene is here to see you."

"Send him in."

The door opened, and Mr. Gruene came in. He was dressed in a dark suit, although Erik wouldn't call it conservative except in its color. It had clearly been tailored to fit the tall, trim frame in a way no off-the-rack suit ever would. His brown hair was just long enough to curl around his ears and the nape of his neck without being too long to be professional. He had a friendly smile and, when he offered his hand, a firm grip.

"Liam Gruene. Thank you for seeing me on such short notice."

"Erik Jansen." He released the hand, then gestured to the chairs in front of his desk and waited until the younger man gracefully settled into one of them before sitting again himself. "How can we help you today, Mr. Gruene?"

"I need to withdraw some funds," Mr. Gruene said. "Actually, I need to withdraw as much as I can without closing the account."

That hadn't been what he'd expected or prepared for, and Erik frowned. "I hope nothing has happened to make you dissatisfied with our services," he said, though the funds' performance had been respectable, if not the best they might be with rebalancing.

"Oh no, not at all. It's just… I need the money for a new venture. My housemate and I are starting a business," Gruene said, leaning forward eagerly. "She inherited some money from her grandmother, but I can't let her take all the financial risk. I need to match her investment. When my parents died, I invested the life insurance payouts, so I could cash those in or take a loan against my 401(k) if that's not enough. Of course I plan to keep investing in my IRA, although probably smaller amounts for a while, so I don't want to close the account, but I also don't want us to fail for lack of funding."

"What type of business are you planning to start?" Erik asked. The client's enthusiasm was obvious, but he knew the statistics about how many new businesses failed within the first six months.

"We're calling it Out and About. We'll organize social events— outings"—he grinned sharply at that—"for LGBTQ singles. A chance for them to meet and mingle with other people who share, or might share, their orientation. It's hard to meet people when you're single and on the spectrum, you know? There's bars and hookup sites, but that's not a relationship. It won't be a matchmaking service. We aren't trying to pair people off. We're just giving people the opportunity to meet other people like them. What comes of it after that is up to them. No commitment, just fun."

Erik almost chuckled at how closely Gruene's description addressed the issue he faced personally. Maybe that was an indication that the idea would fill a real need. Still, he wouldn't be doing his job if he didn't recommend caution. "As I'm sure you know, a large part of any investment's accrual is a function of time. You've done a better job than many of your contemporaries"—and didn't that make him sound ancient in comparison when there were less than ten years between them—"beginning a solid investment plan for your retirement. It would be a shame to lose that, and take even more to replace it later."

"I'm aware," Gruene said, his enthusiasm easing. "It's a risk, but it's a calculated one. We've put together a complete two-year business plan, with best-case and worst-case options." He handed Erik a sheet of paper outlining several different scenarios. "Well, not quite worst-case, because that would be going out of business, but less-good-case anyway. With the money Kate inherited plus what I have in my account here, we have enough to finance the startup plus keep things going for eighteen months before we have to turn a profit in the worst-case option. If things go better than that, we'll be able to either expand or begin putting the initial investment back. And at least for the time being, I'll continue working at the jewelry store. Kate's the event planner. I'm the business side of things, and I can set up a website, plan ad campaigns, file for DBAs and licenses and things like that in the evenings, on the weekends, or during my lunch breaks. So while it is a step backward as far as this one aspect of retirement planning, it isn't as big a risk as it sounds."

Erik studied the numbers for a few moments, then pulled up the account profile on his computer and angled the screen so Mr. Gruene could see it. "Fortunately, the latest returns on your stock funds will cover your planned outlay without having to touch your 401(k) or your Roth account. You'd continue making regular investments from your full-time job?" He couldn't prevent a client from withdrawing funds—at the end of the day, it was their money and their decision—but he had a fiduciary duty to uphold. And if he were honest, he'd be sorry to lose Mr. Gruene as a client of B&F. It would hardly be a good reflection on his customer service skills, after all. "I'd recommend that, as well as increasing the amount as soon as your new venture begins to show a profit. Growing a business is well and good, but you also have to plan for your future personally."

"I haven't forgotten." Gruene's brown eyes sparkled, lighting up his face. "Part of the beauty of the business plan is that it doesn't require anything from either of our current incomes. We'll have the money to live on and pay all our bills from our existing jobs until the business is doing well enough to replace that, so my regular investments will continue. I don't know about increasing them yet, not until Out and About starts to show a bit of a profit. I'm already investing everything I don't need to cover my daily expenses and a little fun money. But we'll start being able to deduct part of our utilities, rent, and other expenses because we'll be running the business out of our home, so that will eventually allow for some redistribution of funds."

"I wish you every success in your venture, then, Mr. Gruene," Erik said, opening a drawer to pull out the necessary forms to begin the funds withdrawals. "I'm afraid there will be a bit of paperwork to complete, but we should be able to get your money to you before the end of the week."

"I'm afraid this will only be the beginning of the paperwork we'll have to deal with," he answered with a wide smile. "And please, call me Liam."

That smile made something in Erik's insides heat up, and he forced himself to look away under the pretext of finding a pen to complete the forms. *Don't even go there*, he told himself firmly. Just because *Liam* was investing in a business catering to LGBTQ clientele didn't mean he was gay or bi himself. *And he's a client, and that means he's off-limits.* He tried for his most professional expression as he extended the pen. "Well then, Liam, let's get started."

Forty-five minutes later he ushered Liam out of the office, having received a promise that he'd contact B&F once the new business was in a position to support increasing his investment deposits. He sank back into his chair with a sigh but made a note in the folder before filing it in preparation for the next client.

Out and About. He hoped Liam and his partner could make it work.

CHAPTER 3

"HOW WAS work?" Liam asked Kate when she came into the kitchen of their townhouse that evening. She looked tired, but she was smiling, so he hoped that meant her current client was pleased with her efforts.

"Some people have no idea what's feasible to do within their budget. The software development firm I'm working with wanted to bring in the entire Texans cheerleading squad to kick off their latest release. Luckily I know one of the members—you remember Keisha Jameson, she played on the volleyball team with me at Rice—and she agreed to come to their meeting and bring a few of her friends." Kate chuckled. "And now the client thinks I'm a miracle worker."

"You are a miracle worker," Liam replied. "And having a client realize it is never a bad thing. That means we have two reasons to celebrate tonight. I'm making veal marsala."

"Sounds delish. What's the second reason?"

"I'll have the money for my contribution to Out and About by the end of the week." He'd finally convinced Kate they'd be able to make more of an initial splash if he added his money to Nana Weaver's bequest. "I met with my new financial advisor today—the old one retired—and all the paperwork is filled out. It's just a matter of getting it processed." Liam couldn't stop the smile that played around his mouth as he thought of the meeting and the delectable Erik Jansen. Of course Liam had no idea if he was gay or if he'd be interested in someone like Liam even if he was, but that didn't make him less attractive. Nor did it hurt how seriously he'd taken his job of advising, not just catering to Liam's whims. Sure, that was a legal obligation, but Liam appreciated competence, and Erik had seemed truly interested in Liam's situation, not just in fulfilling the letter of the law.

"I recognize that expression." Kate waggled her eyebrows. "Someone hunky's caught your eye. Since my own love life's been on life support lately, I need some vicarious thrills. Dish!"

Liam turned back to the stove to check on dinner—and to hide his expression from Kate. He hadn't meant to be quite that obvious. "I told you my old financial advisor retired. The new one pushed all my buttons. I do love a man in a well-cut suit." It was far more than that, as Kate knew him well enough to guess. It was everything the well-cut suit implied. Professionalism, competence, success, stability. Everything Liam wanted in a man and couldn't seem to keep, no matter how hard he tried.

"So did you get his number?"

"I suppose you could say yes, since I know where he works," Liam said. If she'd been the one in that office with Erik, she'd have gotten his entire life story out of him, including his orientation, but Liam didn't have the people skills she did. "I don't even know if he's gay, Katie. I couldn't ask him about it in the middle of a business meeting!"

"Maybe I should go with you when you pick up the check," she suggested. "You know my gaydar's always been better than yours. And I can see whether he's good enough for you. Not like the last loser you were serious about." Kate had made no secret of the fact that she'd never liked Todd, which should have clued Liam in sooner than it did. He'd never be able to sustain a long-term relationship with someone who couldn't get along with his best friend.

"You can come if you want, but there's no guarantee he'll be the one to give me the check. I might just pick it up from his assistant." He took a sip of his wine and sighed. "Just let it go for now. With starting a new business on top of our regular jobs, neither one of us will have time for a social life for a while. We have too much work to do."

"You may be right." One thing he loved about Kate was that she knew when to let something go. "Anyway, speaking of our new business, I talked with Shannon at the Wine Cellar like you suggested, and she thinks the tasting party is a great idea. She gave me a couple of potential dates that will work for her, so we just need to let her know which one we decide on. She'll provide the wines, and she suggested I talk with the owner of the tapas shop down the street to provide the hors d'oeuvres. If we let her know what we order, she can pair the wines to the snacks."

"See? Miracle worker," Liam said as he dished up dinner. "If you'll take the plates to the table, I'll grab my tablet, and we can check our lists and do some more planning while we eat." He'd worked on some ideas for the logo that afternoon, but he wanted her input as well. Plus they had to decide where and how to advertise the first event, and they had to plan out the website.

"We should decide on the second event too, so we can publicize it on the website and at the tasting." Kate took a bite of veal and closed her eyes. "Mmmn, wonderful. If we can't find a restaurant or caterer willing to host the cooking lesson, we can just have you teach people how to make this."

Liam took a bite himself. It wasn't the best he'd ever made, but it had turned out well. He hadn't been able to find his usual brand of marsala wine the last time he went shopping, so he'd bought what they had, and it wasn't quite right. "The second event... we talked about mixing things up so we'd appeal to a variety of customers. If we do the wine tasting in March as planned, we'd be talking about April for the second one. That's getting toward the end of the season for the Rockets or the very beginning of the seasons for the Astros. We could do see how much it would be to reserve a block of tickets at one of their games. That might be too big of a commitment this early on, though. I mean, if we ended up with tickets we couldn't sell, that would be out of our pockets."

"It might be better to save that one until we have a few successful events under our belt," Kate agreed. "We'd have a better idea of the numbers we can expect to draw. Anyway, I think the second event should be something a bit more active. Something to get people up and moving and interacting. April's probably too early for beach volleyball, but what about a softball game?"

"You'll have to run that one as well as do all the planning. You know how I am about sports." He'd watch them all day long, but other than running, he didn't participate in any of them. "Are you up for that?"

"Are you kidding?" Kate had made it to Rice University on a sports scholarship, and while volleyball was her first love, she pitched a mean softball too. "I can get Coach Manning to let us use one of the fields on campus, and I'm sure I can get some friends to play if we don't have enough people to fill out two teams."

"I see what you just did there," Liam said with a wry smile. "You're totally planning this so you can meet someone for yourself."

"Like you're not going to pay more attention when we have a night at the symphony or the art museum or something highbrow like that. I know your tastes too. And why shouldn't we be able to reap the same benefits as our customers?" Kate countered.

"No reason, I suppose, as long as we don't neglect our responsibilities to the business." It wasn't like either of them had had any luck meeting people recently. Kate's last relationship—with a man she'd met at a conference for event planners—had ended more than a year ago when they decided the distance between Houston and Dallas was more than they cared to travel anytime they wanted to see each other. He'd had even less luck than her on that front. He hadn't managed to make a relationship last for more than a few dates since college, with the exception of Todd, and that had been even worse. Too busy with work, too serious too fast, too "highbrow," as Kate would call it; the list of reasons was as long as his arm, but none of that changed the fact that he was single and tired of it.

"Of course the business is our top priority, but there's no reason we shouldn't enjoy our work." She tapped the table. "Okay, let's get serious here. What's next on your list?"

He opened a note on the tablet. "Website design. We need the landing page, of course, but what else do we want to have? A calendar with future activities, a sign-up page, a subscribe page for future updates or email blasts...."

"Maybe a reviews page where people can leave testimonials to how much they loved the events they've gone to?"

"That's a good idea. What about a suggestions page? I mean, between the two of us, we'll have no shortage of event ideas, but if people have suggestions for other kinds of events, we can add those to our list. Especially when we get to the point of doing more than one event a month," Liam said.

"And we can offer free admission to the person who suggests it if we use their idea." Kate nodded as Liam jotted another note. "A links page where we can post logos of places we hold events at or are LGBTQ-friendly in general in exchange for promoting us. Shannon's already offered to put up posters for our second event once we have it lined up, so we can give her a bit of advertisement in return."

"Speaking of advertisement, we need to think about where we want to place ads or try to get press coverage," Liam added. "Obviously the *Montrose Star*, but there have to be other places besides that. And we want to make sure we reach the full LGBTQ spectrum."

"I have some mainstream contacts who occasionally cover events we hold at the hotel, but I think we'll do better focusing on media that targets an LGBTQ audience. We should talk to *OutSmart Magazine*.

When our budget's larger, we could even look into local cable advertising to run spots on Logo or HereTV."

"That may take a few events. TV spots are expensive. Radio might be more affordable in the short-term. I'll look into it." He paused and stared at his notes for a few minutes. "You know, there's one thing we haven't addressed yet."

Kate snorted.

"Okay, there are probably lots of things we haven't addressed yet, but the one that just came to mind is how to figure out who to approach. I mean, it's an LGBTQ event, so the worst that would happen if a guy caught your eye is that he'd be gay, not bi, and therefore not interested, but not everyone is going to be comfortable with that uncertainty. On the other hand, we don't want to make anyone uncomfortable by forcing them to self-identify. What do you think?"

"Who'd sign up for a group called Out and About and not want to be open about their orientation? The whole point is for it to be a place where people can be up front and not have to worry about being judged for who they are."

She had a point, Liam admitted. "That's not our call to make, though. Yes, presumably everyone there will be LGBTQ and furthermore out enough to sign up in the first place, but it's still not our place to require that they share anything more about themselves than their names. We could do some kind of opt-in identification. Different-colored lanyards or bracelets or something for people who want to say 'I'm gay' or 'I'm lesbian' or 'I'm bi.' Or maybe that mean 'female company,' 'male company,' and 'anyone's company.' And someone who doesn't want to participate won't have to."

Kate shook her head. "Name tags. That way people don't have to keep introducing themselves, and we can have different-colored borders that aren't dependent on gender identification. Red if they're interested in meeting girls and blue if they're interested in meeting boys, or just solid white for both boys and girls, or for people who don't fit squarely on the gender binary." But she smiled when she said it, so Liam knew she wasn't really upset. She was just so centered that it was hard for her to relate to people who might not be as self-confident as she was.

"We'll see what we can find, but that's a good idea. Now, we need to decide on a logo." He opened a new window on the tablet to show her the possibilities he'd come up with.

CHAPTER 4

ERIK SHIFTED uncomfortably in his seat at the bar and sipped his overpriced beer, the pounding bass of the dance music adding a nascent headache to the awkwardness churning his stomach. He'd known coming to the Six-Pack was a mistake the minute he stepped inside, but when the highlight of his social calendar in the past six weeks was dinner with Billy, his wife, and two toddlers, he was desperate enough to try something new. So he'd pulled on a pair of soft jeans and a black T-shirt—he'd left the sweatshirt he needed against the February chill in the car—and searched "gay nightlife" on his phone for the nearest bar.

He wasn't sure why he'd expected it to be any different than the club scene in SoCal, but he felt just as out of place here as he had in the places Mark had dragged him to. Striking up a conversation with a stranger shouldn't have been difficult, but he hadn't seen anyone who didn't look half his age, and call him a prude, but he'd like to get to know a person before dry-humping on the dance floor or disappearing into the men's room held any appeal.

Face it, Erik. You're an introvert, and no matter how lonely you are, that's not going to change. He drained his beer and placed the empty on the bar, conceding defeat.

"Hey there, handsome. This must be your first time here, because I'd have remembered seeing you before." Erik looked over at the kid—he barely looked old enough to drink!—next to him and smothered a sigh. T-shirt so tight his nipples were visible through the fabric and short enough that a swath of skin showed between the hem and the low-slung waist of the skinny jeans that clung to every curve of his hips and ass as he leaned against the bar. And was that eyeliner around his eyes? If it wasn't, he had the darkest eyelashes Erik had ever seen. The kid preened under Erik's gaze, angling his body to show off the perfect curve of his bubble butt.

If Erik were twenty himself, it would have been his fantasy come true. Now it made him feel ancient. "First time," he agreed. *And last,* though he didn't say that out loud. "I've only recently moved to Houston from LA."

The kid scooted closer, crowding against Erik as another man pushed up to the bar on his other side. He steadied himself with a hand to Erik's chest—a hand that copped a feel through his shirt. Erik doubted he had the physique to impress a kid like this, but he didn't immediately move his hand or back away, so maybe he was wrong. "Well… welcome to Texas. We should have a drink to celebrate. I'm Jace. What's your name?"

What the hell, it wasn't like he'd ever see this kid again. "Erik. Nice to meet you, Jace." As much as he wanted to leave, he couldn't be rude enough to just walk out. He raised a hand to beckon the bartender over. "Another beer, and whatever Jace here would like to drink."

"Sex on the Beach for me," Jace said. He turned so he was pressed up against Erik and kept a hand on his arm, nothing more than a light pressure, but enough contact to keep Erik's attention. The bartender left to make their drinks, and Jace shifted up to murmur into Erik's ear. "There's nothing quite like good sex on the beach, don't you think?"

If Jace had ever actually had sex on a beach, he'd know that it led to sand getting in places sand was never meant to go. But Erik wasn't going to be the one to shatter his illusions. "So, tell me something about yourself, Jace," he countered instead.

"What do you want to know?" Jace asked with what Erik assumed was meant to be a seductive pout. It only made him look younger. "I'm twenty-two, finishing up an English degree at HCC. I'm a part-time model, hoping to break into acting at some point."

Of course he was. Erik had met his fill of waiters/models/actors while living in LA, though he imagined the competition wasn't as cutthroat in Houston as it was in Hollywood. And the twenty-year difference in their ages meant he was old enough to be Jace's father, though while his first sexual encounter had come a few years earlier than that, it hadn't been with a woman.

"I'm forty-two and work in the local office of an investment management firm," he said in turn, sure the combination of age and mundane job would be enough to send the hot young thing running for greener pastures.

It had the opposite effect. Jace leaned even closer into his space, rubbing against Erik like a cat in heat. "I like you more and more. There's nothing like a man with some experience under his belt." As he spoke, he dropped his hand from Erik's chest to the waist of his jeans and traced along the edge of the fabric. "Want to share a little of that experience with me?"

Erik couldn't deny he was tempted. His cock stirred in his jeans at the tantalizing touch. He'd been alone since the breakup with Mark, and he was only human. He'd had his share of one-night encounters over the years, but he wasn't that impulsive young man anymore. A quick fuck would slake his libido temporarily, but tomorrow he'd be just as alone and with a bad case of morning-after regret. He glanced around the club in a vain hope for someone a bit more mature, but only the bartender seemed to be anywhere near his age, and he was smirking at Erik as if to say *You'd be crazy to pass that up.*

Maybe romantic deprivation was making him crazy, then, because he reached down and gently prevented Jace's hand from making its way any closer to his crotch. "I think you're out of my league, Jace."

Jace pouted up at Erik in a way that was certainly designed to tempt him, probably to break him. "Don't put yourself down like that. I know a catch when I see one." He didn't try to pull his hand out of Erik's light grip even though he could have broken free easily. "Handsome, strong, rich."

Erik managed to hold back a laugh at that, just barely. The last thing he wanted from a relationship was to be some young twink's sugar daddy. If that was the only option open to him, he'd stay celibate. "I'm flattered, Jace, but you can find someone much better suited to you than I am."

Before Jace could come up with another bit of wheedling flattery, Erik stood—dislodging Jace's hand in the process—drained his beer, and dropped a bill on the bar to pay for the drinks. Jace looked up at him with kohl-lined puppy-dog eyes, and Erik had to resist the impulse to tousle his hair. "Good luck with your acting career, Jace."

Once outside the bar, he drew in a deep breath of the cool night air and started walking toward his car. That was another mistake he would never make again.

SEVERAL DAYS later, Erik's sense of mortification after the fiasco at the Six-Pack—he couldn't have been more out of place if he'd tried—

had started to fade, though the loneliness that prompted it hadn't. When his phone rang while he was reviewing a report on foreign stock trends during his lunch break, he picked up the receiver, knowing Billy would have held the call if it was business-related. "Hello?"

"Erik, darling, how are you? You haven't called me all week." Erik couldn't stop the smile at the sound of Aunt Marjorie's voice. He'd gone to live with her when his parents died shortly after his fifteenth birthday. His older siblings hadn't needed a guardian, although they'd all joined him at Aunt Marjorie's house for holidays until they'd started families of their own, but it had just been him and "crazy" Aunt Marjorie most of the time until he'd finished college and moved to LA.

"I'm good, Aunt Marj, just busy getting familiar with the staff and clients at the new office. How are you doing?" His uncle Russ had passed away before his parents, and Marjorie's rheumatoid arthritis kept her from doing some of the bigger chores around the house. Erik didn't necessarily miss shoveling snow during Minnesota winters, but he still remembered the hot chocolate and homemade cookies his aunt would set on the kitchen table when he came inside. His older brother Kris's sons had taken over his role now that they were teenagers themselves.

"Oh, you know me. I can't complain. We had a couple of feet of snow earlier this week, but Joe and Brian came over and cleared my drive and sidewalks, and the temperature came back up to zero so I'm not hurting too badly at the moment. Have you met any nice boys since you've been in Houston? I worry about you, all alone down there."

That Marjorie had never had a problem with his orientation was another reason he loved her, even if he hadn't appreciated it when she'd tried to fix him up with the son of one of her canasta club partners back in high school. Some things never changed. "I've made some friends," he said, which wasn't really a lie since he considered Billy and Richard and the other advisors, male and female, who worked at the agency as friends.

"Friends are good," she said. "It's important to have friends, but that's not what I was talking about. I know you always tell people how good it was of me to take you in after your parents died, but you never seem to remember how much I needed you too. It's not good for us to be alone, and after Russ died, I was drifting. You gave me a purpose again, a reason to look forward to coming home from work instead of dreading the emptiness. Houston's a big city. There's bound to be someone who's caught your eye."

"It's a lot bigger than St. Cloud, that's for sure," Erik agreed with a smile. "You should come visit now that I'm settled, since I wasn't able to make it home for Christmas." By the time he'd completed the move to Houston, it didn't feel right to take time off right away, especially since most of the office staff had already made their holiday travel plans and coverage was light. And while he knew Aunt Marjorie would be supportive, he'd still been too raw to face the prospect of rehashing the breakup with his family. "I have a guest room in the apartment, and you'd love all the museums."

"Erik Peter Jansen, don't think for one moment that I can't see right through you. You're avoiding my question, and that means you know I won't like the answer. Have you turned into a hermit? Moving to Houston was supposed to be good for you, turning over a new leaf and all that. Have you *tried* to meet anyone?" Erik winced at her scolding tone. Age hadn't mellowed her sharp tongue one bit.

"It's taken time to settle in at work," Erik answered, though he knew she wouldn't accept that as an excuse. "That has to be my first priority. I've done some things socially," he added before she could call him on it. The wedding and dinner at Billy's counted, and she'd even approve of the futile night at the Six-Pack, not that he was going to share that with her. "It's not easy to meet people who are looking for the same things I am."

"I know it's not, sweetheart. Have you considered a dating site? I know some of them are narrow-minded, but some of them are open to LGBTQ individuals. It would still be hit or miss, but you could weed out the ones who were obviously not what you were looking for, and it's less awkward than going to a club hoping to meet someone." He wondered again, not for the first time, if she could read his mind. She might not have had children of her own, but her trouble detector was as accurate as his mother's had ever been.

"If all I wanted was a hookup, maybe," he told her. He might not have shared all the salacious details, but she knew he'd dated quite a few men in LA before settling into what he'd thought would be a lasting relationship with Mark. "I've been there, done that. Trying to find someone who shares my experiences and values—or even someone with different opinions we could debate—is turning out to be a lot harder than I'd hoped."

"I said dating, not Grindr." He didn't want to know how she'd heard about Grindr. "Not everyone on Match.com or places like that is looking for a hookup. You're selling yourself short. There have to be ways to meet other men your age who are interested in real relationships. Promise me you'll keep looking."

"I promise, Aunt Marjorie." The coffee shop where he bought his beans had a rack of local newspapers; maybe one of them targeted an LGBTQ audience. He could always try online again too, looking for LGBTQ activities or something where he might have a chance of meeting someone looking for more than a night's fun. Something tickled at his memory, but it wasn't a thought he wanted to pursue with Aunt Marjorie. "And I'm serious about you coming to visit too."

"It would be a nice break to get away from all this snow. I bet it's positively toasty down where you are. I'll get down there and you won't be able to get rid of me," she warned.

"You know you'd never leave the rest of the family permanently, but it's in the sixties today here, rather than below zero or even below freezing. You'd like walking around with only a light sweater instead of having to bundle up like an Eskimo," he said.

"That sounds like heaven. Now, I've kept you long enough. I'll let you get back to work, but don't go so long without calling me next time, and get out and meet some people. I expect to hear progress the next time I talk to you."

THE CONVERSATION with his aunt was still on his mind as he got ready to leave the office that afternoon. Marjorie's birthday was coming up, and though she insisted that since she'd stopped counting there was no reason to celebrate them, she was turning seventy, and Erik wasn't going to let that pass unnoticed, especially since he'd missed celebrating the holidays with her. He considered buying her a plane ticket to Houston, but he'd have to coordinate the timing of that with her, and besides, he wanted to give her something as special as she was. Maybe a nice piece of jewelry, something that would remind her of him whenever she wore it.

A thought teased at him. One of his clients managed a jewelry store…. He opened a desk drawer and ran a finger over the hanging files inside. Liam Gruene, that was it. Handsome, enthusiastic, withdrawing funds to start a new business on top of his current job. He pulled out

Liam's file and scanned the information. The Karat Patch, that was the name. And he and a partner were starting an LGBTQ matchmaking service. His lips twitched in a smile. After his conversation with Aunt Marjorie, maybe this was a sign. It was as good a place to start as any, and if he could give Liam some business while he was launching a risky venture, that was an added bonus. He pulled up the Karat Patch on his phone and clicked on the map feature. It wouldn't take him too far out of the way before he headed home.

When Erik walked in the shop, Liam stood behind the counter, dressed much as he had been that day in Erik's office, although the color on this suit was less conservative. The light gray drew attention to Liam's olive skin in a way the other one hadn't. Erik couldn't help wondering if Liam spent enough time outdoors to still be tan even in February or if that was his natural skin tone.

"Welcome to the Karat Patch. May I help—Erik, right? From Bauer & Fitzroy. What can I do for you?"

"I'm surprised you remember me," Erik said. It had been weeks since their one meeting, but he supposed it wasn't every day someone planned to start a new business. "I'm looking for a gift for someone very special, but I'm not really sure what might appeal to her. Maybe you can give me some suggestions."

"I'm happy to offer suggestions, but I'll need a little more information," Liam said, although some of the light seemed to have gone out of his eyes. "Who is it for? Your wife? A girlfriend? Your mother?" The last was said almost hopefully.

"My second mother, I suppose you could say." Eric didn't think Liam wanted to hear his life story, but that needed some explanation. "My parents died when I was a teen, and my aunt Marjorie took me in. Her seventieth birthday is coming up, and I'd like to give her something special."

"Oh, I think we can find something special. All our jewelry is designed and made in-house, so these are one-of-a-kind pieces. We can even do custom designs, although if we did that, you wouldn't walk out of the shop with something today. Does your aunt have a favorite stone? Or we could go with her birthstone. Amethyst if it's this month, aquamarine if it's in March. Or platinum is for seventy. We could look at something along those lines. Does any of that appeal?" Liam leaned forward on the counter as he spoke.

"She doesn't wear much jewelry," Erik mused, looking down at the display and Liam's reflection smiling up at him from the glass. "She and my uncle never had a lot of money, so other than her wedding rings and a necklace or two, I don't think she has much. So nothing too ornate— she'd call it 'fussy.'" He shook his head, hearing her voice in his head. "But I like the idea of platinum and her birthstone. Her birthday is March 30, so I don't know if that would give you enough time if we went with something custom-made."

"That's less than six weeks away, so probably not, but we could definitely modify an existing piece, change out stones, for example, or possibly even add a few. We have a number of platinum pieces already made up, although most of them have diamonds in them. They're over in the case on the far wall. If you see something you like, we can switch them out for aquamarines."

"I don't really know what I'm looking for," Erik admitted. "What would you recommend? Something you'd pick out for your mother to let her know how special she is to you."

"You said she had a few necklaces, so you could go that route," Liam said as he walked over to the case. "Something like this one, for example." He pulled out a slender chain with four diamonds that dropped, pendant-like, from the necklace. "Very classic, very elegant, but not showy. If that's still too fussy, you could go with something like this, with just a simple diamond pendant. Or, we can go a little fancier if that's not enough."

"I can't imagine her wearing that to play cards or go to the casino with her friends. Maybe a ring or a bracelet would be better? Something she can see that will remind her of how much she means to me."

"We can definitely look at those. My mother loved necklaces, so I tend to think of that first as a gift, but we have a sizable collection of rings. The simplest would be a single stone in a four-point setting, but those are most commonly designed as engagement rings. Obviously they don't have to be used for that purpose, but maybe something like this one? It's still very simple and could be given as an engagement ring, but the slight twist to the band makes it less traditional."

The uncluttered, elegant design, a single twist of platinum framing the stone on a diagonal, would appeal to Marjorie, he was sure. "I like it. Would it be possible to put her birthstone in the center, and maybe two smaller diamonds on either side?"

"Putting an aquamarine in is easy. That's just a question of switching out the stones. We should be able to add two small diamonds, but I'll have to check with our designer, both about the timeline and the price for doing that. Having the large stone as an aquamarine will lower the cost, but there will be added labor." Liam pulled out a pad of order forms from below the counter. "If you'll fill out the top so I have a way to contact you, I'll discuss it with our designer when he comes in tomorrow and call you with the information. Whatever number would be best to reach you around lunchtime tomorrow."

Erik filled out the requested information and handed the form back. "I appreciate your help. You've made this much easier than I was afraid it might be, since I didn't have a clue what I was looking for other than something special."

Liam gave that bright smile Erik was already beginning to look forward to. "It's all part of the service." He looked down at the order form to start writing in the specifics, then glanced back up. "That's not a Houston number. Where are you from?"

"Minnesota originally, though I worked in LA before moving to Texas." He pushed back the niggle of sadness just thinking about LA still triggered. "You mean I've managed to lose the Fargo accent?"

Liam laughed. "I can identify every Texas and Louisiana accent there is, but if you don't have one of those, I just know you're not from 'round here." He winked as he said it, playing up the Texas twang that Erik hadn't noticed before now. "How long have you been in town?"

"Just a few months. I'm still finding my way around. I remembered you mentioning you manage a jewelry store, so I thought you might be able to help, and I'm glad you did." He ought to head home now that he'd accomplished what he came for, but Erik was reluctant to return to his empty apartment. "How are plans for your matchmaking business coming along?" he asked instead.

"Oh God, don't call it that," Liam groaned. "It's not matchmaking. It's offering people a place to meet other people. Any matchmaking is their responsibility." He glanced down at his watch. "If you'll give me five minutes, the second-shift manager will be here. We can grab a cup of coffee at Agora, and I can bring you up to date on all the details. If you're really interested, that is. If you were just being polite, I won't keep you."

It might have started as a polite question to keep the conversation going, but Erik found he really was interested in Liam's plans. "I'm not just being polite. After all, as your financial advisor, I have a vested interest in your success. Where is Agora? Should I go ahead and find us a table? I can even have your coffee waiting for you if you tell me what you'd like."

Liam laughed. "It's across the street. You're welcome to start ahead if you want, and if there aren't any tables, we can go around the corner to Common Bond. It's a bakery as well as a coffee shop, but they're usually more crowded, plus I like Agora's coffee better. Tell them you're getting coffee for Liam, and they'll make it for you. But you don't need to do that unless you want to." The door chime rang as someone walked in. "Now you really don't need to. Sam won't mind if I duck out early."

The newcomer grumbled a little but waved for Liam to go ahead.

"Let me just grab my things and we can go," Liam said.

"Take your time," Erik answered. "I have no plans for the evening." *Or any other evening, for that matter.*

"My things" turned out to be a backpack Liam slung over one shoulder as they left the shop. The air had gotten cooler as the sun sank behind the buildings, but Erik's suit coat was enough to keep him warm as they dashed across the street and up the cobbled walk. More a café than a coffee shop, he decided when they walked inside. A bar along one wall offered wine and beer as well as coffee drinks, and small tables and cozy-looking chairs invited lingering. "Very nice," he said as the server behind the bar called out a greeting to Liam.

"I like it," Liam said. "I grab coffee here on my break most days, even if I bring lunch from home. And it's a good change of scenery from my dining room table when I need a place to sit and think. What's your poison? Ryan can make you pretty much anything you want."

"I'm fairly boring. I like to taste the coffee, so I don't want a lot of cream or flavorings to overwhelm it." He moved closer to the bar, scanning the list of drinks posted behind it. "Just an Americano, black," he told the barista. "And Liam's usual," he added with a smile.

The man laughed. "I started that the minute I saw him coming up the walk. Have a seat and I'll bring it out to you."

Erik returned to the table. "Now I have to ask. What's your 'usual'?"

"An espresso granita," Liam said, flushing slightly. "I love strong coffee, but I have to cut it with something. Vanilla and whipped cream do the trick."

"So you have a sweet tooth. Nothing wrong with that. My aunt has to put at least three teaspoons of sugar into her coffee before she declares it drinkable."

It only took a moment for the barista to set their cups onto the table. "Let me know when you're ready for a refill or if you'd like to order some snacks to go with it," he offered before turning back to greet another group who'd just entered.

Erik took a sip of his coffee and sighed in satisfaction. "So much better than the break-room coffee at the office." He watched Liam lick a splotch of foam from his lip and glanced away before it felt like he was staring. "So, tell me how plans for the not-matchmaking business are working out."

"We're making great progress," Liam said. "The Out and About website is live, and we've had people start signing up for our first event. We're doing a wine tasting at a place in Montrose. Small enough to feel intimate without being so small that we have to turn people away for the first event. Not that I expect us to reach capacity the first time out. And everyone who's signed up for the wine tasting so far has also signed up for our newsletter, so they'll know about future events. A few of them have even already signed up for April."

If enthusiasm and charm alone could guarantee a venture's success, Erik, thought, there was no doubt Liam's new business would thrive. "It sounds like you're off to a good start."

"I think so," Liam said. "It's certainly keeping both Kate and me busy, but if it grows the way we hope it will, it'll be worth it. I like working at the jewelry store, but there's no possibility of advancement there. I'm already the manager, and the owners have kids who will take over the store when they're ready to retire, so it's either continue in the exact job I have now until I'm ready to retire myself or build something of my own."

"Not everyone has the courage to take that step. I hope things work out, and I'm not just saying that as your financial advisor." He took another sip of coffee and decided to look up Out and About's website when he got home. A wine tasting might be just the thing to help him meet more people—more friends—like Liam.

CHAPTER 5

LIAM MET Kate at the Wine Cellar at five o'clock on the afternoon of their launch event in March. He'd been surprised and gratified at the response they'd gotten to the articles in *OutSmart*, the *Montrose Star*, and the Rice student newspaper. So far they hadn't even needed to dip into their advertising money. They had almost fifty people signed up for the wine tasting, and they'd had to limit it to sixty because of fire codes—and budgeted so they'd break even at twenty. Now all they had to do was deliver on the event itself.

"Hi, Shannon," he said when the owner of the Wine Cellar came out carrying a box of wine bottles. "Let me help you with that."

"Thanks, Liam." Shannon handed him the case of rioja and pointed toward one of the several tasting stations set up around the wine shop. "If you can put it behind that table, I'll get the last of the cava. Then we should be all set until the people from Sabroso get here with the tapas."

Liam set the carton down behind the wooden bar against one wall of the main room of the store. He wasn't a true wine connoisseur, but he loved coming here. Shannon always had new things for him to try. Kate had certainly approved when he brought her to evaluate the site. Shannon had created a rustic, welcoming feel in the shop, with wines in wooden crates or stacked in square cubbies along the walls rather than on cold metal racks. The second room was more open, with cases of wine stacked along the walls, a combination of extra storage and decoration. With several tables set up in that room for the tapas, Liam figured most people would congregate there, but they'd have the run of the whole shop since the event didn't start until after regular business hours.

God, he hoped it was a profitable event for Shannon too! They had so much riding on this.

Kate looked up from where she was arranging colorful plates and napkins on one of the tables they'd serve the tapas on. "Liam, relax. I can feel you vibrating from over here. Everything is going to be fine. We've planned this down to the last detail."

Liam took a deep breath to steady himself. "You're used to this. You organize events all the time. Don't tell me you weren't nervous the first time. I just want it to be perfect for everyone."

Kate came around the table and took Liam by the shoulders. "Trust me, no event is ever going to be perfect for everyone, and thinking you can do it is the best way to make yourself crazy. That's why we're planning so many different kinds of activities, right? Because one size doesn't fit everyone. I can guarantee that someone tonight is going to spill a glass of wine or be allergic to garlic or hate olives. That's why we have extra glasses and labels for the appetizers and a variety of choices. Expect that something's going to go wrong, and when it does, don't make a big deal out of it and do the best you can to make it right, and most people won't even notice."

Rationally he knew all that from managing the store, but this was different. Then it was Karat Patch's reputation on the line, and while the owners wouldn't be happy if he did anything to damage that reputation, it wasn't the same. This was his and Kate's baby. They didn't have anyone else to rely on if there were problems. It all fell on them. "I know you're right, but it's not doing anything to help the nerves. I think it's the waiting. Once people start to arrive and we have something to *do*, I'll feel better."

"Here." She pulled a stack of flyers from her leather tote bag and handed them to him. "Put out the ads for next month's event. And stop worrying! People will start arriving in the next hour or so, and after that we'll have plenty to keep us busy."

Liam took the flyers and tried to figure out how to arrange them artfully next to the displays of tasting wines on the bars. He heard Kate greet the caterers, but that was still her domain. When he was satisfied he'd made them as visible and appealing as he could, he headed to the front of the store where they'd be checking in the customers for the tasting. He had the list, the different stacks of name tags, and plenty of markers for people to write with. He just hoped people liked the idea of the identifying who they wanted to meet. Out of everything they had done, that had been his idea, and if people were bothered by it….

He broke off that train of thought and read the list of names again, trying to commit them to memory. No one would expect him to put faces to names yet, but if he already knew the names, he'd have an easier time remembering people, and that was important. Being able to call people by name and make a connection with them would make them feel important, and that would make them want to come back. He'd picked that little trick up from the retired manager at his store, and he'd had more than one customer thank him for remembering them and their preferences. One person had even said she went out of her way to come to his store rather than one closer to her because of that personal touch.

He couldn't help the smile that formed when he came to Erik's name toward the bottom of the list. Erik had signed up for the tasting shortly after their coffee "date." He'd been surprised at first, since Erik hadn't said anything about coming—or even being LGBTQ—while they were talking, but he wouldn't look a gift horse in the mouth. They'd talked several times since then as they worked out the details of the ring for his aunt. It would be ready for Erik to pick up next week.

The sound of the chime above the door ringing drew Liam's attention, and he smiled as a woman came up to the desk. "Welcome to the Wine Cellar and Out and About. I'm Liam. If you'll give me your name, I'll check you in."

"Sophie Barrett," she said.

Liam found her name on the list and checked her off. "Here's a glass for the tasting." He offered her one of the glasses Shannon had set out for them. "And then here are name tags. Red border if you're interested in meeting women. Solid white if you're open to meeting both men and women or people who don't identify on the gender binary."

"That's a unique way to do it," Sophie said as she reached for a name tag with a red border and wrote her name on it neatly. "What do I do now?"

"Now you take a list of the wines we're showcasing tonight, you help yourself to some tapas or some bread and cheese, and you let the staff of the Wine Cellar tell you all about what you're drinking. Both rooms are ours for the evening, so mix and mingle as people arrive, and have a great time!"

"I'm sure I will," Sophie said with a smile. Liam watched her head in Kate's direction, but the chimes sounded again, claiming his attention before he could see whether they spoke. Blonde and elegant was just Kate's type. He hid his own grin as he checked in the attractive redheaded man who said his name was Dave Watkins.

Within twenty minutes, he'd checked in most of the registered guests, as well as the friend of a guest who hadn't registered in advance. "He needs me for courage," Kurt said in an aside loud enough for his friend Martin to overhear. "He would have talked himself out of showing up otherwise."

"We don't all have your abrasive—I mean outgoing—personality," Martin retorted, though the twinkle in his eyes told Liam this wasn't the first time they'd had this discussion. He handed them both glasses and indicated the name tags. "Blue border if you're interested in meeting other men, and solid white for both men and women, or for people who don't identify on the gender binary." Kurt chose blue while Martin opted for white. "Here's a list of the wines we're tasting tonight. Help yourself to the tapas, and have a great time."

By the time he'd checked off all but a few names from their registration list, the shop was filled with people and the sounds of conversation almost drowned out the soft flamenco music playing over the sound system. Liam searched for Kate and spotted her in a group of people clustered around one of the tasting stations. Interestingly, both Sophie and Martin, as well as a tall, ruthlessly elegant mixed-race woman whose name escaped him, had gravitated into her orbit. Kate caught his eye and gave a thumbs-up. Liam grinned back and picked up a glass, deciding he might as well start to mingle himself.

Shannon poured him a glass of the prosecco with a grin. "Do you want the whole spiel?"

Liam laughed. Shannon had gone through all the wines with him and Kate when she picked them out, so he didn't really need a repeat, but before he could decline, Kurt joined him at the bar. "Why don't you tell us both?"

Shannon poured Kurt some of the prosecco as well. "We're serving a Cavit Lunetta Prosecco Brut tonight," she told them. "It has a bit of fruit to the flavor, but more tropical fruit than the more typical apple or pear. It's crisp and eminently drinkable as an aperitif or with appetizers."

Liam clinked his glass against Kurt's and took a sip. He'd tasted the wine before, but he enjoyed it just as much this time as he had the first time. He stepped away from the bar to allow others to refill their glasses as Kurt took a sip as well. "Is this your first time at the Wine Cellar?" Liam asked.

"Yes, but it won't be my last if this is typical of the quality of their wines," he said after savoring the sip. "And the quality of their customers," he added with an appreciative glance at Liam.

Liam didn't preen under his gaze, no matter how much he wanted to. Kurt was tall, dark, and more than handsome enough to push Liam's buttons, especially with the scruff of a beard along his jawline, and if the way his shirt clung to his shoulders was any indication, he either spent plenty of time in a gym or had a very physical job. "I can't speak to the quality of their customers when we aren't sponsoring an event, but their wine is excellent and a lot of it is very reasonably priced. Wait until you get to the malbec. It's my favorite of the evening. I've already bought a case."

"We'll have to compare notes after I taste it."

Liam wouldn't be averse to that at all, even if he didn't expect to find someone special at their very first event. There was nothing wrong with a little casual flirting, and judging by the lilt in Kurt's voice and the way he'd teased his friend when they arrived, he wasn't the type to take things too seriously either.

Before Liam could respond, the bell over the door jingled again. "Oops, I need to get back to my post," he said. "Let me know what you think of the malbec when you try it."

"Count on it." Kurt wandered toward the group Martin was part of, and Liam turned toward the check-in table, smiling immediately at the sight of Erik standing there in a denim shirt and khakis, his sandy hair smoothed to perfection. "Erik, sorry," Liam called as he hurried over. "Didn't mean to keep you waiting. It's good to see you again. I'm so glad you came to see what you helped make possible."

"I can't take any credit. Your money and your efforts brought this about, and judging by the crowd you have here, it's working." Erik ran a hand through his hair and smiled wryly. "I'm glad I managed to talk myself into coming. I haven't had the best of luck at meeting people since I moved here."

Liam couldn't imagine why, other than the same problem that had pushed Kate and him to start Out and About in the first place. "That's what we're here for. We've got name tags, color-coded to take some of the guesswork out of knowing who you might want to chat with. Blue if you're interested in meeting men, white if you're open to exploring your options. If you want, I can introduce you to a few people."

"At least I seem to have more in common with this group than the last time I tried going out." A hint of color tinged Erik's cheeks, making Liam wonder what that experience had been like, but he didn't know Erik well enough to ask. A tickle of happiness warmed him when Erik selected a blue name tag, and Liam was surprised at his own reaction. Hadn't he just told himself he was only interested in a little harmless flirting? *Well, there's no rule that I can only flirt with one person, is there?*

"Here's a glass for the tastings and a list of wines we're sampling tonight. Help yourself to the tapas, and let me know if you have any questions." He couldn't stop the smile he felt spreading across his face. "I'm really glad you came."

Erik returned the smile with a shy one of his own, making Liam's stomach flutter in pleasant anticipation. He was about to offer to go with Erik to get his first glass of wine when he caught Kate coming his direction. "Excuse me," he said regretfully and went to see what she needed.

"Having fun?" Kate asked when she reached him.

"So far so good," Liam replied. "You seem to have gathered quite the crowd of admirers yourself."

"It's my sparkling personality," she replied with a laugh. "Mostly it's that I'm good at breaking the ice and introducing people to each other." She tipped her glass in Erik's direction. "Who's that? He's yummy."

"Oh no you don't," Liam said. "I saw him first. He's the financial advisor who helped me get the cash for my contribution to the business. And he's wearing a blue name tag, so keep your grubby mitts off."

Kate snorted. "I'll have you know I keep my mitts in perfect condition. They're so clean and well-oiled you could eat off them if you wanted."

"No, thank you," Liam replied. "I'll settle for eating off a plate. Go back to your harem. I'll take care of this room."

Kate swatted at him for the teasing, but she went back into the other room with a charmed smile on her face, leaving Liam free to mingle with the guests in the front room and try to figure out how to approach Erik again without appearing too obvious.

CHAPTER 6

ERIK GLANCED around the wine shop, pleasantly surprised at the number of people gathered. Though he might still be the oldest person there—most of the people mingling seemed to be in their late twenties or early thirties. Soft guitar music encouraged conversation, and the aroma of olives and peppers tempted him toward the tables of tapas and cheeses. At least now the growling in his stomach was due to hunger and not nervousness. He'd paced outside the shop for at least five minutes after parking his car, dreading a repeat of the night at the Six-Pack, before screwing up his courage to venture inside. But the atmosphere, and Liam's welcome, couldn't be more encouraging.

Liam. If it hadn't been for their contact as they worked out the details of the ring Erik had ordered for Aunt Marjorie, he might still have talked himself out of coming tonight. But Liam had been so upbeat and excited about the event that some of the excitement had rubbed off on Erik. At least until he stood outside the wine shop. For all Liam's assurance that Out and About wasn't a matchmaking service, Erik was sure he wasn't the only person here hoping to meet someone special, and the idea had his stomach in knots. If he didn't know Aunt Marjorie would grill him about what he'd done to find "a nice man" the next time she called, he might have turned around and headed back home. Now he was glad he hadn't.

"You're getting a late start," a brunet said with a gesture to Erik's empty glass. "I'm Kurt. Come on, I'll introduce you to the nice lady at the bar. The one with the alcohol." He winked as he led Erik through the crowd to the bar and a smiling woman who did indeed offer him alcohol.

As she was pouring him the first wine—something bubbly, he was still a little too nervous to pay attention to what she was describing—Liam joined them at the bar, a gentleman with salt-and-pepper hair in tow. "I see you two have already met, but have you met Dr. Kelly?"

"Eamon, please. We aren't on campus, Liam, not to mention you graduated ten years ago. I think you can call me by my first name. Although if you don't get back into practicing your piano, I might make you go back to calling me Dr. Kelly."

So Liam played piano? It seemed they had something in common. Erik felt a little like a bobblehead doll, offering smiles to Eamon, Kurt, Liam, and the woman who filled his glass. "To new friends," he toasted before taking a sip. The crisp, dry flavor sparkled on his tongue. "And excellent wine."

"I'll drink to that," Liam said. "Eamon, I introduced you, but I didn't introduce Kurt and Erik. Erik works in financial management, and I haven't had time to find out what Kurt does yet."

"You're falling down on your job," Eamon teased. Erik couldn't help smiling at Liam's flustered expression.

"You're not missing out," Kurt said with a bit of a grimace. "I'm an actuary at State Farm. It pays the bills, but it's nothing exciting, let me tell you."

"I'm glad I'm not the only one with an unexciting office job," Erik said. "But you must work out—you don't get muscles like those sitting at a desk all day." As soon as the words left his mouth, he wondered if it was too forward to say something like that to a guy he'd just met. He was so out of practice at this!

"It pays the bills, but it's not all I do," Kurt said. "I play soccer with one of the Houston Football Association teams and softball when it's not soccer season. It keeps me in shape. What about you? Any passions outside of financial management?"

"I play the piano myself—or I used to. I haven't played since I moved to Houston." Mark had complained so much about the time Erik spent on lessons and practice that he'd stopped playing, and he hadn't bothered to look into finding a studio near his new apartment.

"That won't do," Eamon said with a frown. "Liam didn't mention it, but I teach in the music department at Rice. We have rehearsal halls available 24-7, if you're interested in starting again."

"I've never met anybody who could play like Dr. Kelly," Liam enthused. Before he could say more, someone at the door caught his attention and motioned for him to join her. "Excuse me. I need to see what Kate wants."

"I'm sure I'm not up to the quality of your students," Erik demurred, though the offer was tempting. Eamon seemed to be the oldest man at the gathering, and he was clearly in his element, which gave Erik hope that his own age wouldn't be an issue. "I'm strictly an amateur."

"I wouldn't be assessing you for a grade," Eamon answered with a chuckle. "We music lovers need to support one another. And I can show you some of the places around the university that aren't overrun with barely legal students—not that there's anything wrong with that, when one's in the mood to deal with them."

"Just because I'm not a fan of classical music doesn't mean I'm not a music lover, Eamon," Kurt said with enough of a teasing edge to make Erik suspect they'd had this conversation before, though he did wonder how they knew each other. "I consider Eric Clapton or Stevie Ray Vaughan as much of an artist as Van Cliburn or Yo-Yo Ma." He turned toward Erik. "What about you, Erik? What kind of music do you like?"

"Can I say both?" He glanced between the two men—two new friends, he hoped—with a smile. "There isn't much I don't like to listen to, except maybe very loud heavy metal."

"A very progressive attitude," Eamon said. "Kurt is just still perturbed with me for ruining his 4.0 the semester he had to take a music class with me."

That explained how they knew each other and when they'd had the conversation before.

"Asking a numbers person to take music is just cruel," Kurt insisted. "I can tell the difference between classical and jazz, but asking me to distinguish one classical composer from another? Lost cause, I'm telling you. If you two are going to talk music, I'm going to get more wine and see how much trouble Martin has gotten into with the pretty brunette in the other room."

Erik felt a bit guilty about excluding Kurt from the conversation, but he could always find him to strike up a conversation on another topic later. That was the purpose of the event, to mingle and meet lots of different people, right? And it had been so long since he'd known anyone who shared his interest in music. "Nice to meet you, Kurt. You'll have to introduce me to you friend Martin too." Kurt clapped him on the shoulder before heading away, and Erik finished his glass of wine. "Are you serious about my being able to practice at Rice?" he asked Eamon.

"Of course. I never joke about music," Eamon assured him. "Let's try some of these delicious-looking patatas bravas, shall we? I believe they're pouring a tempranillo to accompany them."

Erik followed Eamon back to the bar and watched in quiet surprise as Eamon turned his charm on the young woman serving the wine, despite wearing a blue name tag.

"Ah, thank you, my dear. Now tell us all about what you've just poured for us,"

The young woman gave him her best smile. "This is the Zuccardi Q from Argentina. It's a hundred percent tempranillo, lightly aged in oak before being bottled. A prime example of what a tempranillo should taste like—dark and juicy with a dry, spicy finish. It's a 2012 vintage, so it's had a bit of time to age, but it could easily sit for another few years and only improve in taste."

"It sounds like just the thing," Eamon said. "Have a taste, Erik. Tell me what you think."

Erik took a sip of the wine she'd poured him and let it sit for a moment on his tongue before swallowing. Smooth, with enough dryness to counter the spiciness of the sauce on the potatoes, but without a strong tannic finish. "That's excellent. I think I need to take a few bottles of it home with me. It would go perfectly with snapper Veracruz."

"You've moved on to the reds, I see. And run Kurt off." Liam's grin as he approached softened his words. "Not your type?"

"I think it was more an issue of my not being his type," Erik said, the twinge of guilt returning. Mark had always hated it when his excitement about a topic overtook the conversation. "He wasn't interested in talking music with Eamon and me."

Liam laughed, a bright, cheery sound that made Erik want to smile in response. "It takes a music aficionado to keep up with Eamon. I have someone else I need to introduce Eamon to, if you don't mind me dragging him away. Kurt is by himself over at the bar. You shouldn't leave a good-looking guy like that to his own devices. Someone else might snap him up."

Eamon's eyes twinkled. "In case I decide to run off with the person Liam's keen on my meeting, let me give you my card." He pulled one from his wallet and handed it to Erik. "Give me a call and we can discuss times for you to come practice."

"I'll do that, thanks. Great to meet you, Eamon." Erik watched him walk away, guided by Liam's hand on his arm to another group of guests. He'd definitely take Eamon up on his offer. He enjoyed the older man's quirky humor as much as he looked forward to getting his hands on piano keys again.

When he glanced over at the tasting station where Kurt was chatting with the server, Kurt raised his glass and winked. Erik finished the tempranillo—he really was going to have to arrange to buy several bottles—and made his way over. "Is the wine here as good as the last one?"

"I suppose that depends on your taste in wine, but I like it," Kurt said. "Then again, I tend to go for younger, fresher wines rather than heavier, aged ones."

Erik wondered whether that was a veiled dig at Eamon, but Kurt's smile seemed too genuine to harbor a sarcastic meaning. "I'll have to give it a fair evaluation, then. I don't like to make judgments ahead of time—I've been pleasantly surprised before."

"Keeping an open mind is never a bad thing," Kurt agreed as Erik took a glass from the server. "Have you been in Houston long?"

"About four months." He sipped the wine—a rioja, according to the server—and let it linger on his palate before continuing. "I transferred from our LA offices to manage the branch here. It's been a bit of an adjustment."

"Just four months? You've got some catching up to do, then. I hope your coworkers have been introducing you to the finer points of being a Houstonian," Kurt said with a grin. "Or I'd be happy to show you around, if they haven't. No expectations or anything. Just a couple of finance guys hanging out."

"Not a lot of singles among my coworkers," Erik admitted. "That's partly why I'm here. I hope to make some friends and get to know more about the city at the same time." That didn't make him sound too desperate.

"Yeah, this was a great idea they had. I mean, the wine tasting, but just in general as a chance for people to meet. I'm looking forward to the next one already. I like wine as much as the next guy, but the softball game is much more my style. But that's a month away. I'm sure we can find something to do between now and then if you're interested. The Rockets are still playing, or there's always stuff going on at the Wortham or the Alley—downtown theaters, in case you aren't familiar. The Museum of Fine Arts has a big exhibit of Flemish paintings right now. Houston is really a great city to explore, but it's kind of overwhelming at first, until you get to know what's out there." Kurt looked at Erik hopefully. "What do you say?"

"I've never been much of a jock," Erik said, hoping that wouldn't end their potential friendship before it started. In fact he'd usually been among the last picks for team activities during gym, especially before he switched from glasses to contact lenses in junior high. "But I used to catch at least a couple of Laker games every year. How do your Rockets stack up to them?"

"We'll see how this season finishes out, but they had a better record than the Lakers in 2016-2017," Kurt replied. "But if sports aren't your thing, there's plenty else to do. Houston has some amazing community theater, if that's more your style. Let me give you my number, and we'll figure out something that appeals to us both. It's a big city. I know we can come up with something."

"That sounds good." Erik took out his phone and typed in the number Kurt gave him. Once it was programmed, he sent Kurt a quick text so he'd have Erik's number too. He wasn't quite sure how to read Kurt, but getting together with him to watch a basketball game or a play with no expectations sounded good to him. He hadn't come expecting to meet a soul mate the first time around. He'd be happy with making a few new friends.

"Kurt, it's getting late and I have an early flight in the morning." A man Erik hadn't met came up to them with an apologetic look on his face.

"Sorry, Martin, I got caught up. Martin, this is Erik. Erik, this is Martin. I came with him tonight as moral support, but that also means I have to leave when he's ready. Call me, okay? We'll plan something before the next Out and About gathering."

"Nice to meet you, Martin. Sorry we didn't get a chance to talk tonight," Erik said.

"Next time for sure." Martin took Kurt's arm a bit possessively, making Erik wonder whether he had the same idea of "moral support" as Kurt did. He sipped his wine contemplatively while the two men worked their way to the door, then glanced around to see which tasting stations he hadn't visited yet.

"Don't tell me Kurt abandoned you," Liam said from behind Erik before he could decide which wine to taste next. "But since you're alone, there's someone I want you to meet."

Erik turned, and Liam's infectious grin called an answering smile to his face, even though he wondered whether he appeared so incapable of mingling on his own that Liam had to take him under his wing. But he'd noticed Liam moving among groups throughout the evening, making introductions and encouraging interaction. *He's just doing his job*, Erik told himself. *He's not taking any special interest in me.*

"Are you enjoying yourself?" Liam asked as he led Erik toward the other room, the one Erik hadn't been in yet. "We tried to pick a variety of different wines so there would be something for everyone."

"I haven't tasted anything I haven't enjoyed, and I'm definitely going to take some bottles home with me." There was an even larger selection of tapas in this room, and Erik promised himself he'd make a plate for himself after he met whoever Liam was delivering him to. Drinking too much on just a few nibbles of potato would be a bad idea.

"I'm glad to hear it. I'd hate for you not to come back." He made his way over to a large group near the back wall. When they approached, a tall, elegant woman with long dark hair pulled away and joined them.

"Hi," she said before Liam could introduce them, "I'm Kate, Liam's partner."

"Business partner," Liam interjected. "Because, no. Just no."

"Yes, his business partner," Kate said with a wink in Liam's direction, which he returned with a frown Erik wasn't sure how to interpret. "I wanted a chance to meet you. Liam told me all about you after your meeting, and I had to say hello."

Erik was surprised Liam had mentioned him to Kate, but he must have come up in the context of Liam's funds withdrawal. "The two of you have made an impressive start. If this is any indication of the kind of response your events will draw, your venture has an excellent chance of success." And could he sound any more like a boring financial analyst if he tried?

"We're hoping you're right," Kate said brightly. "Your plate is empty and so is your glass. Liam's falling down on the job. Let me get you set up." She took his plate and glass and slipped away before he could reply.

"Sorry about that. I really did want you to meet her, but I didn't get a chance to warn you that Kate packs as much punch as a small hurricane," Liam said. "If you don't want what she brings you, you don't have to eat it."

"The tapas look delicious, and I planned to have more, but I'm really not as incapable of taking care of myself as I apparently seem."

"What? Oh God, is that how we're coming across to people?" Liam asked, looking stricken. "Kate is the consummate hostess. Event planning is her job, so she flits around these things greasing the wheels and making sure everyone is taken care of, and I've just been trying to find people who weren't in a group and introduce them into one. After all, if the idea is for people to meet, they can't do that in a corner by themselves, but if we're making people feel like we're being condescending…. *So* not what we intended."

And now he'd succeeded in making Liam feel bad. Erik shook his head. "I didn't mean that the way it sounded. I'm just so out of practice at getting out and meeting people, I keep second-guessing myself. I know you're only doing your job, and you're great at it. I might be one of those people standing in a corner by myself if you weren't. It isn't something I like to recognize about myself, but I hope it will get easier with practice."

"Hey, you're not as bad as all that. I saw Dr. Kelly—Eamon—give you his card, so you met at least one person tonight who liked you well enough to want to continue the contact, and you spent quite a while talking with Kurt, and he's already signed up for the next event, so you can see him again then for sure," Liam said. "This is a safe space. Maybe not everyone will be interested in everyone else, even as friends, but you don't have to worry about being ridiculed or worse for being yourself."

"Here you go, Erik," Kate said as she handed him a full plate and a glass. "Plenty to eat and a lovely glass of malbec to go with it. And now I have to steal Liam away. I can introduce you to some people before I do, if you'd like."

Erik glanced toward a cluster of people gathered at the next tasting station. He hadn't spoken with any of them yet, so it would be a good place to start putting his words into action. "Thanks, Kate, but I'm good." He drew in a breath and smiled at them both. "I have some new friends to meet."

CHAPTER 7

LIAM FLOPPED onto the couch in their townhouse and toed off his shoes. He'd never realized running an event could be so exhausting. "How do you do this all day, every day?" he asked Kate.

"I'm not usually the one hosting the event, just the one coordinating backstage," Kate said. "It's still exhausting, but not like this." She joined him on the couch and propped her feet in his lap. Taking pity on her—she'd been in heels—he rubbed the arches of her feet gently.

"I think it went well. I didn't hear any complaints."

"And Shannon was thrilled with how much wine people bought after tasting it. She said we're welcome to hold an event there every quarter if we want." Kate hummed in pleasure as Liam increased the pressure of his massage. "Maybe not that often, at least while we're only doing one a month, but we could plan another one in the fall."

"Let's see what kind of feedback we get from our attendees, but I think doing another one is a good idea," Liam said. "It was easy for people to mingle, and I heard a lot of conversation around the wine, so that worked as a way to break the ice. And of course as we get to know people who come to multiple events, we'll be able to help introduce people more easily."

"I noticed you were especially solicitous in making introductions with all the cutest guys. Scoping out the booty?"

Liam tickled Kate's insteps, wringing a squeal from her.

"Like you weren't checking out the girls just as hard," he retorted. It had made sense for him to facilitate those introductions. That was his story and he was sticking to it. If it had given him an opportunity to have a few interesting conversations himself, well, that was the point of the event.

"There's no reason we can't enjoy the fringe benefits of the job. And the name tags were a good idea. I was a little worried that people might only want to mingle with their own colors, but I didn't see that happening." She wiggled her toes happily. "I was glad to see Eamon showed up. He'll spread the word at Rice as well as any ads we could run."

"And everywhere else he goes. That man is the biggest gossip in town," Liam said with a shake of his head. "But he also knows more people than any one person should be able to remember, so I won't complain if he gives us a little free publicity." Eamon had been in his element, holding court in every group he joined over the course of the evening. Liam hoped he'd come to other events and that he'd meet someone. If he remembered correctly, Eamon had lost a long-term partner to a sudden heart attack. Liam would probably never be able to see past the patina of Dr. Kelly, but for anyone else, Eamon would be quite a catch. "I doubt we'll see him at the softball game, though. Not exactly his style."

"Are you kidding? A chance to ogle all the other players, especially if they're buff? He'll be there," Kate stated confidently. "I hope he brings lots of friends too. The wine tasting didn't require any physical exertion, but I talked to a few people who weren't sure about playing softball. I told them it would be fun, and no one expected them to be José Altuve, but I'm not sure I convinced them."

It took a minute for Liam to place the name of the Astros' top hitter. Kate talked baseball at him all the time, but he usually tuned her out. "It's a risk we knew we were taking when we planned such a different kind of event. We'll have to hope we attract a different crowd for the softball. Maybe we should start planning the May event so we can get it up on the website when people come back to leave feedback on the wine tasting. That way even if they aren't interested in softball, they might see something else to catch their attention."

"The Astros will be playing by then, but we don't want to do two sports events in a row. What about something cultural? We could look at the symphony calendar, or maybe a play? I'd like to have some more specifics on the number of attendees we can expect before I start talking to the museums about some kind of after-hours party."

"What about something where numbers wouldn't matter?" Liam said. "A show at Miller Outdoor Theatre or appetizers in Memorial Park… something where the only reason numbers would matter would be for the catering. We wouldn't even have to reserve space at Miller. We'd just show up early enough to save a section of the hill."

"And it shouldn't be hot enough yet in May to make it too uncomfortable to sit outside for a couple of hours, at least at night. We can check and see who's performing, but honestly, I'm not sure it matters.

The people I talked to were thrilled just at the idea of meeting people in a safe atmosphere."

"Or if we don't want to have a performance limit interaction, we can do a park in town, or even head out to Brazos Bend. Although they were hit pretty hard by Hurricane Harvey, so maybe we'd be better off with somewhere in town," Liam said. "One of the nice things about the wine tasting was that people could eat and chat and move around the whole time instead of having to give their attention to some kind of entertainment. Or maybe you're right and the entertainment would be part of the draw. You know more about this than I do."

"Speaking of moving around, what about laser tag? No one has to be an athlete to enjoy that, and it's indoors so weather wouldn't be an issue. And a lot of those places have group rooms. We could have light refreshments available," Kate suggested. "That would give people a chance to interact when they take a break. You know, so they can make plans for after the event or later," she added with a smirk.

"You and your one-track mind," Liam teased. "Not that there's anything to stop people hooking up at our events, of course, but we're supposed to be about more than that."

"And we are, but do you really think some people aren't going to hook up? Honestly, Liam, that ex of yours messed you up worse than I thought. Time was you'd be right there looking for someone to hook up with yourself."

"Todd was a long time ago, and I'm not the same person I was then," Liam said. It was even the truth. Just not the whole truth. He'd been so sure they were building something real, and finding out that Todd just wanted him for the sex had left him off-kilter. He had no issue with other people having all the sex they wanted, but the disappointment had soured that scene for him completely. No, if he was going to have sex with someone, he wanted it to mean something.

He must not have done as good a job of hiding the bitterness as he thought, because Kate sat up and put her arms around him. "I hate that he made you doubt yourself. You're a better person without him, and one day you'll meet someone who recognizes all your sterling qualities." She dropped an arm down to poke at his ribs. "But there's no reason not to enjoy yourself while you're looking."

"I enjoyed myself plenty tonight," he protested as he arched away from her bony fingers. "Really, Katie. I did. I met a lot of really interesting people, and even if all that comes out of it is a few new friendships and a successful business, that's still more than I had before. What about you? How many phone numbers did you bring home?"

"A lady never tells." Kate stretched out her legs and sighed contentedly. "Let's just say I might not be waiting until next month's event to see some of our guests again."

Liam grinned at her. "You're incorrigible. And I wouldn't have you any other way." If his thoughts drifted to a certain financial planner and whether he'd attend their next event, that was no business but his own.

"MORNING, ERIK," Billy said when Erik got to work on Monday. "You're looking very relaxed this morning. Did you have a good weekend?"

"I did," Erik said, stopping at Billy's desk. "I tried something different on Saturday and went to a wine tasting sponsored by a new group called Out and About. It's actually run by one of our clients and his partner. They'll be putting on events geared for LGBTQ singles." Billy knew he was gay, but Erik still watched to gauge his reaction. It hadn't been an issue when he wasn't doing anything to actively look for a relationship, and he hoped that wouldn't change now.

"Well, look at you, getting a social life," Billy said with a wink and a grin. "Meet anyone interesting?"

"Quite a few people, actually. There's a music professor at Rice who offered me the use of their practice facilities to play piano, and an actuary for one of the big insurance firms who wants to commiserate about our boring office jobs. Not that I'd know anything about that, with all the excitement going on around here."

Billy laughed. "It's not usually this exciting, I'll tell you that. Your arrival and then Rick's wedding are more excitement than we've had since I started here five years ago. But that's cool about the Rice professor. I've met a few who were really friendly and a few who were… convinced of their own importance. Then again, that's probably true of people in general. I didn't know you played piano."

"I used to be fairly decent, though I haven't played in almost a year. It didn't seem worth it to move my upright here from California, and I don't know that my neighbors would appreciate it if I tried to put one in my apartment."

"If you change your mind, let me know. I have a friend—well, an acquaintance—who works at the Houston Piano Company. I can put you in touch with him. He might be able to get you a deal. Now you just need to follow up with that actuary and have an actual date or two."

"If you can call two guys having a beer and griping about work a date," Erik said dryly. He'd enjoy Kurt's company, but he wasn't expecting it to turn into anything more. Kurt had made it pretty clear he wasn't looking for any strings, and Erik wasn't sure he wanted to chance getting serious about anyone who didn't share his love for music. He'd had enough of Mark complaining every time he practiced.

"It's still more of a social life than you've had up until now," Billy pointed out. "And if it doesn't work out, you can always go to the next event. I'm sure as they get more established, there will be new people at the events. You are planning to go to their next event, right?"

Erik hesitated long enough that Billy raised an eyebrow and repeated, "Right?"

"I'm not sure the next one is my speed," Erik said. "They're hosting a softball game at one of the university fields. Competitive sports have never been my strong suit." That brought to mind one of Mark's last comments when they broke up—about how his lack of physical skills carried over to the bedroom—and he felt himself flush. "I think I'll pass and see what they have planned after that."

"Really? Come on, Erik, live a little. Even I know pickup games like that are just an excuse to get together, drink beer, eat hot dogs, and flirt, and if it's an event aimed at singles, the softball game will be the least important part of the event," Billy said. "I mean, it's your choice, but you shouldn't just write it off. If you hate softball on principle, that's different, of course, but not just because you're not a star athlete."

"I think it's obvious I was never a jock, even when I was younger. I'm pretty sure my middle-aged ineptitude wouldn't contribute much to the game." He knew he shouldn't let Mark's parting taunts get to him, but he also knew his talents were intellectual, not physical.

"Beer, hot dogs, flirting," Billy repeated. "Pick a team and cheer for them. Hang out with the batters when they aren't on the field. There's plenty of ways to have fun without actually playing. And you're assuming everyone there will be any better than you think you are. You're seriously overthinking this."

Billy was probably right, but the upbeat mood Erik had come into the office with was all but gone. He'd hoped to leave his self-doubts behind when he left California, but they weren't that easy to shake off after all.

"I'll take it under consideration," he told Billy with a tight smile and headed into his office. At least he knew he was good at his job.

CHAPTER 8

"AH, GOOD, I caught you before you left," Eamon said, breezing into the practice studio where Erik was just packing up after an hour of playing like he hadn't since longer than he cared to remember.

"I can't thank you enough for this, Eamon," Erik answered. "I knew I'd be rusty after not practicing for so long, but on an instrument like this, it all came back to me." He wished it were an option to fit a piano into his apartment. There was no way playing once a week would be enough. All the petty irritations of the day had fallen away the moment his fingers touched the keys and coaxed out the first notes. Why had he let Mark deny him this joy for so long?

"You're very welcome. Next time I'll try to get free a little faster so I can hear you play. If you don't mind, that is. But I have other plans for tonight, and I hope you'll join me."

"I'd appreciate your opinion. My last instruction was several years ago, and I'd like to be sure I haven't picked up any bad habits." He ran a grateful hand over the keys before closing the lid. "My only plans after this were heading home for dinner and maybe a glass of wine to celebrate being able to play again. What do you have in mind?"

"A glass of wine sounds perfect. There's a lovely French café in the Village where we can have a glass of wine and a good meal and a chance to talk without getting interrupted," Eamon proposed.

"That sounds wonderful, but it will be my treat." Before Eamon could protest, Erik continued, "It's the least I can do to thank you for reminding me of what I'd been missing."

"That's hardly necessary, but I won't say no to having a handsome young man buy me dinner," Eamon replied. "And yes, I know it's not a date. I don't think either of us wants it to be, but I'm old enough to get away with being outrageous when I feel like it."

"There aren't that many years between us." Erik picked up his jacket from where he'd folded it over the back of a chair. "Would you like to walk? Even a newcomer like me knows how hard it is to find parking in the Village, especially after seven."

"A walk sounds like just the thing. It's the perfect evening for it. And you can't be more than forty, which makes me a good twenty years older than you. Being around college students keeps the spirit young, but the flesh ages no matter how youthful the company," Eamon said as they walked out of the Shepherd School and onto Rice's campus.

Erik glanced up at the dark sky, but the lights from the city were too bright to see all but a few stars. Not that he'd seen many in LA either. "I wouldn't have guessed you were more than ten years older than me. Whatever you're doing to stay young, it's obviously working."

"They say love keeps you young," Eamon replied. "Of course losing the love of your life is a recipe for aging, and Patrick would shave me bald if he thought I was sitting around moping because he's gone, so I'm doing my best to get back out in the world again. The opening of Liam's Out and About was just what I needed."

Losing Mark had been hard enough. He couldn't imagine what Eamon had gone through. "I'm sorry for your loss. Can I ask how long you and Patrick were together?"

"Twenty-nine years," Eamon said. "He died two months before our thirtieth anniversary. His heart simply gave out. We didn't have the slightest warning. We went to bed as usual one night, and when I woke up, he didn't. But enough of that. What's a good-looking man like you doing single?"

That certainly puts my situation in perspective, doesn't it? Erik shook his head. "I was… dating someone in LA"—because Mark obviously hadn't considered it a relationship the way Erik had—"but it didn't work out." Because Mark found someone younger and more exciting. More capable of managing the social whirl Mark thrived on. At least Eamon had almost thirty of years of his Patrick's love, though that must have made losing it even worse.

"I'd say that's a shame, but if it had, you might not have moved to Houston and we wouldn't be enjoying this lovely evening," Eamon said. "You'll love Café Rabelais. They have some items that are fairly stable, but they don't have printed menus. Everything is on a big chalkboard, depending on what they can get fresh that day. And the wine list… ah, it's a thing of beauty. All French, of course, which isn't to some people's taste, but there's just something about a finely aged Bourgogne that calls to the wine lover's soul."

Eamon's comment gave Erik pause. If he hadn't broken things off with Mark, he'd still be in LA, and if he were honest with himself, he was glad he'd moved to Houston. He enjoyed his job responsibilities, he liked and respected his new coworkers, and he was discovering more to do in his new city every day. A little loneliness was a small price to pay in return, and the new friends he was making would help with that. "You're absolutely right," he said, realizing the answer applied to both Eamon's statements. "I bought some excellent wines at the Out and About tasting."

"They did have some lovely wines," Eamon agreed as they left the Rice campus and navigated the streets toward Times Boulevard, where the restaurant was located. "I'm definitely looking forward to their next event as well."

"Do you play softball?" Erik asked, hoping he didn't sound surprised. It wasn't a question of age; he just couldn't imagine Eamon fielding a pop fly or sliding into a base.

"Oh heavens no, but the scenery, Erik… just think of the scenery!" They reached the restaurant as Eamon spoke, giving Erik enough light to see Eamon's wink and the mischievous twinkle in his eyes. "I'll have far more fun watching than should be legal for a man of my age and stature."

Erik couldn't help but chuckle as they walked inside. "There's that, I suppose. I'm not sure I could pull off watching from the sidelines with you."

Eamon didn't reply until they'd been seated at the little round café table in the quaint restaurant that would have done justice to any Parisian bistro. "Why not? There's no shame in being more artistic than athletic. The point of Out and About is to be social. The softball or the wine tasting or whatever is after that is just the vehicle. I wouldn't be surprised to find quite a few people in attendance but not playing."

"There will have to be at least enough players to make up two teams, or it'll be nothing but socializing." Erik paused as a waiter approached their table to describe the night's specials and drop off a wine list. The topic of softball didn't come back up the rest of the evening.

"ERIK, OVER here!" Kurt called as Erik walked into Buffalo Wild Wings. He'd agreed to meet Kurt to watch the Rockets away game on the big screens.

"Sorry I'm late," Erik said, peeling out of his jacket and loosening his tie before dropping into a seat across from Kurt. "We had a corporate conference call, and the West Coast people always seem to forget how much later it is for the rest of us."

"I feel you. I'm not high enough up to have many of those, but I've seen it happen to my bosses more than once. But you're here now. You want a beer? Or something stronger?" Kurt signaled to the waitress as he spoke.

"Beer sounds great. Anything local you'd recommend?" Erik asked.

"I don't know about local, but you can't go wrong with a Shiner Bock," Kurt said. "I don't have fancy tastes. I tend to just go with what I like."

"I know more about wine than I do beer, but the West Coast is all about microbreweries, so I tried a lot of different brands and styles. Two Shiners," he told the waitress. Once she walked away, he let out a sigh and rolled his head until his neck cracked. "This is great. The end of the accounting year is coming up, so it's been crazy busy with compiling the year-end reports for our office and reviewing them with senior management and making decisions about changes in direction going forward. I need a night to relax."

"God, tell me about it. It's like everyone sees tax season as a reason to revisit their insurance needs. And I'm not complaining, in a way. I mean, we need people to buy the insurance we offer, but they couldn't do it in, I don't know, August? When we can go days without an appointment? But we can forget about all that tonight and enjoy some good basketball. The Rockets are on fire this season."

"That'll be a nice change after the lousy teams the Lakers have had lately. They haven't been the same since Jackson retired."

"Keeps things interesting." The waitress came back with their beers. Kurt tapped the neck of his bottle against Erik's. "Are you planning on coming to the softball game next weekend?"

Erik took a sip of his longneck and sighed. "I might wait and see what they have planned for next month. I'm not much of a jock."

"Oh, come on, Erik," Kurt said. "You can't be as bad as all that, and even if you are, that's not what it's about anyway. Come hang out with us, if nothing else. You can be my cheering section."

"Your personal cheerleader? Something I should know about?" Erik raised an eyebrow. "You did have on a blue name tag at the wine tasting."

"Not like that," Kurt said with a roll of his eyes. "But if you aren't going to play, you can cheer on those of us who are. And there will be a cookout along with the game, so hot dogs, beer, an afternoon outside before it gets too hot to breathe during the summer. We won't have many more nice days before summer hits."

"That's going to take some getting used to. A warm day in LA was if it hit 90. Nothing like the temperatures I've heard it can reach in Texas."

"Wait till you live through it," Kurt said with a shake of his head. "Ninety-five degrees and ninety-five percent humidity from sunup to sundown. I have to get all my outdoorsy stuff in from October to April because after that, it's just too damn hot. And don't think I didn't notice you avoiding my question."

"I'm sure I'll be complaining that 'it's not the heat, it's the humidity' by midsummer." Erik set down his beer as the waitress returned to take their order. "I'll start with a dozen wings with the Asian Zing sauce."

"A dozen for me too, Desert Heat," Kurt said. "And another round of beers. Cheering is thirsty work."

"Then I hope they have plenty at the softball game. Don't expect me to dress up in one of those little skirts, though." Erik grinned. Between Billy, Eamon, and now Kurt, it was clear he wouldn't hear the end of it if he skipped the softball game. He just hoped he could steer clear of actually having to take the field. "So what other kinds of outdoorsy stuff is there to do around here?"

"In the city itself, not a whole lot. I mean, it's the city, but the Hill Country is just a couple of hours away for hiking and camping, and you can go kayaking on Buffalo Bayou or pretty much any of the rivers around here depending on how difficult you take your rapids. If you want to go skiing, though, you've got to go into New Mexico or Colorado. I try to do that a couple times each winter, just to keep my skills up, but it's not a regular thing."

"I'm used to having to travel to ski. I'm not black-diamond level, but I'd spend a few weekends every winter in Tahoe or one of the resort towns in Colorado." Mark was the avid skier, but he'd been too much of a hotdog. Erik would rather be safe than have to untangle himself from around a tree.

"We'll have to make plans for next winter," Kurt said with a wink. "If we're both still free by then. Wouldn't want to make anyone jealous."

Kurt had said up front they'd get together with no expectations, but Erik was still relieved that Kurt didn't seem interested in pursuing anything more serious—at least with him. He enjoyed Kurt's company, but he didn't feel a twinge of romantic attraction, any more than he had with Eamon. Which wasn't a bad thing. He'd made two new friends thanks to Out and About, and that alone made it a success as far as he was concerned. Enough to give even the softball game a try.

"Who knows?" Erik replied. "We might both have someone to invite with us by then."

Kurt clinked their bottles together again. "I'll drink to that."

CHAPTER 9

LIAM LOOKED around the area they had reserved for the April event. The field was immaculate, as Kate had promised it would be, but that was her domain. He was more concerned with the rest. He'd been nervous about the relatively low number of repeat attendees from the first event to the second, but he could hardly argue with the overall turnout when they had nearly fifty people registered for the day—almost the same turnout as the first event. Even if some of them—like him—didn't play, they should have more than enough to put together two teams. And everyone else could enjoy the cookout and drinks and company while they cheered on the people who were playing.

He'd relied on Kate to keep things flowing during the first event, but this time a lot of that would fall on him since he'd never manage to keep Kate off the field. Then again, he didn't want to. Softball was one of her first loves.

"Worrywart," Kate chided as she slung an arm around his shoulder. "I told you plenty of people would show up. I didn't even have to call in favors from the varsity teams to get enough players, though a few of them may stop by just to watch."

"I know, I know," Liam said with a roll of his eyes. "You told me. If this were more my scene, I'd have a better sense of how people would react to it, but since it's not, I was afraid we'd lose people's interest. As it is, I'm surprised by a few of the names on the list. But you were right about Dr. Kelly being a softball enthusiast."

"Speaking of 'just to watch....'" Kate chuckled. "He'll cheer equally hard for both teams."

Liam had to laugh at that. He could imagine it already. "I suppose you're right."

Before he could say more, the first attendees started to arrive, and he was busy passing out name tags, explaining the color system to those who were new, and explaining the overall setup for the event to everyone. He recognized Travis Cummings as one of Kate's exes when he stepped up to get his name tag.

"Hey, Travis," Liam said, handing Travis a white name tag and explaining the color system. "Unless you've sworn off women again?"

"You know I like to keep my options open," the tall blond replied with a grin. "Katie love, it's been too long! Remind me again why we stopped seeing each other?"

"Because you like playing the field too much to settle down with any one person, even one as perfect as me," she answered, stepping into his hug. "Which doesn't mean I don't still appreciate your other assets. Can I count on you to coach one of the teams tonight?"

Travis straightened after kissing her cheek. "I assumed you and Liam would coach."

"She's coaching, but what in the world made you think I would?" Liam retorted. "You know my only interest in softball is watching Kate wipe the field with the opposing team. I'd consider it a huge favor if you coached the other team."

"So she can wipe the field with me? Not gonna happen." Travis patted Liam's shoulder. "But you can owe me one anyway."

Kate rolled her eyes, then glanced at her watch. "We'd better get started. Okay, people, listen up," she continued in a voice that didn't need any amplification to be heard. "Travis and I are going to pick teams. Liam, do you have a quarter to flip to see who gets the first choice?"

Liam fished in his pockets until he came up with a quarter. "Call it, Travis," he said as he flipped it into the air.

"Tails," Travis said with a grin and a leer as Liam bent to see which way the coin had landed.

"Tails it is," Liam called. "Travis picks first."

Travis hooked his thumbs into the pockets of his shorts and strolled through the cluster of participants. Liam glanced over the group, trying to guess who Travis would choose first. To his surprise, he saw Erik chatting with Eamon and Kurt. He must have arrived while Travis had claimed Liam and Kate's attention.

"Kurt, glad you made it." Travis took him by the shoulder and turned him toward the left side of the field. "I'm counting on your arm to keep Kate's team from getting on base."

"I wouldn't miss it," Kurt said. "Hey, have you met Erik yet? He's convinced he's just going to sit and watch."

"Injury?" Travis asked, and something about the way he raked his green eyes over Erik made Liam's skin twitch.

"No, I'm afraid it's chronic." Erik offered his hand to Travis with a smile. "Ineptness, that is."

Travis seemed to hold on to Erik's hand longer than a simple greeting required.

"Bull, man. Anyone can play slow-pitch."

Erik shook his head. "I was always the last guy picked in gym class for a reason. Trust me, you don't want me on your team."

"Ah, but you never had me coaching you." Travis clapped his shoulder. "If Kate doesn't snatch you up first, I want you."

Liam frowned at Travis's choice of words, but he stayed out of the conversation. If he didn't, he'd end up getting dragged on the field too, and that wasn't happening. He left Travis and Kate to pick their teams and went to check with the caterers to make sure the drinks were set out along with snacks for now. They'd serve the hot dogs and hamburgers after the game was over.

ERIK WASN'T surprised when, after Kate—looking much younger without makeup and with her hair tucked under a ball cap—selected Miranda, the elegant black woman he'd seen her with at the wine tasting, Travis was back tapping him on the shoulder. To continue to protest would be churlish, and Travis didn't look like the kind of guy to take no for an answer. "As long as you know going in how badly I'm going to suck at this." He regretted the unintentional innuendo as soon as the words left his lips, but Travis just raised an eyebrow and nudged him toward Kurt.

He hoped his face didn't look as warm as it felt, but if it did, Kurt didn't mention it. "So you and Travis have played together before?" he asked, then bit his tongue. Travis was the type to press all his buttons, at least hard enough to disconnect the higher motor controls from his mouth.

"Yeah, we played on the same team in Houston's men's league a couple of years ago," Kurt said. "He's a great guy and a great player. I didn't put it together until just now, but he and Kate dated for a while. I got the impression she was too independent for him. He likes to be needed."

"Well, I'll need all the help he can give me if I'm not going to embarrass you and the rest of the team." Kate and Travis had completed two more rounds of selections while he and Kurt spoke, and a blonde woman Erik recognized from the wine tasting and a lanky black man he didn't recognize joined them on their side of the diamond. Erik was about to introduce himself when Liam jogged over.

"Hi, Erik, I didn't see you arrive. I brought you a name tag. Blue again since that's what you had last time, although I can get you a different one if you prefer."

"Blue's fine." Erik printed his name on the tag, then peeled off the backing and pressed it to his chest. At least he'd worn a polo shirt and khaki shorts in deference to the already warm weather, though if it were a weeknight and he'd come straight from work, he'd have had a better excuse for begging off. "Are you on our team too?"

"Travis and Kate know better than to pick me to play softball. Besides, someone has to coordinate everything, and I wouldn't dream of keeping Kate off the field," Liam said. "I'll cheer you on from the sidelines between checking on everyone and making sure the caterers have dinner ready on time."

As if on cue, Erik's stomach growled, though he hoped no one else could hear it. Lunch had consisted of a carton of yogurt he'd munched while on mute on another corporate conference call. Saturday calls were uncommon, but the senior VP wanted to get an early start on planning for the annual corporate meeting. Still, if he was going to have to play softball, it was probably better he didn't have a full stomach. "I guess I'll see you later, then," he said as Travis made beckoning motions to pull their team into a huddle.

"There are snacks out if you're hungry now. And drinks. I can bring you something while Travis gives his pep talk," Liam offered.

Damn, he must have heard Erik's stomach growling after all. "Thanks, but I'd better listen up. I need all the tips I can get." Erik turned toward the rest of the group, wondering if Liam was going to offer drinks to anyone else. He was just in time to hear Travis assigning positions. He'd hoped to be able to stand as far in the outfield as possible, but to his horror Travis told him to man third base.

"Uh, Travis, maybe you should put a better player—someone with more experience—there?" He hoped that didn't sound as much like a whine as it felt.

"Don't worry, with Kurt pitching, no one will ever get that far around the bases," Travis assured him with a grin.

"No pressure or anything," Kurt said, but his grin matched Travis's, so Erik figured Travis's assessment was fairly accurate.

A few minutes later, the remaining players were divvied up and the two teams moved to their respective sides of the diamond. Erik had met enough of the others on Travis's team to feel comfortable chatting with them before it was time to take the field. Since Travis had won the toss to pick first, Kate's team got the first turn at bat.

Erik felt a bit awkward standing beside third base, though he spotted Eamon among the small handful of people who weren't playing and got a wink and a thumbs-up. Then Kurt threw the first pitch and Erik dragged his attention to the game.

Travis hadn't been exaggerating about Kurt's talent, from what Erik could see. The first two batters on Kate's team struck out, and the third popped up an easy fly to the outfield that Sophie, the blonde Erik remembered from the wine tasting, caught easily.

The teams switched places, and Erik saw Liam waiting for them in the "dugout" with bottles of water and a marker. "I thought you'd like something to drink," he said, clearly addressing the whole team for all that he continued to look straight at Erik. "If you want to put your names on the bottles, I brought a marker."

"Thanks, Liam." Travis plucked a bottle from Liam's arms and marked it with a large *T* before twisting off the cap and taking a deep swig. "Won't do for anyone to get overheated or dehydrated."

Erik took a bottle in turn, smiling at Liam. He'd started to offer his thanks when a shout rose from his teammates. Kurt, the leadoff batter, had connected with a pitch that sailed over the heads of the infield and landed between the outfielders, making them race for it. He trotted into second base with a broad smile.

"He's good," Liam said. "I'm surprised Kate didn't know him before last month. I thought she knew all the really good softball players in the city."

"He said he met Travis in the men's league. I guess he doesn't play in the coed league."

"That would explain it," Liam replied. "Do you need anything else before I go check on Kate's team? She'll never let me live it down if I play favorites with the opposing team."

Erik took the remaining water bottles from Liam's arms. Of course he'd offer water to everyone. He must have been imagining that Liam's gaze had lingered on him. "This is good, thanks." He set the bottles on the bench and turned his attention back to the field, where Kurt was rounding third base after Travis had tapped a single. *Better her than me*, he thought as the Latina woman manning the base missed the toss from the shortstop and Kurt raced for home to score.

"You're up, Erik," another team member called. Erik sighed and took his place at home plate, hoping he wasn't about to make a fool of himself.

It had been so long since he'd held a bat that he didn't trust his judgment, swinging at every pitch. Before he could strike out, he caught the ball with the tip of his bat, sending it dribbling down the first-base line. He was tagged out before he made the base, but Travis trotted to home plate to score their second run. Erik accepted the backslaps from his teammates with a bemused smile.

"And you told me you couldn't play softball," Travis said with a grin. "I think you underestimated yourself."

"Game's not over yet," Erik answered, but as the innings went on, he saw that except for a few exceptional players like Travis, Kurt, and Kate, most of the others were no more talented than he was. He didn't manage another hit in his remaining at bats, and no one from the other team threatened to reach third base, though Kate smacked a home run that tied the score before Travis did the same the next time he was up. Going into the final inning, their team held on to a one-run lead.

Kurt retired the first batter before Kate came back to the plate.

"Nice and easy," Kate called. "Just like the last time, so I can hit it out of the park."

"In your dreams, Weaver," Kurt retorted and threw the ball toward the plate. While Erik wouldn't have said Kurt was going easy on the other players, even he could see the difference in Kurt's pitch when Kate was at bat. Then again, she was so much better than most of the rest of the players that she could handle it.

"Strike!" the umpire called.

"Just a little lower," Kate called, tapping her bat on the plate.

The next pitch didn't look any lower to Erik, but Kate must have liked what she saw. The hit didn't make it past the outfield, but it was solid enough to land her on base.

Kurt had two strikes on the next batter before giving up a pop fly that let Kate make it to second. Miranda came to the plate, and while she might look harmless, Erik had seen enough of her play to know how deceptive that could be.

"C'mon, Miri, knock one out so we can wrap this up," Kate called from second.

Miranda let the first two pitches go by, one a strike and the second a ball. As soon as she swung at the next pitch, Erik braced himself. The hit bounced just behind Kurt, and Kate was racing toward him when Kurt scooped up the ball and tossed it his way. One foot on the base, Erik raised his arms and somehow, miraculously, the ball dropped into his grasp. He managed to hold on to it as Kate plowed into him, sending them both tumbling to the ground, but it was clear she was out.

Kurt whooped and raced toward Erik. Travis did the same from the sidelines, then offered a hand up to Kate before pulling Erik to his feet and wrapping him in an embrace.

"Told you you'd underestimated yourself," Travis said while Kurt pounded his back and the rest of the team surrounded them.

"Must have been your inspired coaching," Erik said when the hugs and backslaps eased enough to let him draw a breath.

"I think this calls for a beer or two to celebrate."

"Pretty sure the university doesn't allow alcohol on the fields." At least, Erik hadn't seen anything more than water and soda when he'd passed where the caterers were setting up as he arrived.

Travis's smile made his eyes twinkle wickedly. "We'll just have to find somewhere after this breaks up, then."

CHAPTER 10

LIAM KEPT his smile in place as he approached Travis, Erik, and their team, even as he heard Travis suggest doing something after the event with Erik. Liam reminded himself firmly that he had no claim on Erik's time, no matter how attractive he found him, and that the whole point of Out and About was for people to meet other singles they might find interesting. He didn't wait for Erik to reply to Travis before he announced, "Food's ready when you are. And winners eat first."

Erik still looked a bit stunned at having caught the ball to end the game and give their team the win, but he followed Travis, Kurt, and the rest of the team to the tables where the caterers had set up burgers, hot dogs, and all the fixings. "I couldn't eat before the game," he admitted to Travis while filling a plate with a burger and chips. "And now I'm starving."

"Help yourself," Liam said when he overheard Erik's comment. He ignored the odd look on Travis's face. There were plenty of other people here Travis could go meet. He didn't have to monopolize Erik's time. "There's plenty. And nice catch. I may not play softball myself, but I know a great play when I see one."

"That was pure luck," Erik said, shaking his head. "But I have to admit, even not knowing what I was doing most of the time, I had fun."

"All thanks to my skilled coaching," Travis said with a grin.

"And my pitching," Kurt chimed in.

Of course Travis would take credit. "I'm glad to hear you had fun," Liam said to Erik. "I wasn't sure when Kate first suggested it. I mean, not everyone can be as athletic as she is. But it's turned into quite the afternoon. Very different from the wine tasting, but still enjoyable."

Before he could say more, one of the caterers caught his attention. "Excuse me. I need to go see what's going on."

The issue was a simple question about the veggie burgers Kate had ordered in case any of the attendees didn't eat meat. By the time he'd checked around and determined they wouldn't need to cook any, Erik had taken a seat at a table with Kurt, Travis, and several others from the team.

Liam had to smile when he noticed Eamon had joined them, but that meant there wasn't an empty place for him. There wasn't any space at Kate's table either, so he made up a plate for himself and joined several guests who'd watched the game but hadn't played.

Fortunately they'd all enjoyed watching and were talking about how much fun it had been to cheer on the teams without anything riding on the game except who got to eat first. Liam let them talk and marveled at how exhausting the afternoon had been, even without playing. He didn't know how Kate did it, but his admiration for her talents increased with each activity they organized.

Next month's event—laser tag—was already set and announced, although they had plenty of work to do on it still. That led him to thinking about the month after. It would be too hot in June to plan anything outdoors unless they did something water-related, but after two physical events in a row, something more cultural, maybe. They'd talked about a night at the museum. That might be a good June event. He'd have to talk to Kate about it.

He'd gotten so caught up in his thoughts that when he looked up again, the table around him was empty. Just like his life. He gave himself a firm shake and stood to take care of his plate.

Before he could make it to the trash can, Erik walked over, his own empty plate in hand. "I want to thank you for another great time," he said. "I'd struggled with whether or not to come today, but I'm really glad I did. I had a great time. It was good for me to do something outside my comfort zone."

"I'm glad to hear it," Liam said. "You're a lot braver than I am, getting out on the field like that. Not that Travis gave you much choice, I imagine, but even so, you did it."

"I would have said no if I had a real reason not to play, but remembering how awkward I was in middle school gym class seemed like a pretty lame excuse. I like to think I've matured a bit since then."

Liam laughed. "We'll hope we all have. Have you been pleased with the events so far? Gotten what you came for?"

An expression Liam couldn't identify flashed over Erik's face before a small grin replaced it. "Absolutely. I was hoping to get out and meet people who weren't looking for an immediate hookup, and it's only the second event and I've already made several friends. And had a good time even when I didn't expect to, like tonight. I'd say you're doing a great job."

Liam couldn't stop the relief at Erik's word choice—friends, not boyfriends. "We aim to please. And I really am glad you're making friends. Sometimes I think friends are even harder to come by than lovers when you're in a new place, especially if you're single."

Erik's smile widened. "Well, you know what they say—friends make the best lovers." His cheeks pinkened, as if he'd embarrassed himself with the comment, and he cleared his throat.

Liam took pity on him and changed the subject. "How did your aunt's birthday go? Did she like the ring?"

"She loved it." Erik's smile lit his blue eyes, making Liam wonder what he'd need to do to make Erik smile that way again. "She scolded me for spending too much, but she said it fits her right hand perfectly and she hasn't taken it off since it arrived."

"I'm so glad to hear that. When I sell jewelry as a gift, I don't usually get to hear what the reaction is from the person it was for, but it's important to me that people like what they get from the store." He patted Erik on the shoulder. "Thank you for telling me. You've made my day."

Erik's blush deepened, and he shrugged, dislodging Liam's arm. "I'd better go—I promised Travis we'd have a beer to celebrate my miraculous catch. I'll see you next month, whatever you have planned."

"Have fun," Liam said because he couldn't figure out a way to keep Erik with him longer. He was glad Erik had made friends, even if Kate's experience with Travis made Liam want to warn Erik off. He'd just have to see about spending a little more time with Erik next month.

"GOOD GAME," Liam said to Kate when they got back to their house later that evening. "Even if Travis's team did win."

"One more inning and we would have had them. Kurt's arm was starting to go." She was smiling as she said it, though—no one could accuse Kate of being a bad loser. "And who knew he had a ringer in Erik? I'm wondering now if that 'I can't play' talk was just to keep me from picking him for my team."

"I'm sure it wasn't," Liam said. "I talked to him afterward, and he seemed pretty surprised that he'd made the catch or even that he'd had a good time playing. You know, like me, only he actually went out and played instead of dealing with the caterers and stuff. Although Travis sure monopolized him after the game was over." He grimaced a little. Travis had been okay. He hadn't been mean to Kate or anything, but they had not been a good fit. She'd been way too independent for him.

"You aren't still down on Travis, are you?" Kate slapped him on the arm. "I told you, he didn't do anything wrong while we were dating. We just didn't click. We both like to be in charge too much. He needs to find someone who actually wants him to make all the decisions and solve all their problems."

"Then Erik definitely isn't what he's looking for," Liam replied. "He moved here on his own without knowing anyone. He's not looking for someone to run his life."

Kate's eyebrows rose. "And how do you know what Erik's looking for? I noticed you had a lot to say to him after the game."

Liam flushed. "I just asked him if he was enjoying our events. He said he'd made several new friends, which was what he was hoping for. And I had to make sure his aunt liked the ring I helped him pick out for her. Then Travis dragged him off, and I didn't get to ask him anything else."

"Oh ho!" Kate crowed. "You're interested in him, aren't you? That's why you're acting pissy about Travis all of a sudden. You think he's making his own move on Erik!"

"It sure looked that way from where I was sitting," Liam grumbled. "And there's nothing wrong with being interested in getting to know him better. If I can ever find five uninterrupted minutes to talk to him again."

"Well, you're not going to find it at our events, Liam," Kate said as if she was explaining things to a five-year-old. "You're working then, and you're too conscientious to let anything slide so you can spend time with Erik, no matter how interested you are in him. You need to call him and ask him out, one-on-one."

"And where am I supposed to get his number? I have his work number, but I'm not going to call him there to ask him out," Liam retorted.

"Why not?" When Liam frowned and shook his head, she continued, "He probably wouldn't have put his work number on the Out and About registration form. Look it up from there. Or I know you got a contact number when he ordered the ring. Use that to call him."

"That's confidential, whether I get it from work or from Out and About," Liam said, fighting not to blush at having called Erik from the

Karat Patch at his personal number. He'd used the work phone anyway, so the number wasn't in his cell. "I mean, sure, we have it on file in case we need to contact him about a change in an event, but we can't use it for personal reasons."

Kate's expression said she wouldn't have any problem pulling someone's home number from the database, but that didn't make Liam feel right about it. "Next month is laser tag. Since you handled all the arrangements so I could play today, I suppose it would be only fair for me to manage that one so you can make some time for a tête-à-tête with your new crush."

Liam scowled at her, but that wouldn't stop him from taking her up on her offer. "I'm going to hold you to that." Now he just had to hope one of Erik's new friends hadn't snatched him up between now and then.

He excused himself and went into his bedroom to sort himself out, because if he stayed in the living room, Kate would just keep poking at him. She'd ask what made Erik special, why Liam had fixated on him instead of any of the other men who had come to the events, and he'd be stuck trying to explain or even justify his tastes, which were vastly different from hers. Liam wasn't necessarily looking for the most handsome or ripped man out there. He didn't need someone who could keep up with him on the softball field. He needed someone steady, someone who would enjoy a quiet evening in as much as dinner out followed by a show. He might be reading more into Erik's reliance on Out and About to make friends than was actually there, but combined with his hesitancy to play softball today, Liam's gut told him Erik would appreciate the same things Liam did. Certainly the way he talked about his aunt reminded Liam of his own relationship with Nana Weaver. Not to mention that while he wasn't outrageously handsome, his kind smile and quirky features appealed to Liam. And that sexy dimple on his chin didn't hurt either.

And maybe he was misreading everything, but with Kate's promise to take care of things at the next event, at least he'd have the chance to find out.

CHAPTER 11

"I'M NOT very familiar with this part of town yet," Erik admitted as he followed Travis to the Rice athletic fields' parking lot after the softball game broke up. "Eamon's been letting me use the music department pianos for practice, and we had dinner together one night, but I think we're a bit underdressed for the place he took me." He actually felt a bit too sweaty for even a casual spot, but it would take too long to drive back to his apartment to change, and he had no idea if Travis lived nearby.

"I wouldn't worry about that," Travis said with a grin. "Valhalla doesn't have a dress code, but they have a great selection of beer, and we can watch whatever's on at the bar."

"Yeah, Valhalla's great," Kurt agreed, jogging up beside them. "They serve some tasty buffalo wings too. I can drive if you don't know how to get there."

Erik thought Travis's expression tightened for a moment before he smiled and clapped Kurt on the shoulder. "Glad you can join us. I'd be happy to drive us all there if we only want to take one car."

"I'm sure I can find the directions on Google Maps," Erik answered. "That way you don't have to come back here later." And he wouldn't be dependent on either Travis or Kurt to get back to his car if he wanted to call it an early evening.

"Parking might be a bit of a trick," Kurt warned.

"You sure you don't want a ride?" Travis chimed in. "Even if you want to leave early, it's close enough you could walk back to your car."

"If it's in walking distance, why don't we all walk?" Erik suggested. "That way we won't have to find parking, and we can always catch an Uber if we have a little too much to drive safely."

"Works for me," Kurt said. "Travis?"

"If you really want to walk after all that softball, I'm game," Travis said. "Let's go."

The live oak trees shadowed the sidewalks as they headed across campus to the bar. The evening was cool enough to feel good against Erik's sweaty skin. They reached the bar and headed inside.

"What are you drinking, guys? First round's on me."

"A ZiegenBock for me," Kurt said.

"Do they have Shiner Bock?" Erik asked.

Travis nodded. "On tap. Grab a table while I get the beers."

Kurt found an empty table facing a screen tuned to Fox Sports Southwest. "You should sign up for the Houston Parks men's softball league," he told Erik while they waited for Travis to put in their order at the bar. "We're always looking for good players."

Erik laughed. "I don't think so. One lucky play doesn't make me a good player. And honestly, I'd much rather watch a game than play in one. But if you tell me when you're playing, I'd be glad to come cheer you on."

"I'll make sure to send you the schedule," Kurt said. "I'm glad you decided to play today, winning catch aside. You're a great sport."

"Thanks," Erik replied.

Travis returned with their drinks before Erik could say more. "Cheers," Travis said, tapping their glasses together. "And here's to winning the game, and to new friends."

"New friends," Erik agreed. "Do you play on the same team as Kurt, Travis?"

"Not this season. Are you thinking of taking up softball?" Travis asked.

"I already tried," Kurt said, "and if he changes his mind, I get first dibs. I met him before you did."

"I'm the one who recruited him to play today," Travis retorted.

"I'm really not good enough to fight over," Erik said with a grin, "but it's nice to feel wanted."

"There's more to life than softball," Travis said. "What do you do with yourself when you aren't hanging out at Out and About events and catching winning plays?"

"I work in investment management. I moved here from Los Angeles a few months ago. What about you, Travis? What do you do when you're not roping innocent bystanders into softball games?"

"I work at one of the refineries," Travis said. "Not on the floor. I work in middle management. It's nothing fancy, but it pays the bills. I learned to find fulfillment in other ways a long time ago."

"That's one way to put it," Kurt said, snickering. "Travis has 'found fulfillment' with just about everyone on the city coed league."

"Not my fault I've still got it at thirty-eight," Travis replied. "I'm single. There's no harm in considering my options."

"Divorce final?" Kurt asked.

"Two months ago," Travis said with a grin. "No more ball and chain."

Kurt chuckled. "So you're free to play more field than just softball."

"How long were you married?" Erik asked. Liam had mentioned that Travis and Kate had dated, and now he found out Travis had been married until a couple of months ago. He could overlook a lot of things, but cheating wasn't one of them.

Travis snorted. "Not long. It was an impulse, a bad one as it turns out. We married a year ago and realized in less than six months that it was the wrong choice."

"Not the first time either," Kurt said. "Maybe you *should* stick to men, Travis. You don't have the greatest track record when it comes to women. Of course, now that same-sex marriage is legal, your luck could be just as bad with men too."

"Fuck off, Schneider," Travis retorted, though his smile didn't waver. "Just because I haven't found the right person yet doesn't mean they aren't out there."

Liam hadn't said how long ago Travis and Kate had dated. It was possible it had been while Travis was between marriages. Erik would give him the benefit of the doubt unless he learned otherwise.

"Yeah, yeah, you keep telling yourself that," Kurt quipped. "What about you, Erik? You ever been married?"

He'd hoped that was where his relationship with Mark had been leading, but the pang he felt was surprisingly muted. Erik shook his head. "I thought I was close once, but it didn't work out."

"That just means you're free to enjoy yourself now," Travis said. He tipped his beer in Erik's direction. "If that's your style, of course."

"Sure is yours," Kurt said with a smirk as he took another sip of his beer.

"How am I supposed to find my one and only if I'm not out looking?" Travis asked reasonably. "You may be willing to wait for your prince to come to you, but I believe in taking a more active role. I'll bet Erik agrees with me, don't you?"

"As long as both people have the same expectations," Erik said slowly. "If neither of you expect the relationship to be exclusive, that's fine." *And doesn't that sound preachy?* he thought, but Travis had asked.

"Nah, it's not like that," Travis said. "I believe in monogamy when I find someone I want to be monogamous with. In between times, I've got to keep looking, right?"

"Of course," Kurt jeered. "You look them right into bed."

"And what's wrong with that?" Travis retorted. "It's not as if you're exactly a monk yourself. I mean, look at Erik here. Can you tell me you wouldn't take him to bed if he was willing?"

"I'm glad I get a say in this." Erik wasn't sure if this was some sort of strange come-on, but while he found Travis's rugged looks appealing, he wasn't buying. At least not yet. "Sorry to disappoint you, but if I was interested in jumping in bed with any hot body, I'd go back to Grindr or a pickup bar. I'm looking for more than that."

"If you aren't looking to meet someone, why are you at the Out and About events?" Travis asked.

"There's more than one reason to want to meet new people," Kurt said before Erik could reply.

"I want to meet friends," Erik answered. "Maybe someday one of those friendships might grow into something more. I hope that happens, but even if it doesn't, I'd rather have a friend than one night with someone I'll never see again."

"You can count me as one of those new friends," Kurt said.

Travis rolled his eyes at Kurt. "Nothing wrong with making friends. It's like you said. As long as everyone knows what they're getting into, there's no harm, no foul."

Kurt's phone buzzed on the table, drawing the attention of all three men. Kurt frowned as he glanced down at the text message. "I hate to cut things short, guys, but I need to go. I'll call you, Erik. Travis, I'll see you on the softball field."

"You bet you will," Travis said with a sharp grin.

"Take care, Kurt." Erik wondered whether the text was some sort of problem, judging from Kurt's somber expression as he left the bar, but before he could say anything, Travis drained his beer and set the empty on the table.

"Another round?" he asked.

"Okay, but it's my turn to buy." Erik threaded his way to the bar— the place had gotten significantly more crowded since they'd arrived— and ordered two more beers. Travis was checking his phone but put it away when Erik returned carrying their drinks.

"Schneider's a good guy, but I didn't think he'd ever leave," Travis said when he sat back down. He raised his glass in Erik's direction. "Here's to making new... friends."

The gleam in Travis's eyes hinted that he was interested in more than just friendship. He was an attractive guy, his short blond hair cut in a casually tousled style, the stubble on his chin accenting a strong jaw and thin lips that were currently quirked into a smile. His sense of humor appealed to Erik's own whimsical side, one he usually kept to himself at work to maintain a professional demeanor. He could see something developing with Travis if he let it; the question was whether he wanted that to happen.

Based on several of Kurt's comments, and Travis's responses to them, Travis liked to play the field and wasn't interested in settling back down, which would be fine with Erik if all he wanted was a good time. He had no doubt Travis could give him one—but would that be any better than the pickup he'd rejected from Jace? He felt a physical attraction to Travis he hadn't with Kurt, and they'd probably continue to see each other at Out and About events, but Erik wasn't sure that was enough. Still, he wasn't ready to reject it out of hand.

"New friends," Erik echoed and took a sip of his beer.

"You don't play softball, and from a couple of other comments you made, I'm guessing you don't play a different sport either, but you're in too good shape to spend all your time behind a desk," Travis observed as he gave Erik a thorough look. "Running? Or swimming? What's your poison?"

"There's a workout center in my building that I use a few days a week," Erik answered. "I enjoy swimming, but the complex doesn't have a pool. I used to run in California, but I tried it here a few times and darn near keeled over. Unless I want to get up and run before the sun comes up, the heat and humidity together are too much for me."

Travis chuckled. "Yeah, and it's not even hot yet by Houston standards. If your building workout center isn't up to snuff, I can recommend a couple of places around town, depending on what you like. There are a couple of clubs that cater specifically to gay men. And if that isn't your scene, I know a few good ones with a more... general appeal."

He hadn't thought about gay fitness clubs, but that could be another place to meet people. Though he was happy with the friends he'd met so far through Out and About. "I might have mentioned I'm not much of a jock," Erik answered. "I work out because I've gotten to the age that I need to keep in shape, but I'm not obsessed with chiseling my abs or bulking up my pecs. Not that it's any hardship to check out guys who are, but the center in my building has enough variety of equipment for my needs, and since I sometimes put in late hours at the office, it's convenient since it's available to residents 24-7. Thanks for the offer, though. How do you like to spend your free time other than softball?"

"During the softball season, that pretty much takes all my free time. When I can't find a game somewhere, I run and lift to stay in shape, and cook to make it harder," Travis replied. "I like experimenting with recipes. Different spices, combining two recipes to come up with something completely new. That sort of thing. What about you? Enough of a workout to stay in shape can't possibly fill all your free time."

He hadn't pegged Travis as a cook. "I do well enough in the kitchen to keep myself fed, but I'm not much of an experimenter. I like trying new foods, but when it comes to making it myself, I tend to stick with things that are simple and quick. I haven't got a lot of hobbies, other than reading. Oh, and I think I mentioned I play the piano—strictly amateur-level, but Eamon has been kind enough to let me use the instruments at the university, so I try to practice there at least once a week."

"Perfect," Travis declared. "You can be my new guinea pig. I've got a couple of recipes I'm eyeing. What are you doing on Wednesday?"

"Having dinner at your place, apparently," Erik said with a grin. Travis clearly had hidden depths, and Erik wanted to get to know him better, even if nothing more came of it than another friendship. "Do you live around here? And what kind of wine can I bring to complement your cooking?"

"I live in old Pearland," Travis said. "South of Beltway 8 between 45 and Cullen. And probably either a pinot noir or a shiraz, something with some body but not overpowering. Wine should go with food, not beat it over the head. If you give me your number, I'll text you the address. Text me when you leave work so I know what time to have everything ready. I work one day each weekend and take Wednesdays off, so whatever time you get there is fine."

Erik recited his number to Travis, who punched it into his phone and then hit an icon to dial Erik. "Now you have my number too."

"I left my phone in the car," Erik said in answer to Travis's raised eyebrow when he didn't hear the call ring. "I didn't want to take a chance on damaging it or losing it during the game." And it wasn't as if he'd expected anyone to call him; there were no pending crises at the office, he'd spoken with his aunt Marjorie the night before, and all the friends he'd made in Houston other than his coworkers had been at the game. "But I'll text you Wednesday to let you know what time to expect me, and you can give me your exact address then. And I know just the shop to pick up some wine to go with the meal."

"Just because we have plans for Wednesday doesn't mean you have to rush off now," Travis said as he settled back in his seat and took another sip of his beer. "I worked enough overtime this week to have tomorrow off too. Or we could get out of here and find another way to spend the rest of the evening."

"What did you have in mind?" Erik asked. He'd expected to have a quick drink or two and then head home, but he was intrigued enough to see where the night might go.

"We could catch a movie or see what's going on downtown. There are almost always shows of one kind or another with tickets still available. Or if that's not your speed, we could go to Hermann Park and see what's going on there this weekend, and that's free. Or… we could go back to my place. I've got a great bottle of scotch I've been wanting to share with someone."

Erik glanced down at his shorts and T-shirt, still streaked with dirt from when Kate had bowled him over in the game's last play. "They might have let us in here dressed like this, but I don't think many other places would. Next time I'll know to bring a change of clothes with me."

Travis laughed. "My place, then? There's no dress code on my couch."

At least he hadn't said bed… and Erik couldn't stop the grin spreading across his face. "I do like a good scotch. But I'll have to limit it to one, or I won't trust myself to drive home."

"I have a guest room too, but that's your call," Travis said. He grabbed his phone and sent a quick text. "There, now you have my address as well as my number. Let's get out of here and you can follow me home."

ERIK FOLLOWED Travis up the sidewalk of a bungalow. Travis unlocked the door and held it open for Erik to go inside. No sooner had Travis closed the door behind them than Erik felt something furry glide past his ankles.

"Hello, Mouse," Travis said, bending down to pet the largest orange tabby Erik had ever seen. "I should have asked if you were allergic to cats, but Mouse doesn't usually come out when I have guests. He must like you."

"Give him time. He hasn't gotten to know me yet." Erik squatted down and held out a hand for Mouse to sniff. The big cat took a step closer and bumped Erik's palm with his head. "Glad to meet you, Mouse. My aunt in Minnesota used to have a tabby like you, but he wasn't as big." Erik rubbed Mouse's head, and when he was rewarded with a rumbling purr, stroked the length of the long orange body.

"He wasn't this big when I got him either," Travis said with a laugh. "I found him when he was a kitten, way too young to be weaned, eyes barely open yet. That's where the name came from, because he looked like a mouse, he was so small. Obviously he grew, but by then the name had stuck."

"You must be feeding him some of your cooking." Erik tried to stand, and Mouse made his displeasure at the loss of attention known with a piteous yowl. Erik knelt to give him a few more rubs and then stood again, ignoring the resulting protest. "I came to visit your owner, attention hog."

Travis laughed again. "No, my sister is a vet. Nothing but doctor-approved kibble for him." Mouse meandered between the two of them, trying to get more attention. Travis bent and scratched behind his ears before gesturing to the couch. "Have a seat. I'll get the glasses and the scotch."

Erik took a seat on the deep leather couch and smiled when Mouse jumped up next to him and rubbed against the back of his hand. He imitated Travis's scratching while he looked around at the open space. From where he was sitting, he could see Travis in the kitchen, pulling tumblers from a top shelf and giving them a quick rinse. The kitchen gave way to an eating area. The other wall was a huge bank of windows looking out onto a big backyard with a pool at the far end. Erik could imagine that getting a lot of use in the summer months, which he was learning were March through November in Houston. A fireplace was tucked in one corner with a pile of logs next to it. Erik didn't imagine it got nearly as much use, but he had fond memories of long winter nights spent curled up in front of the fire at his aunt's house. Maybe if they had a cold night next winter, he could convince Travis to let him light a fire.

"Here you go," Travis said, breaking into Erik's reverie as he set a glass down on the mosaic-topped coffee table.

"Tell me about the scotch," Erik said, lifting the tumbler to his nose but not drinking. The tawny liquid smelled peaty with a toasted undertone. "My boss in LA was born in the US but has relatives in Scotland, so whenever he'd go over for a visit, he'd bring back a different kind of whisky to share with the senior managers."

"It's called Cardhu. It's a single malt from the Speyside region. The distillery was founded in 1824 by a distant relative, though legend has it they'd been brewing illicitly for longer. My sister got fascinated with genealogy a few years ago and traced our family back to a little town called Knockando, so last year we all went to Scotland, met some distant cousins, drank some great scotch, and had a blast. So now I always keep a bottle of the family scotch, but I've also started branching out. Occasionally I'll find a dud, but for the most part, I just keep finding more favorites."

"Your family has good taste," Erik said after taking a sip. "I'll have to find a bottle of this to take back to my aunt Marjorie at Christmas. She enjoys 'a bit of a nip,' as she calls it, to keep the chill off on cold nights."

"Specs," Travis said. "They're the only place in town that carries it regularly. Sometimes the liquor store up the street carries it, but it's not a popular enough brand for a small store like that." He took another sip of his drink and set the glass down before scooping Mouse up and depositing him on the floor. "Scram, Mouse." He turned back to Erik with a grin. "Worst cockblock ever."

The knowing smile prompted Erik to answer in kind. "No, that would be my aunt. One time she walked in on me going down on the cutest guy on the JV hockey team. All she said was that she hoped we were being safe, but he jumped up, nearly tripped on his jeans, and took off. He wouldn't look at me again the rest of the year."

Travis's eyes twinkled as he laughed. "Oh, that's a great story. Sounds like she's quite the character if that was the extent of her reaction. My mother would've had a fit if she'd walked in on me like that."

"She's pretty special," Erik agreed. "My parents died when I was fifteen, and she took me in. My uncle had passed away and they never had any children, so she's been like a second mother to me. And no matter what outrageous thing I did as a teen, I was never able to shock her."

"I'm sorry about your parents, but I'm glad you had someone like that to take you in. My parents know I'm bi, but they generally cope with it by ignoring it when I'm dating a guy," Travis said ruefully. "Fortunately my sister makes up for it. Do you have siblings?"

"Two brothers and a sister, but they're all older than me by quite a few years. I was a bit of a surprise to my parents, apparently. And Aunt Marjorie took my being gay completely in stride. She might have an opinion on the guy I was dating if she didn't think he was a good match for me"—she never had taken to Mark, which should have been a sign to Erik from the beginning—"but she's never been anything but supportive."

"When I was a kid, all I ever wanted was a brother, but my sister has been my rock." Travis knocked back his scotch and poured a second glass. "And if we're going to get this serious, I need more alcohol." He tipped the bottle in Erik's direction in silent offering.

"I shouldn't." Erik shook his head. "I have a feeling you're going to be a bad influence on me."

"That's the best kind," Travis replied with a cocky grin, "but I won't pressure you. I really did mean it about the spare bedroom, though, if you want to have another. We're close enough to the same size that I can lend you something to sleep in."

"One more," Erik said, holding out his glass for Travis to fill. "It's been a long time since I've had a scotch I enjoy this much—or since I've done something I probably shouldn't."

"That sounds like a challenge." Travis pushed off the back of the couch and leaned closer to Erik. "What else can I tempt you into doing?"

Erik's good and bad angels held a quick debate, but he consciously shut them down. He'd been alone for more than six months, and there was nothing wrong with giving in to his longing. This wasn't Jace trying to pick him up in a bar. This was someone he was getting to know and already liked. How would he find someone new if he never took a chance? He swallowed the second shot of scotch in one gulp for courage. "This," he murmured, bending forward until he was near enough to brush his lips softly over Travis's.

Travis returned the kiss, keeping the contact light at first, but it didn't take long before he lifted one hand to cup Erik's jaw and deepen the kiss. Erik flicked his tongue against Travis's lips, an invitation Travis accepted immediately. He tasted like scotch, unsurprisingly, and smelled like sweat and an aftershave Erik didn't recognize. The thought made him smile into the kiss.

"What?" Travis asked, lifting his head.

"Nothing. Just thinking how good it feels to be close to someone again. It's been a while."

Travis arched an eyebrow at him. "Really? Why?"

It would be so easy to sidestep the question and just enjoy kissing Travis, but if there was a possibility of what he felt developing into more, he owed Travis honesty. "I was in a relationship in LA," he began, sitting back. "Mark worked at the same investment firm I do. We were together almost a year, until I found out he was seeing a client behind my back. When the chance to manage the Houston office came up, I jumped at it as much because it would get me away from LA and Mark as for the opportunity to run my own branch." If he left out the damage Mark's comments had done to his self-esteem, that was no one's business but his own.

"Bastard," Travis muttered. "My track record when it comes to relationships pretty much sucks, but even I know you don't cheat. I'm sorry that happened to you. We're both on the rebound." He ran a hand down Erik's sternum. "Want to rebound together?"

"What are you offering?" Erik asked. "I'll be honest, Travis. From what I heard earlier, you just got rid of a 'ball and chain.' I'm not interested in being your rebound guy. I'm past the age of wanting to screw a different guy every week. I want someone I know is always going to be there for me the way I will for him. And if that's not what you want too, we're better off stopping this right now, while we can still be friends."

Travis leaned back against the couch cushions. "You're right. The divorce was only final a few months ago, and I'm not ready to commit to anything yet. Are you sure you aren't up for some fooling around?"

Erik shook his head regretfully. While it hurt a little that Travis wasn't interested in a serious relationship, at least he was honest about it up front. *Not like—* He shut down that thought. "I wish I could, but I'm not built that way anymore."

Travis huffed, but he was smiling. "Why are all the good ones too honorable for me?" He winked and held out his hand for Erik to shake. "Friends?"

Erik summoned a smile and took Travis's hand. "And you're too honorable to string me along, so your bad-boy act isn't working on me. Friends."

"I guess I'd better make up the guest bed, then. You've had too much to drive safely."

CHAPTER 12

"LOTS OF new people this time," Liam said as he skimmed the sign-ups for the laser tag event they'd organized for the May outing, pretending he wasn't looking for a specific name. "That's a good sign. Word is getting out."

"Lots of repeaters too." Kate bent over his shoulder and tapped the list with a manicured fingernail. "He's right there."

"I wasn't looking for him in particular," Liam said, hoping his cheeks didn't look as red as they felt. "I was looking at overall numbers and trying to see how we're doing with the growth we'd forecasted so we can decide when to add a second event a month."

"And I'm moving to Washington to work in the Trump administration." Kate pulled out the chair next to Liam's and sat. "You can run the numbers, but just based on attendance I think we're ready to start thinking about it. The interest is there, and you'll have another chance every month to moon over your crush."

Liam sighed. "Travis is on there again too. You know they left together last month. My luck, they've gotten together by now and have decided this will make a good date night."

"They won't be spending much time together, in that case. Running around in the dark trying to shoot each other? Travis might manage to cop a feel or two, but there won't be much chance for conversation."

That only made Liam feel marginally better, because while Travis might not get to spend much time with Erik, Liam wouldn't either, for all the same reasons, plus the fact that they always had so much organization to make sure the events ran smoothly. "I suppose you're right. We need to decide on a June event too. Did you ever hear back from Archway Gallery?"

"They have a new exhibit promoting local artists and would love to host us. They offered us any Friday night or two of the Saturdays." Kate pulled up the calendar on her tablet. "I'm thinking the second Friday, so if we decide to plan another event too, we can aim for the last weekend."

"That works. Reserve that Friday. I'll get the info up on our website, and that way we can make sure people know about it at laser tag," Liam said. And Travis wouldn't be caught dead at an "artsy-fartsy" event like a gallery show, so Liam might actually get a chance to talk to Erik without Travis interfering.

"Don't worry, Li." Kate patted Liam's shoulder. "Even if Travis is putting the moves on Erik, he'll move on to someone else soon enough, or Erik will get tired of Travis's overbearing ways like I did."

"You're right, I'm sure. We'll just have to see how things go. And you'll have a great time. This is right up your alley too."

Kate grinned. "I promise to get in a few shots at Travis for you."

If only that would draw Erik's attention to him.

LIAM DID his best not to slump against the wall as he said goodbye to their guests as they left the laser tag facility. He'd been right about it being exhausting, and he'd only played one round, but he'd been busy the rest of the time making sure the snacks and drinks were kept replenished and that everything else was under control.

He smiled and waved as Kurt left, but the smile went stiff on his face when he saw Erik and Travis coming toward the door, laughing together. They weren't touching, but they were standing close enough that they could have touched at any second. They looked good together, he admitted to himself. About the same age, both with that certain maturity that could have been thirty-five or fifty-five, on the cusp of middle-aged but all the finer for it.

What would Erik want with Liam when he could have a man like Travis?

"Did you have a good time?" he asked them both because he had a job to do, no matter his personal feelings.

"Top score," Travis said, slinging an arm around Erik's shoulder. "And if we'd been on the same team, we might have set a new record."

Erik didn't move out of Travis's embrace, though he didn't put an arm around him in return. Liam wondered why he was bothering to look for reasons to believe the two weren't together. If they weren't yet, it was just a matter of time.

"You took altogether too much pleasure in blasting me," Erik told Travis with a grin. "At least I was able to even the score before the end of the game."

"I like a man who can give as good as he gets," Travis replied.

Yeah, just a matter of time.

"I'm afraid next month won't be as exciting," Liam said, "but I hope I'll see you there anyway." Of course the point of Out and About was for LGBTQ singles to meet, not to provide date night for people who were already together, but Liam wasn't churlish enough to point that out.

"That's the reception at the art gallery, isn't it?" Erik sounded interested, though Travis rolled his eyes behind his back. "It'll be interesting to see local artwork. I supported a small gallery in LA that focused on finding and developing new artists."

"You'll love Archway Gallery, then," Liam said, hoping maybe Erik would come without Travis. "They're entirely artist owned and operated, and the displays change regularly so there's always something new to see. The date's on the website, of course, but I can send it to you if you want?"

"I've got the dates for all the Out and About events on my calendar," Erik admitted, and Liam thought his cheeks turned a bit pink.

"C'mon, Erik," Travis said, moving his arm to thump Erik on the back. "Loser buys the first round, remember?"

He's still new to town, Liam reminded himself. *He's probably looking for ideas of things to do as much as he is people to meet. Just because he's got all the dates on his calendar doesn't mean he's thinking about you.*

"Enjoy your drinks and thanks for coming," he said as they walked out the door together, but not quite *together*.

He shook his head at himself as he said goodbye to the remaining guests and headed in to wrap things up with Kate. "Did you have fun?" he asked when he found her.

"We've got to do this again." She dumped the pile of guns into a bin and wiped her hands on her jeans. "Everyone I talked to said they had a great time."

"I hope they're as excited about the gallery event next month." Liam sighed.

"You said yourself we need a variety of events to appeal to all kinds of people," Kate countered. "And it won't take as much oversight on our part, so you'll have more free time to *mingle* with the guests."

Liam smiled, or tried to. "Sorry, I don't know what's wrong with me today."

"I do," Kate said. "Erik spent the whole time with Travis. Listen, Liam, I know you like him, but if he's the kind of man who's happy with Travis, then he's not the kind of man who would make *you* happy. Travis is a great guy, but he needs different things out of a relationship than you do. If their needs match, you and Erik would be as much of a disaster as Travis and I were."

Liam knew she was right. Travis had needed someone to take care of, someone who would need him in a way Kate never could. If Erik was looking for that, then Liam's desire for an equal partnership wouldn't suit Erik.

"I guess I just have to wait and see what happens."

"In the meantime, let's start pulling the numbers together," Kate suggested. "If they're as good as I think, we can start planning for a second event each month."

THE DOOR chime sounded when Erik walked into the Wine Cellar the Friday before Memorial Day weekend. Billy had invited him to a cookout on Saturday, and while beer would be the beverage of choice for most guests, his wife, Carrie, preferred wine, so Erik had offered to bring some. He'd been impressed by the Wine Cellar's selection at the Out and About wine tasting and had returned several times since to stock his own modest wine cabinet.

"Welcome back," Shannon said when he walked in. "If you have time, we've got a few bottles open for tasting in the back room."

"I'll never say no to tasting anything you're pouring, but I'm looking for something light and refreshing for this weekend. Maybe a vinho verde or something along those lines? I'm going to a cookout, and I have a feeling it's going to be too warm for anything very heavy."

"Vinho verde is always a good choice, as are several of our rosés, especially if you serve them chilled. And before you wrinkle your nose at me, rosés don't have to be sweet to be light. The Côte du Rhône ones especially are quite dry," Shannon said. "Go on back and taste what's open. I'll pull a few things I think might work for you."

"I appreciate it." And that was why Erik would definitely leave with several bottles of wine. Shannon didn't hesitate to open a bottle for tasting if she thought a customer would appreciate it. He picked up a bottle of the tempranillo he especially enjoyed before heading into the back room.

"Erik, what a surprise," he heard as soon as he walked into the room. He looked around until he saw Liam standing against the bar with a glass in his hand.

"Liam, hi. Are you planning another wine tasting?" Since he'd come straight from work, Erik still wore business attire, though he'd left his suit jacket in the car, but Liam must have had the day off or left work earlier than Erik had. Instead of the suit he'd worn at the Karat Patch, Liam had on slim, worn jeans and a faded Rice T-shirt. It was a more relaxed outfit than Erik had seen him wear even at Out and About events, and he liked the way it fit his slender figure. Everything about Liam seemed more relaxed than Erik could remember seeing him before.

"Not immediately, although we've gotten the highest ratings on that event so far," Liam replied. "We want to incorporate more variety before we start repeating anything. We'll plan another one before Thanksgiving, maybe, so people have an idea of what wine to serve with dinner. Shannon said we could come back anytime, she's gotten so many new regulars from the event. Does that include you?"

"I'm not sure I qualify as a regular yet, but I definitely shop here whenever I'm looking for wine. It has a great selection, and being able to taste anything I'm interested in is a real plus. What about you? Do you live around here?"

"Up in Midtown, so this is on the way home from work," Liam replied. "Kate and I bought a condo there just as the neighborhood revitalization was starting. I don't know that we could afford it now. But obviously I come here, even when I'm not on my way home." He glanced down at his casual clothes. "And since I always leave with at least one bottle of wine, Shannon hasn't banished me yet."

"What's your favorite?" Erik asked, curious how Liam's taste compared to his. He set the tempranillo he was carrying down on the bar and glanced at the open bottle, a French variety he wasn't familiar with.

"You mean besides all of them?" Liam joked. "It depends on what I'm eating and what season it is, but if I had to pick one wine that I couldn't do without, it would be a Meursault for white or a Morey-Saint-Denis for red. What about you?"

Erik gestured to the bottle at his elbow. "I found a tempranillo I really like at the wine tasting, and I've been back several times for more of it. I'm looking for something light that can be served chilled to take to a cookout tomorrow. But my wine knowledge is definitely at the 'I know what I like' level. Shannon's been great about expanding my horizons."

"She is definitely good at that," Liam said. "A cookout sounds like fun, although make sure you wear light, loose clothes if you're going to be outside most of the time. As I'm sure you've noticed, summer has arrived with a vengeance."

"Billy has a gazebo in his backyard with misters to help keep things cool, and I suppose I could always go inside if it gets too hot and sticky. Though depending how many other people are coming, it could get pretty crowded inside if we all have the same idea." Before he could continue, Shannon stepped behind the counter carrying several bottles of wine.

"I brought two vinho verdes and a rosé for you to try." She pulled several glasses from the rack hanging over the tasting station. "It's got a little more body than a white, which would be good with barbecue or steak, without being heavy or sweet."

"Oh, I've had that rosé before," Liam said. "It's a good one, but I don't know either of the vinho verdes. Shannon, have you been holding out on me?" He turned to grin at Erik. "She's been holding out on me."

"You're usually not interested in whites." Shannon uncorked one of the bottles and poured some into two glasses. "Vinho verde has a little bit of fizz, not as much as a champagne or cava, but enough to give it some liveliness."

"Liveliness is good," Liam said, bumping against Erik's shoulder. "Shall we give it a try, Erik?"

The contact sent its own fizz along Erik's nerves, but Liam was touchy-feely with everyone. It was part of his charm. He handed a glass to Liam before picking up his own and clinking them lightly. "To liveliness."

A crisp, fruity flavor tingled his palate. "Oh, that's good," he said, taking a larger sip. "What do you think, Liam?"

"Very nice," Liam said without ever taking his eyes off Erik. "Just the right amount of bite to offset the sweetness."

"I'll make a convert of you yet," Shannon said, reclaiming Erik's attention as she poured two more glasses from the second bottle. "See what you think of this one. It's made from a single grape rather than a blend."

"It's a little drier," Eric observed after tasting it. "I like it, but the person I'm buying it for might prefer the first one."

"This grape tends to be a bit more acidic. It's great with fruit or desserts."

"Maybe I should take one of each. I can always keep the drier one for myself."

"It never hurts to have a few bottles on hand in case of unexpected guests or a hard day at work," Liam said. "I'll take two of the second one."

Shannon shook her head as she grinned at Liam. "You and your 'unexpected guests.' How often does that *really* happen to you?"

Liam shrugged. "Not often, but I've also never been caught without a bottle of wine when I needed one. It pays to be prepared."

"Let's try the rosé first," Erik suggested. "I've never been a fan, but Shannon hasn't steered me wrong yet."

"It is a good rosé," Liam replied. "I have a couple of bottles of it at home already, but I won't say no to a glass since Shannon's pouring."

"It sounds like you have quite a wine cellar," Erik said, taking the glass Shannon offered. "I wouldn't have guessed you were an oenophile."

"It's my one vice," Liam admitted. "I have a small cellar, enough to keep a dozen or so bottles. Between us, Kate and I usually split a bottle or two a week, but it's nice to have extras on hand so we can choose something that goes with dinner instead of having to run out at the last minute to buy something."

"Because you've never run in here asking for something to go with a particular dish," Shannon teased.

"It's a *small* cellar," Liam repeated.

"Since it's not quite as convenient for me to run in whenever I need a bottle, I think I'll take a few of each of these," Eric said. "I have a feeling I'll appreciate a cool glass of wine more than once this summer."

"What part of town do you live in?" Liam asked. "I know you work near the Galleria."

"I have an apartment in Meyerland. The complex has a workout room on-site, which is convenient since I'm more likely to use it than if I had to drive to a gym, and the commute to the Galleria isn't bad. Of course, even Houston traffic isn't as bad as LA, but I wanted something that wouldn't involve an hour drive each way." It was getting easier to talk about LA without Mark's shadow materializing. The new friends he'd made through Out and About deserved at least some of the credit for that. "What are your plans for the weekend?" he asked. "Something big, or are you looking forward to a chance not to have to deal with lots of people needing your attention?"

"Kate's new girlfriend, Miri—you might remember her from the wine tasting. Tall, long black hair, gorgeous dark skin—is coming over for dinner. We'll probably pick up Goode Company barbecue. I'm a decent cook, but I don't have the patience for barbecue."

Erik laughed. "Up in Minnesota, 'barbecue' meant sloppy joes on hamburger buns, and it wasn't much of a thing in LA, but I've acquired a taste for smoked brisket and sausage since moving to Texas."

"Yeah, Texas barbecue is a food group unto itself. As hot as it gets here, you'd think a meal with that much meat would be a winter dish, but it's definitely a sign summer is here," Liam said. "I mean, we eat it all year round, but if you asked people to associate it with a holiday, it would be Fourth of July or something like that."

"Billy—he's my admin at B&F—has his own smoker. He's been bragging all week about the spread he's putting on tomorrow. And I'm sure his wife is busy getting all the side dishes and desserts together. That's why I wanted to bring her a wine I'm sure she'll enjoy."

"She'll appreciate that," Liam said. "I can't imagine putting all that together from scratch."

"We never went to a party empty-handed when I was growing up." Erik grinned. "But I don't know how Texans would deal with a tater tot hot dish or ambrosia salad. I thought wine would be a safer choice."

Liam laughed. "You're probably right." He glanced down at his watch. "Damn, I'm going to be late. Will I see you at Archway Gallery in a couple of weeks?"

"I'm looking forward to it, even if I haven't been able to talk Travis into absorbing a little culture." Erik picked up his bottle of tempranillo. "Shannon, I'll take two bottles of each of the wines we tasted too. Liam, enjoy your weekend. I'll see you at the gallery."

Liam snorted. "Good luck with that. Kate certainly never managed to get him anywhere near culture."

"He doesn't know what he's missing. Say hello to Kate for me." Erik settled up at the front counter and hefted the carton of wine, smiling at Liam's cheery wave as he headed to his car. Running into a friend was a great way to start the long weekend.

CHAPTER 13

LIAM SNAGGED a glass of champagne from a passing waiter and tipped it in Kate's direction at five minutes to seven. She'd been right about both the overall growth of Out and About and about the benefits of having events to appeal to a variety of attendees. He'd been thrilled when Erik said he hadn't managed to convince Travis to come to the gallery exhibit, but a few days later Travis's name had shown up on the list. Liam couldn't decide what to make of that. Nothing in their conversation at the Wine Cellar had suggested they were together, but if they weren't together, how had Erik convinced Travis to attend? Kate hadn't managed to drag him to anything like this even when she'd had sex to bargain with.

He pushed the thought aside as the front door opened and their first guest—someone new—walked in. He fell into the routine of explaining the name tags. He could wonder about Erik and Travis on his own time.

He didn't have to wonder for long. Ten minutes later, Erik and Travis walked in together. *If they were* together, *Erik would have said something about Travis going to the barbecue with him*, Liam reminded himself.

"Good to see you both," Liam said, nodding toward the name tags but not bothering with his usual spiel. Erik and Travis both knew the routine by now.

"Wouldn't miss it." Erik filled out both name tags and handed one to Travis, a white one, much to Liam's relief. "I had to do a little arm twisting to get this one to come along, though."

"If they served beer and nachos instead of champagne and tidbits…." Travis shrugged. "We're going to have to find somewhere to eat after this is over."

Liam met Erik's gaze and rolled his eyes. Erik just shrugged in reply, as if to say *What can you do?* The exchange, minor as it was, helped Liam relax. He and Erik were still on the same wavelength. "They're pretty good tidbits. Give them a try before you knock them entirely."

"It's not the taste, it's the amount." Travis's eyes twinkled. "It takes a lot to keep all this going. Bigger is always better, right?"

"As my dad always said about his car engines, size has nothing to do with performance." Erik slapped his name tag on his chest. "Come on, Travis. Let's go absorb some culture."

Liam shook his head as they moved deeper into the exhibit and turned back to the guests filtering in a few at a time. He greeted those he knew by name and welcomed the newcomers. After about half an hour, he'd checked off everyone on the list, so he switched his empty glass out for a full one and went to check on the artists who had agreed to be there for the evening. Everything seemed to be under control, leaving him free to mingle with the guests. He ignored the desire to head straight to where Erik stood talking to one of the artists and focused instead on people he didn't know.

He spent a few moments making sure everyone had met someone to talk to and then headed toward the back to check on the hors d'oeuvres when he realized Erik was standing by himself. "Did Travis abandon you?" he asked.

"Kate wanted to talk with him about something." He tilted his head toward where Liam could see Travis and Kate in an empty corner of the gallery, heads together. For a moment he wondered what Kate could have to talk about with Travis before the penny dropped. *She's giving me time to talk with Erik alone.* Liam wasn't about to let that opportunity go to waste.

"Then I'm glad I saw you. I'd hate to leave a friend standing alone with no one to talk to. How was the cookout?"

"It was good. Carrie liked the wine. I have to thank you for putting the Wine Cellar on my radar."

"You're welcome. Everyone can find the big chain stores, but I prefer local shops whenever possible. You'll find more of them as you get to know the city," Liam said.

"No one will ever mistake me for a native Texan, but I'm starting to feel more at home here."

Liam laughed. "Good luck trying to find a native Houstonian. We'd be lucky if there's one in the group here tonight. A lot of people move here because of the job opportunities."

"It's definitely not for the climate," Erik said with an answering smile. "And I hear I haven't experienced the worst of it yet."

"God, no. It's only June. Wait until August when the temperature at night doesn't even drop below 80 and humidity hovers around 95 percent. We don't get as many days over 100 as Dallas does, but the humidity makes it miserable all the same," Liam replied. "Still, there are compensations. No snow in the winter, no scraping ice off the windshield. We just move our athletics inside in the summer."

"Not that I had to scrape ice off my windshield in LA, but growing up in Minnesota, I know what it's like to have to shovel your way to your car in the morning so you can start it ten minutes before you leave so it can warm up inside. I certainly don't miss it." He shook his head. "I have to admit I had a West Coast opinion of Houston before I got here, though. I wasn't quite expecting cattle roaming the streets, but I never anticipated the quantity and variety of arts here either."

"Houston is incredibly cosmopolitan. We actually have more performing arts venues than anywhere in the US except New York," Liam said. "People forget that the oil industry brought people from all over the world, and all the money that accompanies it. We may be a younger city than Chicago or Boston, but we're no slouches." He laughed a bit. "I might be a bit protective of my adopted city. I could show you some of the smaller places that aren't really good options for Out and About if you're interested."

"I didn't know you weren't from Houston," Erik said. "The way you talk about the city, I would have pegged you as a native."

"I moved here to go to Rice, about fifteen years ago. I grew up in Beaumont, which isn't that far from Houston. We came here a few times a year, usually for school trips or band competitions, and I always loved it, so there was no question I'd stay after I graduated. Even so, I'm not quite a native." He'd clearly taken the wrong tack in asking Erik out. He'd have to try something else.

"Is Kate a native Texan too?" He glanced over his shoulder to where Kate and Travis still stood talking.

"Yes, we grew up together," Liam replied, wanting Erik's attention on him, not on Travis. "Her grandmother lived next door to my parents, and she spent all her time there because her parents worked such crazy hours, and Nana Weaver never minded when I invaded either. She's the sister I never had. What about you? Any relatives besides your aunt?"

"I actually have two brothers and a sister, but they're all older than me and we're scattered all over the country, so I don't see them very often. That's why I appreciate how Out and About helped me connect with people here. I didn't know anyone and hadn't met anyone other than my coworkers. I missed…." He shook his head. "Having friends."

"I get it." Liam set a hand on Erik's forearm. "It's hard being in a new place. Coming here in college helped because everyone was new and expecting to meet people and make friends, but even then, I don't know what I would have done without Kate. And the older you get, the harder it becomes to meet new people. I've said this so often you're probably sick of hearing it, but it's the whole reason we started Out and About. We might not be new to the city, but we were still struggling with a lot of the same issues."

Erik smiled but drew his arm back. "You'd never know. You and Kate are both so at ease with everyone. I'm still working on that."

"That's because they're here. It's not talking to people that's our problem. It's finding people to talk to, you know? Customers at the store or clients at the hotel for Kate are great, they keep us in business, but they aren't friends, much less people we'd be interested in dating," Liam replied.

Erik's expression froze, making Liam wonder if bringing up dating had been a mistake, but he smiled a moment later. "I've met quite a few people I consider friends."

Friends. That was a start, but not entirely what Liam wanted. "But no special someone yet?"

Erik shook his head. "That isn't the purpose of this, right? You've said all along it isn't a matchmaking site. And having friends is important. I wouldn't be enjoying Houston nearly as much if I hadn't met people through your activities."

"It's not a dating site in the sense that we aren't trying to match people the way so many dating sites do," Liam agreed "But at least part of the point of the colored name tags is so that people who are looking for a relationship can meet someone who has a chance of being interested in them." He looked at the blue name tag pointedly before glancing down at his own, also blue. "I know you have plans with Travis after the event tonight, but I was thinking we could get dinner some other night?"

"Did you say dinner?" Liam hadn't seen Travis approaching until he slung an arm over Erik's shoulder. "Good, I'm starving."

He'd think Travis was trying to get revenge on him for something, but Liam had always been sure to take himself elsewhere when Kate and Travis were at the condo together.

"Yes, we've all heard your opinion about the hors d'oeuvres, Travis." Erik nudged him, dislodging the arm Travis had slung around his shoulder. "Sorry, Liam, I need to get this barbarian fed before he starts chewing on the furniture."

Liam forced a laugh because Erik clearly expected one. He only hoped it meant Erik didn't want to say anything in front of Travis, not that he wasn't interested. "He's certainly a barbarian," he replied, giving Travis the stink eye. "Get him out of here. And maybe he'll think twice next time about what he signs up for."

Liam hoped for some final acknowledgment from Erik that he'd heard the invitation and was interested, but Erik's attention was firmly on herding Travis toward the door. Liam should have known that an event would be too chaotic to ask Erik out. He should have gone for it at the Wine Cellar, except Shannon had been there. Next time he wouldn't make the same mistake.

CHAPTER 14

"LUPE TORTILLA still okay with you?" Travis asked as he steered Erik out of the gallery toward his car.

"Sure," Erik answered distractedly, still replaying Liam's words in his head. He wasn't really hungry, so whatever Travis wanted was fine with him.

Travis shot him a glance but didn't say anything during the short drive to the Mexican restaurant other than to grumble about Erik not appreciating a Houston institution. That lasted until they were settled at a table with menus in hand and drinks on the way.

"Who put a stick up Liam's ass?" Travis asked. "I've never been his favorite person, but I thought he liked you."

"I think it was something I said," Erik said slowly. *Or didn't say*, he added to himself. He hadn't missed how Liam's face fell when he'd ignored his offer to show him some of the places in Houston that weren't part of Out and About's schedule. It had taken him by surprise, and he hadn't known how to answer, so he'd changed the subject. That wasn't completely true—he knew how he'd like to answer, but since that wasn't an option, he'd sidestepped.

"What did you say? It couldn't have been that bad. You're too nice of a guy to say something obnoxious," Travis said after the waiter had dropped off their margaritas and left again.

"What does Liam have against you?" Erik countered, taking a sip of the icy drink even though his stomach was roiling uneasily. "Don't tell me you hit on him?" The idea made him even more uneasy.

"No, I dated Kate for a while. It ended with us still on speaking terms, but I think he's never forgiven me for things not working out," Travis replied as he took a sip of his own drink. "Never mind that she was the one who ended things, although if she hadn't, I probably would have before too long. She's great, but we weren't right for each other. But you didn't answer my question."

Erik frowned, though the server delivering their sizzling fajitas saved him from having to answer immediately. He really didn't want to talk about it, but he'd known Travis long enough to realize he wouldn't let go easily. And wasn't this why he'd wanted to make friends in Houston? To have someone to talk to about both good things and bad ones? Even if he wasn't sure himself which category this fell into.

"He… he asked me out," he said softly once the waiter had walked away.

"Damn, you lucky dog. He's a looker for sure. Where are you going? Besides straight to bed."

"Nowhere," Erik said with a sigh. "I didn't answer him. He caught me by surprise, so I commented on something he said instead, and when he asked a second time, you came up."

Travis winced. "Sorry for the cockblock. I would have talked with Kate longer if I'd known. But I'm sure he'll ask again. He's been flirting with you at every event."

"Flirting? No way." Erik shook his head. "I mean, he's talked with me each time, but that's just because I was new to Houston and he wanted to make sure I was meeting people."

"You keep telling yourself that if it helps you sleep at night," Travis said, "but I know flirting when I see it, and he was definitely flirting. He asked you out, didn't he? Now, what are you going to do about it?"

"Nothing." At Travis's incredulous expression, Erik shook his head again. "Liam is my client at B&F. And I don't date clients."

"That would put a damper on things," Travis replied. "It's not that big a deal, is it?"

"I've seen—" Erik forced himself to take a deep breath and lower his voice. He didn't want to dump all his issues on Travis, especially in a public setting, but apparently the scars from Mark's betrayal weren't as healed as he'd thought. "I've seen too many bad situations come out of people mixing their business and personal lives. It's never a good idea, and I like Liam—and Kate—too much to make that mistake."

Travis shrugged. "It's your life, but you're a better man than me for passing up a chance at that ass."

Which would make me no better than if I'd let Jace pick me up at the Six-Pack. Erik gave Travis a wry smile. "If all I'd wanted was a piece of ass, I could have had yours, if you remember."

"You still could," Travis said with a waggle of his eyebrows. "Eat up. Fajitas don't taste as good cold."

They didn't taste like anything but ashes to Erik, but he must have put up enough of a front to fool Travis, since he didn't bring the subject up again.

"I WAS surprised not to see you at the gallery event last weekend," Erik said to Eamon after his next practice session. They'd gotten into the habit of going out to dinner together at least once a week. "I thought that would be something to interest you."

"It's exactly the kind of thing that interests me," Eamon said. "I'm a regular patron of Archway Gallery, but I had a departmental function I couldn't get out of. Did you see anything that caught your eye?"

Erik could feel his cheeks heating and hoped it was too dark under the streetlights for Eamon to see it. "I really liked the work of several of the artists. I was thinking of going back to see about maybe picking something up for my apartment. But it wasn't really Travis's thing, so we didn't stay very long."

Eamon laughed. "I can't believe you convinced him to go in the first place. How do you feel about Indian tonight? And then you can tell me about what just made you blush."

"Indian sounds great. I assume you know someplace nearby?" Maybe by the time they got to the restaurant, Eamon would forget about the rest of his comment.

"Yes, there's a lovely North Indian restaurant in the Village," Eamon replied. "We could even walk, if it's not too warm for you."

"I might say no if it was the middle of the day, but it's cooled off enough for us to walk. Maybe I'm starting to get used to the heat."

Eamon laughed again. "Tell me that in August."

They walked across campus and into Rice Village in companionable silence. The host at Shiva seated them immediately and left them to peruse the menu. "The lamb korma is excellent, as are the chana masala and the malai kofta if you don't want meat. I eat here pretty regularly, so I can tell you about most of the dishes."

"Chana masala and maybe some aloo gobi. You're welcome to share if you'd like. I think the best part of eating Asian food is being able to try several different dishes in one meal."

"Definitely," Eamon said. "I'll get the malai kofta because it really is my favorite, and we can share the three. That will be more than enough food for the two of us with plenty to take home for lunch tomorrow. Now, what happened at the gallery show?"

Eamon might be less blunt than Travis, but he was no less dogged. And Erik had the feeling he'd be more understanding than Travis had been. "Liam asked me out."

"That's wonderful," Eamon said. "Such a nice young man, and so serious about things. He's an old soul. Where are you going?"

"Nowhere. I know, Travis already told me I'm an idiot for passing up the chance," Erik said before Eamon could speak.

"That's perhaps a stronger term than I would have used, but that's not important. If you aren't interested in him, you aren't interested. Or is something else going on here? Something I've missed?"

"It isn't that I'm not interested," Erik admitted. "But since I didn't answer him either time he offered, he probably regrets asking in the first place."

"Perhaps," Eamon replied, "but if you're interested, let him know. He cared enough to ask you twice. I'm sure he'd be willing to give you a second chance."

Before Erik could answer, the waiter arrived to take their order. Once he'd set their glasses of water on the table and promised to bring their food soon, Erik decided talking to Eamon might help. "Travis says Liam's been flirting with me. I'm not sure he's right, but maybe I just didn't let myself see it because… well, I noticed him the day he came in to the office to talk about cashing in some of his investments to help finance Out and About. Which makes him a client, and I don't date clients."

"That's reasonable," Eamon said. "If Travis is right and he's been flirting with you, you need to tell him that. Gently, of course, but you shouldn't lead him on. That said, we both know chances at happiness are rare, and if he's as interested in you as you are in him, you owe it to yourself to see issues as problems to solve rather than roadblocks."

"I've seen too many instances where someone dating a client or a coworker led to disaster." Erik took a sip of water, but it didn't ease the burn in his throat. "My first job after college was a small, family-run firm. The owner and his wife seemed happily married, but I'd been there about a year when he started an affair with one of the female reps. When the wife found out, she filed for divorce, and the company wound up being liquidated so they each got a share of the proceeds."

"That's a sad situation for sure, but it's not necessarily typical," Eamon replied. "And if I learned anything from my life with Patrick, it's that you have to take your happiness where and when you find it. Solutions, Erik. That's what you have to focus on."

"It's not just that, Eamon." He took a breath, but the pain still cut into him. "I told you I'd been in a relationship in LA that didn't work out. Mark—my ex… I found out he was cheating on me. With one of my clients."

Eamon grimaced. "That certainly complicates things now, but is the issue really the client part or the cheating part? Would you be any less hurt if Mark had cheated on you with someone else?"

Erik shook his head. "I don't know. Maybe. At least I wouldn't have felt as if I'd lost both my partner and my sense of security at the office. The client pulled his account when he found out Mark and I were… together. Of course, I broke things off with Mark, and he resigned from the firm soon after that. I started second-guessing all my business relationships, wondering if the guy I found out about had been the only one. When our branch manager here in Houston retired, I jumped at the chance to get out of LA, but if that hadn't happened, I might have left the firm anyway. They couldn't move on while I was there, and neither could I."

"And security is important to you. I can't tell you what to do, Erik. It's your life, not mine. Patrick wasn't a client, he was a colleague, and we had a lot of people question that as well, especially thirty years ago when it was a lot harder to be open about being gay. We hadn't come to Rice yet. That happened later, actually, because we weren't sure we'd be able to keep our jobs and be together. So I do know a portion of what you're feeling, and for me, that loss of security was worth the life Patrick and I had together. But that's me. You have to decide what's most important for you."

"I've never seen a relationship with a coworker or a client end well. It will either cause problems on the job while it lasts or lead to all kinds of ugliness when it ends." He was the poster boy for that, though Eamon didn't know the half of it.

"You really should discuss it with Liam," Eamon replied. "After all, he's involved in this too."

"A part of me thinks it would be a good idea to stop going to Out and About events so I wouldn't have to face him again," Erik admitted.

"I know that would be childish, and I'm not willing to give up the enjoyment I get and the friends I've made through it. But I don't want things to be awkward with Liam either, and if he asks me out again and I turn him down, I'm afraid they will be."

"All the more reason to talk to him," Eamon said. "And things might be awkward for a bit, but you're both adults, and worst-case scenario, as Out and About continues to grow, there will be plenty of people for both of you to talk to without having to worry about talking to each other."

"I know you're right," Erik answered, and just then the waiter arrived with a tray full of steaming dishes, and he forced himself to put the topic aside so he could enjoy the meal.

ERIK'S PHONE rang as he walked in the door from work a few days later. He tossed his messenger bag on the couch and looked to see who was calling him. He hoped it wasn't Travis calling to cajole him into going out. He really just wanted a quiet night in. When he saw his aunt's name instead, he smiled and slumped onto the couch as he answered.

"Hi, Aunt Marjorie."

"Hello, sweetheart. I haven't talked to you in a few weeks. How are you doing?"

"I'm good," Erik answered automatically. "Things are busy at work, prepping for the annual meeting. We'll have some strong results to share. How are you?"

"I'm well. Enjoying the weather. I've been out in the garden trimming back all my roses and putting in the annuals, although this may be the last year I do. Maybe some hydrangeas instead, so I have flowers all summer without the work of planting new things. I'm not as young as I used to be. What about outside of work? Are you finding ways to meet people?"

"It's just as well I don't have a garden with my apartment," Erik said, though he'd always enjoyed helping his aunt with hers, especially the small plot she devoted to fresh tomatoes and other vegetables. "It's already getting so hot here that anything I'd plant would wither away."

"Erik, love, you avoided the question. You only do that when something is bothering you. Is something wrong?"

Erik ran a hand through his hair. It seemed everyone wanted to talk about his social life lately. Even Billy had teased him when he'd changed from his business suit into something more casual before leaving work for the gallery reception last week. "I told you about the group I joined, Out and About?" he reminded her. "They sponsor a different event every month, and I've made several friends through them."

"Yes, you mentioned it. It sounds like quite a bit of fun, actually. Ah, if only I were twenty years younger, I might go and meet someone myself. What did they do this month?" Marjorie asked.

"A private reception at a gallery featuring local artists. You would have enjoyed it. And you're not too old to go out and meet people yourself, you know."

"I actually joined a bridge club again—and they all commented on the ring you gave me, and how lucky I was to have such a devoted nephew. I'm not the hermit you were trying to turn into. And the gallery sounds fascinating. When I come to visit this winter, you can take me to see it. I'd like to meet your friends."

"I'm not such a hermit anymore. I'll be able to take you around when you get here." Liam's voice, offering to show him places he hadn't been to in Houston, sounded in his mind, and he fell silent.

"I've been very patient, Erik. What's bothering you? You don't have to hide from me." The compassion in Marjorie's voice reminded Erik of all the times she had stood beside him, supporting him through whatever life had thrown at him—from losing his parents through losing Mark and everything in between.

"I wouldn't dare. You've always seen right through me." He remembered how he'd agonized over how to tell her he was gay, only to find she'd known almost before he did. "I think one of the founders of Out and About is interested in me. He's also a client, and after Mark…."

"Oh, Erik," Marjorie said with a sympathetic sigh. "I can only imagine how that makes you feel, but you are not Mark. You're a good man, unlike that worm you were involved with in Los Angeles, so I know whatever you decide to do, it will be the right thing. Just ask yourself this, though. What do you want? In an ideal situation—and yes, I know this is anything but ideal—but in an ideal situation, what would you want?"

Erik had done his best not to let himself think about Liam in any romantic sense, not that he'd always been successful. "If he were just another guy I'd met at an event, I'd go out with him. He's kind and intelligent and good-looking, and I'd like to get to know him better. But I swore after Mark that I wouldn't make the mistake of dating a client."

"I know you did, but that wasn't what I asked. I asked what you wanted, not just from him but in general. Every time you talk about Out and About, you talk about wanting to make new friends, which you know I think is a wonderful idea. Are you looking for another serious relationship? Or do you need more time?"

As much as Marjorie assured him he could tell her anything, he couldn't bring himself to admit he'd turned down offers for no-strings-attached sex because they felt empty. "The way things ended with Mark hurt, and in retrospect I can see we weren't the best match, but I want what I'd hoped we were building—a committed partnership. I had great examples in my parents, and you and Uncle Russ, and I don't want to settle for anything less. It's just my luck that the first guy to light the same spark in me that Mark did is off-limits." He shook his head, though he knew his aunt couldn't see it. "Besides, I have no idea if Liam wanted more than a date. I haven't seen him with anyone, but that may not mean anything. He could be seeing plenty of guys outside Out and About events."

"You have to follow your conscience," Marjorie said, "and you have a good one. The only way to get the answer to your questions is to ask him, but asking at all implies an interest in possibly pursuing something with him if the answers are what you want to hear. I'm not going to tell you what to do because you don't need me to. I'll just say this: don't lead him on. And, well, you know this, but you can call me anytime you need to talk. About anything."

For a moment Erik felt like a teen again, pouring his adolescent woes into his aunt's understanding ear. "Have I told you lately how lucky I am to have you in my life?" he said. "We need to get you to Houston so you can give me one of your hugs. They always make everything better."

"I can be on a flight tomorrow if that's what you need," she offered. "My bridge club can do without me for a few days."

"I wouldn't be selfish enough to take you away from your ladies just because I need a hug. I'd rather bring you down when it means getting you out of bad winter weather. Just save them up for me because when you do come to visit, I plan to collect."

"It's a promise."

Erik smiled as they said their goodbyes and set the phone on the couch next to him. Talking with Marjorie was always bittersweet, since it left him missing her, though he couldn't have the life he lived now if he'd stayed in Minnesota. And other than his loneliness, he was happy with his life. Making friends like Kurt and Travis and Eamon had gone a long way toward remedying that. Shouldn't that be enough? Besides, it was likely Liam would take Erik's avoidance as lack of interest and he was worrying about nothing. He could go to the next Out and About event, and Liam would chat with him like he did with everyone else, and that would be that.

And only Erik would know how much he wished it could be more.

CHAPTER 15

LIAM DOUBLE-CHECKED his calculations because he didn't want to bring them to Kate without being sure, but when the numbers came up the same, he grinned and hit Print.

"Katie, darling," he called. "Do you have a few minutes?"

"It depends on what time you want dinner," Kate replied from the other room. Liam laughed and grabbed the papers from the printer.

"Dinner can wait. This is important." He walked into the kitchen and pulled her into a modified dance hold to waltz her around the room.

"I take it the numbers look good?" Kate asked after a short struggle over who would lead that ended with her dropping Liam into a dip.

"*So* good." He straightened and handed her the papers. "Two events a month is easy. We could maybe even look at three, if one of them didn't have a lot of overhead—like the softball game. Renting the venue space is the biggest variable in event costs. Food and drinks are fairly consistent per person from event to event."

Kate studied the numbers for a minute and broke into a huge grin. "I knew we could make this work! Look how the attendee count has been growing, even though we haven't spent anything on advertising. Just think what could happen if we did more than free ads and word-of-mouth recommendations."

"Exponentially," Liam replied, matching her grin. "Time to put on your thinking cap. We need more events if we're going to commit to twice a month. We could start looking at attending some of the pro sporting events. The Astros are playing now, and after their World Series win, people want to attend their games. I was also thinking about experience-type events. Horseback riding, hot-air ballooning, parasailing, hang gliding, that sort of thing. We'd see if we could get special group pricing, and then the cost would be whatever that is plus a little extra for food and drinks."

"We can work out a budget aiming for one low-overhead event and one costlier one a month." Kate's expression grew thoughtful. "It could be interesting to analyze where the people who've come to the various events live. I suspect a good number in West U and Montrose—the word-of-mouth thing and the flyers we put up around the Rice campus. If we use some of the advertising money we built into the budget, we could target some other areas to widen our reach in the community."

"That's a good idea. We've had great Facebook interaction and sharing. We could look at some targeted ads there too. I think we can narrow it down by location as well as by interests, so we wouldn't be getting hits from people who live too far away to actually attend an event. What do you think about sending out a survey to people who've attended at least one activity asking for feedback on the events but also on whether they've met people? If we can claim success in people meeting, even if it's anecdotal, that's also something we can use in our promotions." Liam grabbed a pen and flipped over one of the financial sheets to jot down notes.

Kate nodded. "Ask about the type of events they're interested in attending too. Though I think we should be careful about how we promote the 'meeting people' aspect. We don't want to come across as just another dating site. The feel I get from talking with people is that they like that there's no pressure to hook up with someone."

Liam didn't flinch despite the pinch in his heart at Kate's comment. He'd met someone, but it hadn't managed to go where he wanted it to. Not yet, anyway. He wasn't giving up hope until he got a firm no from Erik. "That's a good point. Just because we started it because we were having trouble meeting people doesn't mean everyone who attends feels the same way, although meeting people doesn't have to mean dating. Maybe a more open-ended question. Something about whether their expectations of the event were met and how or how not. That would let people tell us what they hoped to get out of coming as well as whether we were successful in providing it." Liam added to his notes, amending the question about meeting people.

"Are you up for putting in twice as much work every month?" Kate asked. "Double the planning, twice the time commitment for the events themselves, and even more participant inquiries to deal with? Plus researching and setting up an advertising strategy… it's going to take some serious extra hours. It might not leave much time for a social life."

Liam snorted. "You know I don't have a social life to begin with. I haven't had a date in…. God, I don't even know when I last had a date." He scowled at the thought of why he still didn't have a date. One more thing to blame on Travis. "At least our events get me out of the house and interacting with people. My next set of numbers to run is how much of a cut in income I could take if I stopped having expenses associated with working somewhere else—gas, work clothes, eating lunch out, that sort of thing. Unfortunately being the store manager makes it hard to cut back hours slowly, but that way we'll have a goal to work toward."

"Right," Kate said with a grin. "Giving up our day jobs to focus a hundred percent on Out and About."

"And not a moment too soon," Liam replied. "And then maybe we'll have time as well as opportunities for a social life."

"I thought you were going to make your move on Erik at the gallery. I managed fifteen minutes of civilized conversation with Travis to give you a chance to talk with him. Don't tell me you chickened out?"

"No, I didn't chicken out. I just… didn't get an answer. It's like he didn't even hear me ask." Liam still couldn't figure out what had happened except that he didn't have a date with Erik. "We were talking, it was going great. I slipped in an offer to show him around Houston more, and then… nothing. He went right on with the conversation like those words hadn't even come out of my mouth. And then Travis came over right as I asked a second time and dragged him off."

"I kept him occupied as long as I could, but you know Travis. Short of getting physical, there wasn't much else I could do, and I wasn't going down that road again even for you. Besides, I don't get to spend enough time with Miri as it is."

"Yeah, yeah, rub it in," Liam drawled, happy to move the conversation away from his failed attempt to ask Erik out. "Did you get to spend some time with her?" Miranda, he'd learned, was doing her residency in sports medicine at Houston Methodist, and her frequent calls kept her from making all the events.

"Not enough, but we're going to see the Astros play next week. I've got a meeting with the group sales director before the game to talk about renting one of the luxury suites for an event, so it'll be a working date, but we had to schedule around Miri's rotation at the hospital."

"As long as she doesn't mind sharing you with work, I'll just be grateful for your efficiency. Hopefully I'll be able to find a little time with Erik at the next event so I can try asking again."

"Why don't you give him a call?" Kate suggested again. "We've both seen how hard it is to have a meaningful conversation at an event.

We have too many responsibilities and too many other people we have to interact with. It's almost impossible to spend any significant time with just one person."

She was certainly right about the challenges of spending much time with any one person during an event, but he still felt skeevy about using confidential information for anything other than business. "You sure it wouldn't be unethical to pull his private number from our business files? I don't want it to feel like I'm stalking him."

"You have his business card from when you cashed in some of your portfolio, don't you? Call him at work since you don't want to use his home number."

"I could do that," Liam said. "It would still feel a little funny, calling him at work about a personal matter, but at least it wouldn't feel like I'm stalking him." Now he just had to convince himself what happened at the gallery was a matter of miscommunication and being interrupted. Then again, if he called and Erik said no, at least he'd know and would be able to move forward.

"So do it." Kate tapped the papers Liam had printed out. "Because both our lives are about to get a lot busier."

LIAM STARED down at the business card in his hand, the one Erik had given him months earlier. He still felt odd about calling Erik at work for a personal matter, but it was the only contact information Erik had provided him personally. If he was going to do this without abusing his own professional ethics, this was the only way. He scrubbed a hand over his face, took a deep breath, and dialed the number on the card.

"Bauer and Fitzroy, Erik Jansen speaking."

"Hi, Erik, it's Liam Gruene. I'm sorry for calling you at work, but I work the closing shift tonight, so I'm not at the store to get your cell number."

"Liam, hello." Erik was clearly surprised to hear from him. "Is this about your portfolio? I didn't think… I hope you don't need to withdraw more funds?"

"No, everything is going great financially. Out and About is doing better than we projected, and we're actually going to expand the number of events we offer each month. I had a more… personal reason for calling. We got interrupted at the gallery, and I was hoping we could continue our conversation sometime. Maybe over coffee?"

Erik was silent for a moment. "When did you want to meet?"

Liam pumped his fist but kept his voice level as he replied. "What about Friday after work? We don't have an Out and About event, so I don't have plans."

"I can do that." Erik still sounded tentative. "Would you like to meet at Agora again? Or is there somewhere else you'd prefer?"

"I'll never say no to Agora," Liam replied, pushing aside the worry at Erik's lack of enthusiasm. He'd deal with that when they actually got together. "Or there's a coffee bar called Minuti Coffee on Westheimer that would be closer to your office."

"Let's go with Minuti, then. If I leave the office at five, it should take about half an hour for me to get there. Will that work for you?"

Liam took a minute to calculate his schedule for Friday and the distance between his store and the Galleria. "That should be okay. If I'm a few minutes late, it just means traffic is worse than usual. Don't give up on me if that happens."

Erik chuckled softly. "Even in the short time I've lived in Houston, I've learned never to count on expected travel times. If I get there first, I promise to wait for you if you'll extend the same courtesy to me."

"Of course," Liam said with a sharp laugh. Houston traffic was notoriously unpredictably "And if you've got somewhere to note it down, I'll give you my cell number. That way you can reach me if you need to."

"Go ahead." After Liam gave him the number, Erik said, "I should give you mine again too, so you have it in your cell phone in case something comes up and you have to cancel."

Liam programmed Erik's number into his phone, not that he was planning on canceling. But this way he'd have Erik's personal number and wouldn't have to feel bad about calling again. "Thank you. I'm looking forward to it already."

"I'll see you on Friday, then."

Liam ended the call and slumped back against his headboard, a huge grin making his cheeks hurt. Erik had agreed to a date. Sure, it was just coffee, but it was a chance to spend time together without Travis, or Liam's responsibilities to Out and About, interrupting. If coffee went well, they could easily stretch it into dinner. Minuti just had sandwiches and pastries, but the Galleria area was full of restaurants. They could find somewhere with a table for two. And if it went really well, he could suggest something else after dinner. Dancing or a movie or even inviting Erik back to the townhouse for a nightcap.

That probably wouldn't be the best idea without warning Kate ahead of time, but if it got to that point, he'd text her with an IOU for a favor in the future. She'd enjoy having that to hold over his head.

Now he just had to make it until Friday.

LIAM ARRIVED at Minuti five minutes before he was supposed to meet Erik, a feat he was quite proud of with Friday rush-hour traffic. He took a minute to check his appearance before climbing out of the car and going inside. He grabbed a table to wait for Erik, not wanting to order until Erik got there so he could pay for both drinks.

A few minutes later, Erik walked in. Liam had seen him in business attire the day he'd withdrawn the money to invest into Out and About, but he'd gotten used to seeing him in casual wear. The charcoal-gray suit he wore over a crisp white shirt—surprisingly unwilted after a day in the June heat—and subtly patterned blue tie was somehow more enticing than seeing him in shorts and a T-shirt for the softball game. Liam could imagine slowly peeling off each layer for his delectation. Which was a bad idea when he had to stand and wave Erik over to the table.

"Hey, Erik," Liam said when Erik joined him. He forced himself not to lick his lips at how good Erik looked. He didn't want to make Erik uncomfortable on their first date. "I haven't ordered yet. I wanted to wait for you. What's your pleasure? Black again? Or something different this time?"

"Just black, whatever the coffee of the day is," Erik said. "I told you I was boring."

"I'll be right back." Liam joined the fortunately short line and placed their orders, a Sumatra Mandheling for Erik and a doppio con panna for himself. The barista prepared them quickly, leaving him free to return to the table with the two cups balanced on a tray.

"This is harder than it looks," he joked as he set Erik's cup in front of him. "Can you tell I never waited tables in college?"

"I'll leave you a good tip," Erik said, a smile relaxing the lines of his face. "I never worked in food service either, but I have every appreciation for people who do." He took a sip of the coffee, and his body language relaxed even further. "This is really good. If they sell beans, I'll have to pick up a bag before I go."

"They do," Liam said, relaxing as Erik did. He could do this. He could sit with Erik and chat, get to know him a little better, and work his way up to another date. "I'll drink coffee from just about anywhere as long as it has enough cream and sugar, but I prefer local shops—or at least local chains—like this one to huge international conglomerations. How was your week?"

"Busy." Erik took another sip of coffee. "The firm holds an annual meeting for all the branches in a few weeks, and we have to put together a presentation to review our results and any plans we have for the next year, so I've been working on that on top of the usual business calls and client meetings. What about you? Summer is usually a slower season for retail, isn't it?"

"Yes. We plan sales—Fourth of July is coming up—to try to draw people in, and we usually get spikes around that, but it won't really pick back up until tax-free weekend in August," Liam said. "Not that tax-free weekend applies to us, but it definitely marks an annual uptick in sales again. I can work with that, though. It gives me more time to focus on Out and About."

"You'll need it if you're going to add more events each month."

"That's for sure," Liam replied. "We're trying to keep things balanced. Do one with low overhead and easier planning—something like the softball game—and then another one like the gallery event this month. That way we aren't straining our resources too quickly. And we have plans to start advertising. But I didn't really ask you for coffee to talk about Out and About. We keep getting interrupted at events, and I enjoy spending time with you."

Erik had visibly relaxed as they drank their coffee and chatted, but he paused with his cup in midair. "My social life has certainly improved since I joined Out and About. Eamon and I have dinner or drinks together most nights when I go to Rice to play piano, and I get together with Kurt and Travis every so often for drinks or to watch a game or something like that. And of course when I run into you."

"Not that I don't enjoy running into you, because I always enjoy seeing you," Liam said, forging ahead. "But I was hoping for something a little more planned. I heard about a new South African place that just opened nearby and is getting rave reviews. We could give it a try together. Maybe next weekend?"

Erik sat still and silent for a moment and then shook his head. "Thank you for the offer, but I don't think that would be a good idea, Liam." He drank the last of the coffee and set down the empty cup. "I should probably get going. Thanks for introducing me to a great local place for coffee." He stood, reached out a hand as if to shake but drew it back before Liam could react, then turned and left the shop.

Liam watched him go in shocked silence. Everything had been going so well, he'd thought. Erik had sat and chatted with him, right up until he'd invited him out again. Had he not been clear enough about the coffee being a date? Or maybe he'd misread Erik's signals all along. Maybe Erik really wasn't interested in him beyond the occasional chat when they ran into each other somewhere or when Out and About threw them together. That stung, but Liam was a big boy. If that was the way Erik felt, Liam would deal with it.

CHAPTER 16

"I DON'T know why I let you talk me into this," Erik grumbled as Travis negotiated the Saturday-morning traffic on I-45 early in July. "I have work I could be doing to prep for my presentation at the annual meeting."

"And you have work hours Monday through Friday to put it together," Travis countered. "Besides, I don't know what you're bitching about. I thought you liked swimming. Didn't you tell me you were on the swim team in high school?"

"Schlitterbahn isn't exactly an Olympic swimming pool. It's more like a theme park where the roller coasters have all flooded."

"Yeah, but that's what makes it so much fun," Travis insisted. "Not to mention the chance to look at cute guys in wet bathing suits. You can't tell me that isn't worth the price of admission."

"And a million kids running around so you won't be able to do anything about it." Not that he'd do anything in a public place anyway, and besides, the only person he was at all likely to be tempted by was off-limits. And if he told himself that enough times, maybe it would be easier to accept. "Eamon will be in his element, though."

"He's an old queen, that's for sure," Travis said. "And the kids won't be in the reserved group area, so we'll have at least some adult-only time. Someone could catch your eye enough for you to make a first move."

"Not likely," Erik muttered. Travis had worn down his resistance to attending the Out and About event at the water park in Galveston, but the ninety-minute drive from Houston gave him plenty of time to regret giving in. At least, from what he'd seen on the Schlitterbahn website, the park had several areas, each with attractions such as water slides, a lazy river, a zip line, and something billed as "the world's tallest water coaster." There was even a swim-up bar in one section. Surely he'd be able to avoid Liam in all that space.

Travis rolled his eyes but didn't keep the argument going. "Fine, then I'll make enough moves for both of us."

Erik could imagine that easily enough. Maybe he'd hang out with Eamon so he didn't have to witness it. Then again, Eamon would probably be just as bad. So would Kurt. And how could he blame them? The whole point of Out and About's activities was to help like-minded people get together. It wasn't Travis's or Kurt's or Eamon's fault that his own hang-ups would keep Erik from putting any moves on the one person he was attracted to.

Once again, Erik wondered if he'd have been better to drop out of Out and About completely. He'd made several good friends, which was his purpose in joining to begin with. He didn't think any of them would shun him if he stopped going to events. He could still socialize with them individually and not have to deal with the temptation of seeing Liam and having to give him the cold shoulder.

He was still haunted by Liam's face when he'd refused his offer of dinner at the coffee shop. His gut had told him that meeting Liam at all would be a mistake, but he hadn't been able to come up with a good reason to say no. And he'd hoped to at least manage friendship with Liam, since he couldn't have anything more. It had worked with Travis, but he wasn't nearly as attracted to Travis as he was to Liam. They'd been doing well, he thought, their discussion no more fraught than any other, though in retrospect he was sure Travis would have called it flirting. But when Liam had stopped hinting and asked him out again, Erik panicked. After the gallery exhibit, he'd tried to think of polite ways to turn Liam down on the chance that he asked again, but he couldn't remember a single one of them in the coffee shop. He'd gone into his default mode—avoidance. *Flight*, he admitted to himself.

"What's got you brooding over there?" Travis asked. "You're never *this* quiet."

"I should have brought more sunblock. You're supposed to reapply it every couple of hours."

Travis snorted. "Somehow I don't think that's what's bothering you, but if you don't want to talk about it, I'll let it slide. This time."

"Thanks, Travis." Erik managed a smile. It wasn't fair to inflict his bad mood on his friend. "I'm sure you're right and I'll have a great time once we get there."

THE CROWDS were everything Erik had predicted they would be, but when they met up with the rest of the Out and About attendees, Liam and Kate ushered them through a separate group entrance with no waiting.

Erik made sure to stick close to Eamon, Travis, and Kurt so he wouldn't end up near Liam. Fortunately Liam stayed with Kate and didn't try to approach him, and once they were inside, everyone went their own ways with a reminder from Kate that lunch would be served in the group picnic area at one o'clock.

Fortunately, Erik's hope proved accurate. While Eamon had taken a turn down one of the smaller water slides and declared he would be far happier "seeing the sights" from a float on the lazy river, Kurt insisted they had to try each of the park's attractions at least once. Erik had followed along and found himself losing some of his anxiousness with each splash-filled landing. Travis kept up a running commentary of the best-looking eye candy of both sexes, which Kurt was happy to join. As they waited in line for each slide, Erik couldn't help scanning the crowds for Liam—so he could stay out of his way, he told himself. He spotted him several times, even though his brightly patterned pink-and-purple board shorts, which would have stood out in most other places, were just another spot of color here. As he usually did, Liam flitted between groups of attendees, spending a bit longer with the first-timers but with a welcoming smile for everyone. But he hadn't managed to greet Erik and his friends. *Probably avoiding me, not that I blame him.* From a vantage point while they waited in line for the Massiv Monster Blaster, the park's signature water coaster, Erik spotted Liam chatting with Eamon, who'd apparently traded his float for a lounger alongside Whitewater River. Eamon waved a languid hand, and even across the distance Erik could see Liam throw his head back and laugh. Not even the rides' twists and drops generated as much of a pang in his stomach as the realization that he'd found what he'd been looking for and couldn't act on it.

Kurt stepped up next to him. "What are you—oh. Nice view there." He elbowed Erik in the ribs. "You should totally go for it."

"What about you?" Erik countered. Sidestepping was becoming second nature, he reflected. "See anything that appeals to you?"

"Have you been listening today?" Kurt retorted. "Half the people in the park appeal to me. If you're asking about people I've met through Out and About, yeah, maybe, but I doubt he's interested in return."

"Who?" Erik asked. He'd been so wrapped up in his own head that he'd missed the signs that Kurt might have found someone. "Whoever it is, he'd be crazy not to be interested in a great guy like you."

Kurt bumped their shoulders together. "That's nice of you to say, but we both know it doesn't work that way. If it did, you'd be over there with Liam right now."

As if that were the problem, Erik thought, but better that Kurt thought Liam wasn't attracted to him than urging him on the way Travis had. "It's Liam's job to be interested in everyone. It's part of what makes Out and About so welcoming." And if Kurt had noticed him watching Liam, he'd do better to forget his own attraction and try to figure out who'd captured Kurt's fancy. If he couldn't further his own desires, maybe he could at least help Kurt pursue his.

"You're right. He and Kate have done a great job with everything, not that I'm surprised. Kate has always been a perfectionist, and it's no surprise to find out her best friend is equally detail oriented. I've had a great time at all the events I've attended. I can't tell you how many times I've thanked Martin for bringing me to the first event, even if he hasn't managed to attend any of the others with his insane travel schedule."

Erik vaguely remembered Kurt's friend from the wine tasting, a fair-haired man who'd stood quietly listening at Kurt's side. "You'll have to bring him along the next time he's in town when we get together."

"I'll do that. I keep telling him he'll never have a life outside of work if he doesn't make the time for one, but he never listens." The line for the next water slide inched forward, taking Liam and Eamon out of Erik's line of sight. He relaxed again and pushed the thought of how good Liam looked in a swimsuit out of his head.

Erik lost track of time, but luckily Travis had a waterproof watch and pulled them aside after they'd splashed to the bottom of the ride. "We should probably hold off on getting into another line. It's only just after noon, but we're supposed to meet for lunch at one, and there's no telling whether we might make it down another slide before then."

"Let's kill the time at the swim-up bar over at Wasserfest," Kurt suggested. "We can cool down, and since it's an adults-only area, it might not be as crowded."

"Sounds good to me," Erik agreed. "I'm still not used to being outside for long in this heat, even though the water helps cool things down."

They made their way through the park to the bar area and hopped down into the pool. Being completely submerged took the edge off the midday heat, although Erik already dreaded getting out to go to lunch. "What do you want to drink?" Kurt asked. "First round's on me."

"Whatever they've got on tap," Travis said immediately. "I'm not picky."

"Boring," Kurt teased. "What about you, Erik?"

"What the hell—get me something with an umbrella," Erik said. "Whatever sounds good to you."

A few minutes later, Kurt returned with a cardboard drink carrier. "Shiner Bock for you, Mr. Dullsville," Kurt teased, handing a frosted plastic schooner to Travis. "What'll it be, Erik?" Kurt asked, gesturing to the two remaining drinks—one bright blue, the other a marbled red-and-white frozen concoction, both topped with bright pink paper umbrellas. "Blue Hawaii or Lava Flow?"

The Lava Flow looked like it had coconut milk in it, along with a skewer of pineapple chunks and strawberries. The clear drink might be more refreshing in the unrelenting heat. "I'll try the Blue Hawaii."

The first sip went down like a frozen slushy, cooling Erik from the inside out. He took a bigger sip and grinned at Kurt. "Good choice."

The problem with sweet, slushy, fruity drinks, Erik discovered over the next hour, was that it was too easy to drink them like they were juice, forgetting about the alcohol. He was definitely feeling no pain by the time Travis announced it was almost lunchtime and they should get their sorry asses out of the pool and go see what Liam and Kate had prepared for them this time.

Somehow Erik knew seeing Liam was a bad idea, but with the alcohol keeping the nerves at bay, it sounded like the best thing he'd heard all year.

With Travis leading the way, they made their way through the growing throng of people to a quieter area where several cabanas offered shelter from the midday sun. A spread of salads and sandwiches covered one of the tables, and Kate waved them in with a wide smile, Miranda at her side. "Erik, Kurt, Travis. Grab a plate and help yourself. There are drinks in the tubs in the other cabana."

"You find seats and I'll get us some drinks," Travis offered. By the time they'd found a cluster of open seats at one of the tables, Travis was back with a handful of ice-cold beer bottles. "It was this or soft drinks," he said, plopping one in front of each of them. Erik would rather have had another Blue Hawaii, but when he picked up the sweating bottle and ran it over his forehead, the coolness felt so refreshing that he took a swig.

"This was a good idea after all. I'm glad you talked me into coming," he told Travis.

"You should know by now I'm always right." Travis clinked his bottle against Erik's and Kurt's. "Cheers."

Kurt rolled his eyes but took a sip of the beer and scooted over to make room for Travis next to him. Travis squeezed in so close they had to be touching, which Erik found vaguely interesting in a detached, half-drunk sort of way. He'd have to think more about it when he was sober. He needed food. "What did Kate say they had for lunch?"

"She didn't, but it looks like sandwiches and salads," Travis said, giving him an appraising look. "You'd better eat something to soak up all the alcohol you've been swilling."

Suddenly the drinks he'd downed so quickly made themselves known. "I'd better find a bathroom first."

"I saw one in the walkway just before we got to the cabanas," Kurt offered helpfully.

"Great. I'll be back in a minute." Erik's head spun a little as he stood. He hoped there'd be a water fountain near the restrooms. He needed to do a better job of staying hydrated.

He had almost reached the restroom when he saw the distinctive stripes of Liam's bathing shorts going into the restroom ahead of him. He almost turned around and went back to the table, but he really needed to go, and he could be adult about things.

Liam wasn't standing at one of the urinals, so Erik made his way into the only open stall. Maybe he could hurry and get out before Liam was finished. To that end, he took care of business quickly. The other stall door was still closed when he washed his hands, so he made his exit and stopped for a long drink of water at the fountain outside, grateful for his escape.

"Oh, Erik, I didn't see you." Liam's voice startled Erik enough to make him gag on the water in his mouth. Liam moved to his side and patted his back a couple of times. "Sorry. I didn't mean to make you choke."

Liam wasn't doing anything sensuous, just patting his back, but the touch of his warm hand on Erik's bare skin sent a bolt of pure desire flaring through him. He knew there were reasons he'd been avoiding Liam, but at the moment he couldn't remember a single one of them. He raised a hand to wipe his lips but didn't step away from the fountain, and Liam kept patting his back even though he'd stopped choking. "It wasn't… I must have been drinking too fast," he managed to answer. He wanted to put a hand on Liam's shoulder, to see if his tanned skin, glistening with a light coating of sunscreen, felt as silky as it looked, but he let it drop awkwardly to his side instead. "I should have been taking in more water while we were waiting for the rides."

"It happens," Liam said with a nod. He didn't meet Erik's eyes, but Erik couldn't quite decide if he was avoiding Erik's gaze or checking him out. "It's always a challenge when it's this hot."

Hot didn't begin to describe what Erik was feeling. Wherever Liam's eyes were focused, Erik hoped it wasn't his swim trunks, which were starting to feel decidedly tight. "I suppose you're used to it," he said, just to keep Liam there a little bit longer.

"I'm not sure you're ever used to it, but I'm not surprised by it," Liam replied, his hand still on Erik's back. "Are you enjoying the park?" Erik wasn't sure if he was imagining it, but it felt like Liam was leaning in closer the longer they talked.

"More than I expected," he admitted. Since Liam seemed in no hurry to stop touching him, Erik set a hand on one of Liam's shoulders. He resisted the impulse to stroke—barely. "I haven't come to an event yet that I haven't enjoyed." *Because you're there.*

"That's good," Liam said, his voice low and warm as he leaned toward Erik. "I want you to enjoy what we do."

"I do." Erik assured him, letting his fingers glide over the film of lotion anointing Liam's skin. "Very much."

Liam curled his fingers around Erik's shoulder blade and leaned close enough that their shoulders brushed. The contact of skin on skin arced through him, leaving his head spinning even more than the alcohol had done.

Erik took a deep breath, inhaling the scent of coconut and chlorine and a faint hint of musk from Liam's skin. Liam licked his lips, and the tip of pink tongue peeking between them stole the last of Erik's resolve. He closed the distance between them and touched his mouth to Liam's, gently, tasting iced tea and lemon. He slid his tongue over the moist flesh, thirsty for more, and Liam opened beneath him.

Liam returned the kiss eagerly, meeting Erik's tongue with his own and twining them together. He moaned softly and lifted his other hand to cup Erik's jaw with enough tenderness to ease the rough places in Erik's heart.

Erik drew Liam nearer, caressing the silky skin of his back with both hands, and lost himself in the kiss. Liam pressed even closer, fitting their bodies together from shoulders to thighs, and Erik's cock leaped in response, drawing another low moan from Liam that vibrated against their joined lips.

The sound of raucous laughter drawing near broke them apart. Liam looked up at Erik with flushed cheeks and dilated eyes. "That," he said in a hoarse whisper, "was worth waiting for." He slid his hand down Erik's arm to squeeze his hand. "Maybe we can continue somewhere more private after the event is over."

The cluster of men and women who split around them to enter the appropriate restrooms didn't seem to pay them any attention. He didn't even know if they were part of the Out and About group, but the interruption was enough to yank Erik from the utopia he'd been drifting through to cold reality. What the hell was he doing? "Fuck," he muttered, stepping back and dragging a hand through his damp hair. "I can't do this."

"Well, not here, obviously," Liam replied, "but there's only another hour in the planned activity, and Kate and I drove separately since she had Miranda with her, so we can leave before too long. And then we can do whatever we want."

Erik's traitorous body was all too ready to demonstrate what it wanted, but the small portion of higher brain function that was still operational screamed at him to run. "That shouldn't have happened," he ground out, taking another step away from temptation. "Sorry," he murmured to Liam. "Sorry." He cravenly turned tail and strode up the walkway, determined to get the hell out of the park as quickly as possible. He was halfway to the exit when he remembered he hadn't driven—he'd ridden in with Travis. Given the way the drinks had gone to his head, that was probably a good thing, but now he'd have to hang around until Travis was ready to leave, somehow managing to hide from Liam, and avoid any behavior that would arouse suspicions in his friends or spend the rest of the day hearing them tell him what an idiot he was.

He didn't need to listen to that. He was already more than convinced.

CHAPTER 17

WHAT THE fuck?

Liam stood by the water fountain as Erik all but ran away after their kiss—and damn, what a kiss it had been—but Erik's reaction after left Liam torn between the desire to kiss him again and a deep, urgent need to smack him as hard as he could. Liam still didn't understand Erik's rejection after their coffee date, but he'd tried to respect it. He hadn't called back. He'd left it to Kate to greet Erik and his friends when they arrived. He hadn't sought Erik out during the day at the water park, although he had caught glimpses of him waiting in lines or climbing out of the pools. Despite how good Erik looked in a swimsuit, Liam had kept his distance until he stumbled across Erik outside the restroom. Even then he'd only said something because it would have been rude not to.

Erik was the one who hadn't pulled away, who had continued the conversation and initiated the kiss. Liam hadn't complained since that was what he'd wanted all along, but he hadn't pressured or seduced or whatever. Erik had made the first move. What was Liam supposed to think after that? Erik's tongue down his throat certainly felt like an invitation for more!

Standing there fuming wouldn't solve anything, though, and he had responsibilities to the rest of their guests. He'd put on a brave face and deal with it when the event was over, but if Erik thought he was getting away with this, he had another think coming.

He pasted on his manager smile and headed back to the group picnic area. Most of the guests had finished and wandered back into the park, although Eamon was still sitting there with a glass in hand. "Can I get you anything?" Liam asked.

"I'm quite content to finish my tea before I return to my lounger. I must congratulate you on an outstanding event. The scenery has been quite worth the price of admission." Eamon leaned forward, his brow furrowing. "Has something happened to upset you, my dear boy? That isn't your usually sunny demeanor."

Liam sighed. If Eamon, who only knew him so well, saw through him, Kate would have a field day with him. "Yes, but it's nothing I can do anything about right now. It'll have to wait until the event is over and I cool off enough to decide what to do."

"Not acting in the heat of the moment is wise in most instances, though there are times when it's inescapable." For a moment Eamon's eyes twinkled, but he quickly sobered. "Would this have anything to do with our mutual friend Erik? He appeared a bit flushed when he rejoined Kurt and Travis earlier." When Liam hesitated, he added, "If you don't wish to speak about it, I understand, but I should confess Erik has spoken to me. Of course, I cannot betray any of his confidences, but I can assure you I would hold yours safe as well. And perhaps some of my experience may be of value."

Liam sighed again. He would inevitably go over it with Kate later, but he already knew what she would say. She'd said it when he'd come back from the unsuccessful first date. Maybe Eamon would have something to add. "I like him, and I thought we were becoming friends. We've had coffee a couple of times, and we ran into each other at the Wine Cellar and had a long conversation. But when I suggested dinner, he turned me down. Okay, fine. He's not interested in a date. Then today, after avoiding me all morning, he kissed me. Not that I'm complaining about the kiss itself, but then he ran again with no real explanation. What am I supposed to think? I've got a business to run. I don't have time for this hot-cold shit."

"I don't believe it would be indiscreet to say that Erik is conflicted." Eamon patted the seat beside him. "Please sit for a few minutes. I'm sure Kate has things well in hand."

Liam looked around, but everything was under control, so he took the seat Eamon offered. He wasn't sure what Eamon could or would tell him, but anything would be better than this confusion.

"My advice is to give him time. I'm sure you've noticed that Erik is a master at avoiding questions or situations that make him uncomfortable. If you continue to pursue him, he may feel pressured and retreat even further. The best you can do at the moment is to let him work through his issues at his own pace."

"That's what I thought I was doing," Liam replied. "I haven't called him since the first time. I didn't approach him today. I have done everything I could think of to respect his wishes since he made it clear he wasn't interested in going out with me. And then he kissed me. I mean, I guess that means he isn't as uninterested as he said, but this isn't junior high." He rubbed the back of his neck, ignoring the mixture of sweat and sunscreen that pooled there. "I'd like to think I've made my interest clear, so I guess the ball is back in his court. Is it worth calling or texting him to tell him that? Or is that too much like pursuing him?"

"I suspect that Erik is already regretting his actions." Liam wondered whether Eamon meant the kiss itself or fleeing afterward. "Both his actions," Eamon continued as if reading his thought. "He'll be reproaching himself, and I'm afraid hearing from you would only exacerbate that. I suggest allowing him to regain his equilibrium and approach you again when he's ready."

It wasn't what Liam wanted to hear, but Eamon was probably right. "If he asks and it seems appropriate to say something, you can tell him I'd like him to call me, even if it's to tell me he's decided he doesn't want anything to do with me. At least that way I'll know."

"If I know Erik, he's going to withdraw until he can come to terms with today's events. To use a musical analogy, he's too discordant to sound the notes you're hoping to hear." He patted Liam's hand. "But don't despair, my boy. I've heard Erik play. He may find the right chord yet."

Liam smiled at the musical reference, as Eamon had surely intended, but it gave him hope too. Eamon was a good judge of character. He wouldn't encourage Liam if he thought nothing would ever come of it. "Then I guess I just have to be patient and wait for him to listen to your good advice, since I'm sure you'll give it to him when the circumstances allow." He stood with a nod. "Thank you for listening. I feel a little more like myself now."

"I'm glad I could be of assistance. It's a pleasure to see you smiling again." Eamon stood as well. "And now, I have well-built men to ogle. I'll see you poolside."

Liam laughed at that. Of course Eamon would go back to his ogling. He watched Eamon go and turned back to the group picnic area to make sure everything was wrapped up and cleaned up from their meal. He'd have to decide how long he was willing to wait on Erik to figure out his issues and make up his mind, but he could think about that later. For now he had a job to do.

LIAM'S SHOULDERS slumped as he walked into the townhouse after the outing they'd organized at the Cynthia Woods Mitchell Pavilion as their second July event. The Houston Symphony performance had been fantastic, and attendance had been up. Everyone seemed to have appreciated the cheese-and-charcuterie picnic they'd arranged, and he'd seen more than one couple snuggled up together on blankets during the concert, but Erik hadn't been there. Sure, it had only been two weeks since the event at the water park, and Eamon had made it sound like Erik had quite a lot to work through, but the silence grated on Liam. He wanted to *know*, whether it was good news or bad. The limbo was driving him crazy. Honestly he'd prefer bad news to this. He missed the friendship he'd been building with Erik.

Kate bounced in a few minutes later, having spent the time saying good night to Miranda, no doubt. Liam couldn't begrudge her meeting someone she'd clicked with, but it made Erik's absence all the more hurtful.

"If tonight is anything to judge by, going to two events a month is going to work out just fine," she announced, flopping on the sofa and resting her feet on the coffee table.

"It was a good event," Liam agreed. "And we already have our largest turnout yet signed up for the Night at the Museum in two weeks." Erik's name wasn't on that list either, but Liam pushed that thought aside. Time. He had to give Erik time, both to make a decision and to sign up for the event.

"Don't think I didn't notice your crush wasn't there tonight. Come to think of it, I didn't see much of him after lunch at Schlitterbahn either. What's going on there?"

Liam cringed. He'd avoided telling her what had happened by sheer luck—and her distraction with Miranda—but the time had come to pay the piper. "I wish I knew. He kissed me at Schlitterbahn and then said he couldn't do 'this,' whatever that means, and ran. I haven't heard from him since."

"Screw him, then," Kate said dismissively. "And not in the way you're thinking either." She caught Liam by the chin. "I thought you'd been looking a little down lately, but I figured maybe it was the extra work from adding another event. No one is worth getting yourself down over, Li, not when there are so many more fish in the sea." She patted his cheek. "And swimming into our nets at every event."

"You're right, of course. It's just… I really liked him, Katie." Not to mention the way he'd kissed, like Liam was both the hottest and most precious thing he'd ever seen. "Is it stupid to feel like we broke up when we weren't even together in the first place?"

"Aw, baby." Kate pulled Liam into a hug. "I'm sorry, but if he can't recognize what a treasure you are, he doesn't deserve you, and you shouldn't waste time mourning over him. If he even bothers to show up to another event, he should find you happily on the arm of someone else."

The pet name made Liam smile as he let her comfort him. For not the first time, he wished he could see Kate as something more than the sister he never had. "I guess we'll see who shows up at the museum, because so far, nobody else has caught my eye."

"That's because you haven't been looking. You don't suppose Miri just strolled up to me and asked me out, do you? I spent the time to get to know her and realize how special she is." Kate stroked Liam's hair from his forehead and dropped a kiss there. "You make time to talk with just about everyone. Take a little longer and see if one of them doesn't push your buttons."

"You're right. And the museum is the perfect place to chat with people. Plenty of conversational openers with all the exhibits." He took a deep breath and pushed all thought of Erik and that incendiary kiss out of his mind. It was time to move on.

LIAM GAVE himself one last check in the mirror. Well-cut linen slacks that showed off his ass, check. Snug (but not too snug) polo shirt, check. Artfully tousled hair, check. Welcoming smile… okay, not a grimace, check. He was as ready as he could be. Erik wouldn't be there, although Eamon and Kurt had both signed up for the Night at the Museum, their first August event. He'd greet them as always. He wouldn't ask about Erik. And he'd spend the evening seeing who else he could meet.

And if word got back to Erik about it, that was Erik's problem. He was the one who hadn't called or texted since their kiss. He'd just have to suck it up and deal with having lost Liam.

God, it sucked getting over someone, even someone he'd never really had in the first place.

"Liam, it's time to go. Miri is downstairs waiting for us," Kate called.

Liam switched off the bathroom light and pasted on his best smile. It wouldn't fool Kate, but hopefully it would be enough to keep Miranda from catching on.

"Coming."

"You made me wait for that?" Kate chuckled as Liam walked into the hall. "Maybe you'll meet someone tonight who'd be willing to help you out."

"Ha ha. You're very funny." He gave her a halfhearted glare. "I thought Miri was waiting."

"She knows how important you are to me. Now let me see a real smile before we leave."

Liam gave her his best shot at a smile. If it wasn't the thousand-watt smile that came out when he was truly happy, it was at least real. She could always make him smile, even when he was miserable.

"That's better." Kate beamed back at him. "C'mon, gorgeous. The man of your dreams is waiting for you to find him. And if you don't, you'll always have me."

And that was what gave him the courage to try, and to keep trying. He might not have managed to find the man of his dreams yet, but no matter what happened, Kate would never let him down.

Liam greeted Miranda as he climbed into the back seat of her car, letting Kate sit up front with her girlfriend. The two chatted all the way to the museum, leaving Liam alone with his thoughts in the back seat.

He checked in with the caterers as soon as they arrived at the Houston Museum of Natural Science, knowing Kate would coordinate any last-minute details with the museum staff. By now the caterers knew what to expect from an Out and About event, so he left them to do what they did best and walked back into the entrance hall to get ready to welcome their guests. He knew a lot of them, but a good quarter were new attendees. Maybe he'd find someone in that group who caught his eye.

As he mingled among the guests, he tried to spend a bit more time chatting with each person, even those he'd met before. If no one lit a spark, he learned that Peter volunteered with Meals on Wheels and that Micah was painting a mural on the side of his local elementary school. He'd managed a good thirty minutes of not thinking about Erik until he ran into Kurt and his friend Martin studying an exhibit in the geology hall.

"I didn't know you were interested in rocks, Kurt," Liam said. *I will not ask if he's seen Erik.*

"Martin's the rock hound." Kurt nudged the blond with his shoulder. "He's actually found some fossils on several of our hikes."

"Just ammonites and gastropods," Martin said with a deprecating shrug. "Not hard to find here in any limestone bed in Texas."

"If you know what to look for," Kurt insisted.

"I certainly wouldn't know what to look for," Liam said. He smiled at the pride in Kurt's voice. Martin wasn't Erik, but he was an interesting, attractive man. It wouldn't hurt to get to know him better. "Where do you usually go hiking?"

"Mostly up in the Hill Country," Martin replied. "There are quite a few state parks close enough to drive to for a day of hiking and come back that night, if you don't want to camp. I wouldn't mind camping, but I can't usually talk Kurt into it."

"Not unless it comes with down comforters and room service." Kurt grinned. "What can I say? I appreciate the finer things in life."

"We've been considering a trip to the Hill Country for one of our events," Liam said. "Maybe you can give us some suggestions for places to consider, Martin."

"Sure, if you think it might help. I could write up a few possibilities and email them to you."

"That would be great, although I'd be happy to take you for coffee so we could talk them through in person if you're free," Liam said. "There's so much to be said for the voice of personal experience."

A slight flush ran up Martin's fair cheeks. "I'll be out of town for the next two weeks on business. It's no trouble for me to email you some options. If there's anything special you want the trip to focus on, like climbing or water sports or historical sites, I can narrow down my suggestions even further."

"We haven't gotten that far in our planning," Liam admitted. Martin's blush was charming, and it only added to his attractiveness. This could be worth pursuing after all. "Maybe you could annotate the list, and then if we have questions, I can send them back to you. Or buy you that coffee when you get back in town, if you have time."

"Let me pull together some ideas, and then we can see if anything in particular interests you," Martin said, his gaze moving from Liam back to Kurt.

"Be sure to work in the room service if you expect me to go." Martin rolled his eyes at Kurt's comment, and Kurt grinned. "Or Travis either, for that matter. He's as much of a hedonist as I am."

As far as Liam was concerned, Travis could stay as far away as he wanted. Of course that probably meant he was off consoling Erik somewhere, but that wasn't Liam's problem anymore. "If we do a day trip, we don't need room service. Martin, have a safe trip, and I'll look for your email. Kate is waving at me. I need to go see what she wants."

He excused himself and joined Kate. "What's going on?"

"Nothing. I was giving you a thumbs-up. Who's the cutie with Kurt?"

"His name is Martin. They're friends. He's going to send us some information about places in the Hill Country."

"That's good," Kate said. "Did you ask him out?"

"He's going to be out of town for a couple of weeks," Liam replied. "I'll email back and forth with him and see about meeting up with him when he's back."

"Good for you," Kate said. "See? I told you there were other fish in the sea."

"Yeah, yeah. Mother Kate always knows best."

"Just remember that and you won't have any problems. Now I'm going to get Miri a drink. Don't give up after just one try—if Martin doesn't work out, you should have a backup plan."

Liam shook his head but continued circulating through the rooms. He ran into Eamon in the Asian culture section, examining an intricately embroidered men's kimono.

"The workmanship is exquisite, isn't it?" Eamon asked when Liam joined him at the display. "The silk of the outer layer is a subdued color, like the black one here, with a very subtle pattern woven in. But underneath, on the *juban*, the design of cranes flying over the ocean is breathtaking. So the wearer would appear formal and restrained, but only those intimate enough to know him well could see the beauty hidden beneath." He raised an eyebrow, and Liam had the feeling he wasn't only speaking about Japanese ceremonial garments.

"It's been a month, and he hasn't texted or called. What am I supposed to think?" Liam asked, even as he hated himself for giving in to the desire to ask. "Good things come to those who wait and all, but I don't even know if there's anything to wait for."

"I haven't spoken with Erik recently. He wasn't able to make his usual practice sessions because he had to fly to LA for his company's annual meeting, and then he canceled last week because he had to work late." Eamon's expression told Liam what he thought of that excuse. "He's holed up to lick his wounds, Liam. Only you can decide whether it's worth waiting for him to venture out of his lair again."

That didn't make Liam feel any better when he didn't understand what wounds Erik had to lick or what he'd done to trigger them. He wasn't going to wait idly for Erik to crawl out of his hole. If Erik wanted him, he'd better get his act together before Liam met someone else.

CHAPTER 18

"I HOPE you're doing something fun with your social group this weekend." Billy was closing up his desk when Erik came out of his office on Friday. "Between the annual meeting and expanding your presentation so other offices can share it with their staff, you deserve some downtime."

Erik had been doing his best not to think about anything to do with Out and About or his disastrous loss of control with Liam. Returning to LA for B&F's annual meeting had helped. His mentor, John, had complimented him on the changes he'd instituted in Houston, and he'd enjoyed spending time with his former coworkers, but by the end of the week, Erik realized he was looking forward to returning to Texas. Somehow over the past six months Houston had become home.

Throwing himself into his work to "catch up" had made it easier to avoid anything to do with Out and About, but he'd finished adding his notes to the slide show he'd presented about reaching out to underserved segments of the community and sent it off that afternoon. "I'm not sure if there's anything planned," he lied. Well, not a complete lie—he'd deleted the notification emails for the past month without reading them. "Too much going on around here."

"Maybe last week, but you're caught up and ahead, unless you've got a project on your desk I don't know about." Billy's expression indicated how unlikely he considered that. "I know you've made friends since you've been here. Call one of them and have drinks, even if your events group… what is it called? Out and About?" Erik nodded. "Even if they aren't having anything. Seriously, boss, you need a break."

"I'm looking forward to doing nothing this weekend." Another lie—with nothing to occupy his time, he knew he'd spend it reliving the kiss and its aftermath. He could call Travis, though he might well be attending whatever Out and About had planned, and even if he wasn't, Erik wasn't sure he wanted to open himself up to Travis's questioning. He'd managed to plead a headache brought on by too much sun for his sudden change of mood at Schlitterbahn, but Travis was perceptive enough to notice it still hadn't lifted. "Maybe I'll put some extra time in at the gym. I've been slacking off on my workouts lately."

Billy rolled his eyes. "A break, boss, but whatever floats your boat. Just do something to make yourself feel better. You've been in a mood for weeks. I know you've been stressed, but that's over now, so let off some steam and recharge your batteries, okay?"

It occurred to Erik that no one at the LA office would have noticed that he was stressed, other than Mark's complaining when he put in extra hours. "I hope I haven't taken my mood out on you. I'll try to shake it before Monday." Though how he could do that was the million-dollar question.

"Not at all," Billy said. "I've just gotten used to seeing you smiling, and these days it's all frowns and grimaces. You could come have dinner with Carrie and me tomorrow, if you don't have other plans. I'll even promise no matchmaking."

That would keep him from brooding, at least for a few hours. "I'll bring dessert," he offered, thinking of the cupcake shop he and Eamon had discovered on one of their weekly dinners. He wouldn't be able to plead too much work to resume his weekly piano sessions either. "Thanks, Billy."

"Wonderful. Come around six and we'll eat between six thirty and seven." Billy grabbed his bag and gave Erik a wave before he left.

THE DINNER with Billy and his wife and children succeeded in taking Erik's mind off his situation for the night. The cupcakes were a huge hit, and true to his word, Billy didn't bring up the subject of dating or Erik's dour mood. Erik, in turn, let the happy family dynamic raise his spirits, and he made a mental note to do a better job of keeping in touch with his nieces and nephews.

On Monday he drove to Rice after work and spent a satisfying ninety minutes pouring out his emotions on the keyboard. Eamon opened the door of the practice room and listened quietly for the last few minutes, until Erik closed the lid and pushed back from the piano.

"Good to see you back to practicing, Erik," Eamon said when he was done. "I've missed hearing you play. How are you doing?"

"It was a busy few weeks at work," Erik answered, the excuse coming automatically. "But I missed playing."

"So busy you missed two events at Out and About after rearranging your schedule to allow you to attend all the previous ones," Eamon observed. "One would almost think something had happened to make you want to stay away."

He could have repeated the justifications of his trip and its follow-up, but a month of internal wrangling hadn't made his decision any easier to accept. Even if Eamon couldn't do anything to resolve the situation, it would be a relief just to talk about it, and Eamon would be less likely to judge him than Travis or Kurt.

"I think I'm done with Out and About," he admitted. "I joined it to make friends, and I've done that." He paused, trying to find the words to explain how badly he'd reacted at the water park.

"I count myself fortunate to be one of them," Eamon replied, "but making friends isn't the only goal of Out and About. Nor do I think meeting that goal is your real reason for thinking about leaving. Do I need to get you drunk for you to tell me the truth? Because I have some very fine brandy that would fit the bill perfectly."

Erik dropped his head into his hands. "It was getting drunk that got me into trouble in the first place. No, to be honest it started before that, but I made an ass of myself as a result."

"Somehow I doubt that, but you'd have to tell me what happened first." Eamon tipped his head toward the hallway. "Let's go somewhere more conducive to talking comfortably. Whether it's my office or my apartment is up to you."

"Your apartment," Erik decided. Less chance of being interrupted by a colleague or student taking a night class, and he'd be embarrassed enough confessing to Eamon, let alone risk being overheard. And maybe on the walk there he could figure out what to say that wouldn't make him sound like more of a fool than he already felt. "If you don't mind."

"I wouldn't have offered if I minded," Eamon replied. "Let me just gather my briefcase and lock my office. It won't take me a moment."

Erik followed Eamon to his office and waited silently while he packed up and locked the door. They kept the conversation light as they crossed the campus to the condos on the other side of Rice Boulevard where Eamon lived. Once inside, Eamon stowed his briefcase and toed off his shoes. "Now, about that brandy…."

The temptation to drown his sorrows was strong, but Erik shook his head. "Not for me, but please don't let me stop you from having some."

Eamon shrugged and poured himself a glass. "Can I offer you something else instead? Water, tea? Beer?"

"I'm good," Erik answered. "Actually, I'm not, but alcohol won't make it any better." He took a deep breath and decided there wasn't any way to say it that would sugarcoat the truth. "I kissed Liam, and I shouldn't have. And I don't think I can face him again after that."

"That sounds like three separate issues," Eamon said after a moment's pause to sip his brandy. "Why did you kiss him? And don't tell me it was because you had too much to drink."

"I would have had the self-control not to act on it if I hadn't been drinking."

"That's not the point, and you know it," Eamon said. "If you want to figure out what to do next, you need to admit—to yourself, if not to me—why you acted the way you did."

"Because he's sweet and smart and gorgeous, and watching him run around all morning in that swimsuit was more than I could resist, all right?" Erik shook his head. "I'm sorry, Eamon. I shouldn't snap at you when I'm angry at myself."

"I think those are perfect reasons for kissing someone," Eamon replied as if Erik hadn't snapped at all. "Why are you angry at yourself? I can't imagine Liam was an unwilling participant. I've seen the way he looks at you."

The memory of just how willing Liam had been was enough to make Erik harden. "Because I know better than to start something that can't go anywhere, and when I remembered that, I took off like a coward. Liam's probably furious with me, and I don't blame him."

"I don't know if 'furious' is the right word," Eamon said. "Confused, certainly. But I think the more important question is why you believe it can't go anywhere. You're single, he's single. You're interested, he's interested. I don't see the problem."

"I told you, he's a client, and I don't date clients. What kind of person would I be if I ignored that with the first person who tempted me?"

"How many other advisors work in your office?" Eamon asked. "It couldn't be that complicated to transfer his account to one of them."

"He'd still be a client in my office. Mixing business and personal life is always a mistake. Mark made damn sure I learned that lesson."

"First, you aren't Mark. Second, neither is Liam. Neither of you is cheating, and the fact that Mark cheated on you with a client is less important than the fact that Mark cheated at all," Eamon replied. "But if that's your stand on the matter, then that's it. You simply need to tell Liam what you just told me, more or less, and that will be the end of it. You can still attend events at Out and About. Liam is a professional. He won't make things uncomfortable for you if you give him an explanation."

He didn't need Liam to do anything to make him uncomfortable. Just seeing him, wanting him, and knowing he couldn't allow himself to act on it again would be its own torture. But he couldn't say that to Eamon, though he was right about one thing. "I do owe Liam an explanation." *And an apology.* Calling or texting was too impersonal, and asking to meet somewhere might give Liam the wrong impression. "What is the next Out and About event? I haven't been keeping up with the announcements lately."

"A cooking class, of all things," Eamon said. "At Sur La Table. It's next weekend, so you still have time to sign up, although you might want to talk to Liam first so things aren't awkward when you get there."

Things would be awkward no matter what he did, Erik was certain. "Thanks, Eamon. I appreciate your letting me unload on you like this."

"You're welcome, anytime, Erik. Sometimes you just need someone to listen." He tipped his glass toward Erik. "And sometimes you need someone to give you a kick in the pants."

A genuine smile creased Erik's face. "I can't think of anyone I'd rather let kick me than you, Eamon."

ERIK ARRIVED at Sur La Table just before the cooking class was scheduled to start, glad for the air-conditioning that countered the late-August heat. The less time he had to stand around trying to figure out a way to talk to Liam, the better. He'd linger after the event was over and speak to him then, but he wouldn't start the evening off on a bad foot when Liam had to monitor the event and see to all the attendees' needs.

"Erik, over here," Kurt called when Erik had picked up his name tag—from Kate, thankfully.

"Good to see you, Kurt." Erik walked over to the cooktop Kurt had claimed, glancing around to see if Travis or Eamon had arrived but also looking for Liam, who was talking with a group of people Erik didn't recognize across the room.

"You could have seen me sooner if you hadn't bailed on getting together so much lately," Kurt razzed him good-naturedly.

"I've just finally gotten my feet back under me at work," Erik countered, though the excuse was starting to sound old even to himself. "You should be used to Martin having the same issues."

"Why do you think I'm trying to make new friends?" Kurt replied easily. "He's never around when I want someone to hang out with. Are things better at work now? You still look pretty stressed."

Erik hoped that would improve once he'd cleared the air with Liam. "Getting there," he said. "So what have you been up to lately?"

"Oh, you know me. Softball's about to start up soon, so I've been running to get back in shape. I managed to drag Martin with me to the Night at the Museum event two weeks ago, but he's been out of town since. We're supposed to go hiking in a couple weeks, weather permitting. He might be fine hiking in the rain, but I'm not that committed. I'm looking forward to the class tonight. I've always wanted to learn to make tandoori."

Erik hadn't even noticed what they were cooking when he'd signed up—he'd focused on registering and getting off the site before he could change his mind. "I haven't had an Indian dish yet I don't like," he agreed.

"Erik, you bastard. About time you showed up for something," Travis shouted as he walked toward him and Kurt. Heads swiveled their direction around the room, including Liam's. Erik turned to Travis before they could make eye contact.

"Thanks for announcing that to everyone here," he muttered as Travis pounded his shoulder. "I'm sure it made a good first impression on all the new people."

Travis shrugged. "Then you shouldn't have given me reason to call you out." He looked around the room. "The cooktops are for two, and I see someone I think I should share with."

Before Erik could reply, Travis was across the room like a shot, sidling up to a man with longish dark hair and a smudge of kohl around his eyes. Erik could just make out tattoos peeking out from under his sleeves.

Next to him, Kurt sighed. "Damn, but he's predictable."

"Someone you know?" Erik asked. "I don't remember seeing him at any of the earlier events."

"Never met him, but I know Travis's type," Kurt said. "I've seen it all before. Ten bucks says he's got a sob story about how he's trying to get his life back together and by the end of the evening, he'll be Travis's new best friend. Give it a month, tops, and they'll be sleeping together, and if the guy holds true to form, they'll be married by the end of the year."

Erik was a little surprised at Kurt's tone until he remembered his earlier comment about meeting someone who wasn't interested in him. Could he have meant Travis? But they'd known each other before Out and About, so that couldn't be it. Before he could reply, Kate stepped forward to introduce the instructor, and soon he and Kurt were mixing yogurt and spices to pour over their chicken.

"Ideally you'd let the chicken pieces marinate a few hours to overnight, but even about an hour will give it a nice flavor," the instructor told them. "We're making skewers rather than bone-in pieces because they'll cook faster, but I recommend you try cooking leg quarters at home. And while the marinade is doing its magic, we'll put together some rice and a cucumber raita sauce to serve with them."

"Maybe now I'll figure out why rice always tastes so much better at Indian restaurants than anywhere else," Kurt said as they covered the bowl of marinating chicken. "Nothing I do ever makes it as good."

"What kind of rice do you use?" The instructor stopped at their cooktop, having overheard Kurt's comment, and gave him a warm smile. "Because if it's anything other than basmati, that's part of your problem."

"I use jasmine rice," Kurt admitted. "I can find that at my local grocery store."

"You need to find an Indian grocery store. They have basmati rice as well as a lot bigger variety of spices, often at better prices," the instructor said. "We have a list of ones we recommend that we'll give you at the end of the class."

"That would be great," Kurt said.

"And if you have trouble finding anything, feel free to stop by and ask me," he continued. "I'd be happy to help you with whatever you need."

They thanked him again, and he moved on to the next cook station before instructing everyone to drop the dry rice in a pot and toast it lightly before adding water, chicken broth, and a variety of spices to the mix.

"That's the secret," Kurt said once they had the rice on to boil.

"I think the instructor knows a few more secrets he'd like to share with you," Erik said as he watched him move on to the station where Travis and the dark-haired man were cooking. The stranger sidled up next to the instructor and murmured something that made the instructor laugh and shake his head.

"Do you suppose Kate and Liam check the orientation of the staff too?" Kurt asked, eyeing the instructor with more interest.

"It may be coincidence, but having seen a little of the connections Kate has, I doubt it," Erik answered. The instructor gracefully moved from Travis's station to the next cooktop, and the dark-haired stranger flounced back to Travis with a decided pout.

"Yeah, she's something else," Kurt agreed. "Speaking of connections, I don't know if you've noticed since you haven't been around lately, but she's met someone. She's definitely been spending any free time at events with one person in particular. Not that you'd notice it if you weren't paying attention. She does as fantastic a job as always with running things."

Erik glanced quickly from Travis's station to Kurt, but he couldn't tell if Kurt was making a point at his expense, since his gaze was following the instructor to the next cooking station. "Yeah, Miranda. Liam mentioned her. I hope it works out for them," he said softly and returned his attention to prepping ingredients for the raita.

"Only time will tell, but she certainly seems happier than I can ever remember her being when she was dating Travis," Kurt replied.

Given his suspicion that Kurt was attracted to Travis himself, he took that comment with a grain of salt and held out a spoon. "Taste this and see if it needs more mint."

Kurt leaned forward and took the spoon in his mouth, not bothering to take it out of Erik's hand. "Careful there," he said with a wink when he straightened up. "You're going to make everyone jealous. And it's perfect."

"You told me straight off you weren't interested, Schneider." Erik couldn't help but glance around for Liam, but he was at a station across the room and gave no sign he'd been looking in their direction. "It's not likely anyone else cares."

"Maybe not, but now I know you still want him to care," Kurt replied. "Besides, it's fun making you blush."

Erik wanted to deny he was blushing, but he could feel the telltale heat in his cheeks. He turned quickly and clipped the handle of the rice pan, knocking it off the burner and splashing the boiling cooking liquid onto his hand. "Fuck!"

since she was in high school. "And I couldn't be happier for you. I just have to find my happiness in my own way."

"As long as you find it." Kate squeezed his hand. "Because no one deserves it more.

WHEN THEY got home and Liam finally escaped to his bedroom, he pulled out his cell and scrolled through until he found Erik's number. He pressed Call and rehearsed what he was going to say. Yes, he'd told Erik he'd call, so he was just keeping that promise, but he wanted to get the tone right.

I've got an extra ticket to the Rice football game on Saturday. Kate bailed on me. Want to come along?

That struck a fun, friendly note. Now to keep it when Erik answered.

After a half-dozen rings, the call went to voicemail. Liam pushed down his disappointment. Erik had no reason to be sitting by the phone waiting for Liam to call.

"Hi, Erik. It's Liam. I've got an extra ticket to the Rice football game Saturday evening if you're free. Give me a call back or text me and let me know. Bye."

He ended the call and set his phone on the charger so he wouldn't be tempted to check it every two minutes. It would ring when Erik called back. Then he grabbed his laptop to type up and organize his notes from all the places they'd visited over the weekend. That would keep him from dwelling on Erik and the invitation for too long.

Nearly an hour later, just as he was wrapping up his notes, his phone rang. He couldn't help his smile when he saw Erik's name on the display.

"Hi, Erik."

"Hey, Liam. Sorry I missed your call. I was working out at the gym."

Liam pointedly ignored the image of Erik in shorts and a tank top, sweaty from his workout or damp from a shower. "No problem. I was just working on notes from this weekend."

"Was it a productive weekend? You're looking at sites for an Out and About event, right?"

"It was a very productive weekend," Liam said, letting the question distract him momentarily from his purpose in calling. "Martin gave us a list of hiking trails to consider, so we checked out several of them for difficulty levels and came up with a couple of solid options for day trips or weekend outings. I'm definitely glad to be home, though. It feels good to put my feet up."

"Sounds like my evening. I don't have anything planned but warming up some leftover fried rice for dinner and finishing the mystery I've been reading."

Liam resolutely pushed aside the thought of Erik lounging on the couch or in bed in nothing but a T-shirt and boxers. He cleared his throat and focused back on the reason for his call. "I wouldn't want to keep you from that. I called because Kate dropped me like a hot potato when she found out Miri has Saturday off, so I've got an extra ticket to the Rice game if you're free."

Erik laughed, the husky sound making Liam smile in return. "I don't have any plans for Saturday. What time's the game? Maybe we could hit the South African place before or after. What's the name again?"

"The game is at six, but we could make an afternoon of it, have a late lunch at Peli Peli on our way to the game," Liam replied. "Or we could grab a bite at the Buffalo Wild Wings in the Village to make it faster."

"If that's more convenient. We'll just hit Peli Peli another time." Liam's grin widened. He wasn't sure why Erik was fixated on the South African place, but since it meant another chance for them to get together, he was all for it. "Should we meet in the Village, or would you rather drive in together?"

"The advantage of Buffalo Wild Wings is that everything is together so we don't have to drive from place to place and worry about traffic. We can leave a car at the park-and-ride at Fannin South and walk from the metro stop instead of having to navigate parking both in the Village and at the stadium. And if I pick you up, then we're already together, rather than trying to meet up somewhere," Liam said.

"If it's not too much trouble for you to pick me up, that works for me. I've never given you my address, have I? I'll text it to you in case you want to enter it into Google Maps, though you might know how to get here on your own. I still have to rely on GPS to get around until I've been somewhere a few times."

"No, you told me you lived in Meyerland, but not the actual address. And it's no trouble at all. I've lived here for years and I still need GPS if I'm going anywhere out of my usual route. Houston isn't a city you ever know completely. It's just too big. I can pick you up at three. That'll get us to the Village by four and give us time to eat and walk over to the stadium before the game starts."

"I'll be ready," Erik said. "And Liam—thanks. I—" His voice dropped, and Liam could hear him swallow. "I'll see you Saturday."

The phone clicked in his ear, and Liam wondered if Erik was about to say something else before he hung up. *Friends*, he reminded himself.

He set the phone down and went to see about his own dinner. To his surprise, Kate wasn't in the kitchen, although whether she'd already crashed or if she'd gone out to see Miranda, he didn't know, but that suited him fine. Otherwise she'd want to talk about Erik, and Liam wasn't ready to share. He'd eat quickly and take a long shower before going to bed early. He hadn't been sleeping enough, and it was showing at work.

Thoughts of Erik working out, eating, showering, and relaxing at home stayed with him as he ate and followed him into the shower. He leaned against the cool tiles and groaned. They were friends. *Friends.* He couldn't jerk off to thoughts of a friend. How was he supposed to look Erik in the eye on Saturday if he gave in now? But he'd never get to sleep tonight if he didn't. He'd just think about something else. He had plenty of fantasies that didn't involve Erik.

Except that when he closed his eyes and wrapped his hand around his cock, the only image he could call to mind was Erik's sun-kissed shoulders at Schlitterbahn. Fuck it, he had to get this out of his system. He'd give himself this one night to play the fantasy out in his head and then he'd put it behind him.

He fell into the memory of their one kiss—the smoothness of Erik's skin along his shoulders, the rasp of his chest hair against Liam's own hairless chest, the smell of sunscreen wrapping around them, the taste of Erik's tongue in his mouth. His cock twitched in his grip, so he worked it harder with his fist, imagining what might have happened if they hadn't been interrupted, if they'd been somewhere private.

In his dreams, Erik stripped his bathing suit from him and replaced Liam's hand with his own. It would be soft, he imagined, his grip firm but smooth as he slid up and down the shaft, smearing the precome with his palm to ease the way. With his other hand, he'd cradle Liam's head the way he'd done at the water park, keeping him in place for kiss after kiss, each one hotter and deeper than the last. When Liam started getting close, Erik would pull back long enough to line their cocks up and jerk them off together, keeping the pace torturously slow until Liam was begging him to finish them off.

And when he did, when he finally added that extra twist of the wrist at the head of Liam's cock, it would send him flying right over the edge.

He moaned as he found his release. Reality settled back in as the cooling water ran down his back, reminding him that he was alone in the shower rather than with a lover who knew exactly how to touch him. The release had eased the physical tension, but if anything, his heart only ached more.

And now he had to face Erik on Saturday without blushing.

LIAM PICKED Erik up from his apartment in Meyerland at exactly three o'clock on Saturday. Erik wasn't wearing a Rice shirt, but he did have on blue and gray, so Liam figured that was close enough. "Good to see you," he said when Erik got in the car. "Did you have a good week?"

"Can't complain." Erik buckled his seat belt and shifted to look at Liam. "How are you holding up with the change to two events a month? It's got to be a lot on top of managing the store too."

"I feel like if I stop moving, I'll fall asleep and won't move for a month," Liam admitted, "but it's worth it. We're looking at our first multiday event. We're hoping to get enough people signed up for a Caribbean cruise this fall, probably November, when it's cooled off a bit, so that's going to take a lot of our spare time over the next couple of months, but it will be worth it."

"Wouldn't you have to get people to Miami for a cruise?" Erik asked.

"There are several cruise lines that sail from Galveston. Carnival and Royal Caribbean both offer four-day cruises to Cozumel or San Juan. We wouldn't plan anything longer than that, at least for the first time. If we get a lot of interest, we might consider a weeklong cruise at some point."

"I've never been on a cruise, though I hear they're nice, especially if you like to eat."

"Definitely. I've never gone on one without gaining at least five pounds," Liam replied. "The best part is that the food is all included, so you eat what you want without having to pay extra. The first time I went on one, the waiter asked if I wanted crab or venison for dinner, and I made a comment about not knowing how to choose. He told me I didn't have to, and I thought I'd gone to heaven. There's also plenty of things to do both on and off the boat, so you can stay as busy as you want or spend the whole time reclining by the pool."

"That will be Eamon's choice, I'm sure," Erik said with a wry smile.

Liam laughed. "Definitely. He was in fine form at Schlitterbahn." The moment the words were out of his mouth, he regretted them. He didn't want to make things awkward by reminding Erik of their kiss.

He glanced over, but Erik was looking out the window. "I'll have to double up on my workout if the food's that good."

He almost told Erik he didn't have anything to worry about, but it sounded as if Erik would consider going, and Liam didn't want to say anything that might make him change his mind. "They have gyms on the ships, so you can always work out during the day if you want to," he said instead. "Or you can keep busy with other activities. Swimming on the cruising days, or hiking or scuba on the days we're in port."

"I've always wanted to go diving." That reminded Liam again of Erik in his swim trunks, and he forced himself to concentrate on his driving and not the sudden flush of arousal.

It took about fifteen minutes to get to Fannin South from Erik's neighborhood. Liam managed to keep up a flow of light chatter about Out and About's upcoming events until he pulled into the park-and-ride lot. "The train will take us up to Rice, and we can walk over to the restaurant from there. That way we don't have to worry about finding parking later."

They rode the light rail up through the Medical Center and got off at Hermann Park across from Rice University. The shaded walks from the live oak trees kept the sun off their shoulders as they crossed over to the Village and the restaurant. It was crowded already, but they got the last table without having to wait. "What kind of wings do you like?"

"Nothing too hot. Would you like a beer?" Erik asked when the waitress came to the table.

"Only if you're having one," Liam replied.

Erik shook his head. "An order of Asian Zing wings and an iced tea for me, please. Liam?"

"Iced tea for me too and an order of Caribbean Jerk wings," Liam said. When the waitress left, he turned back to Erik. "You'll have to get used to spicy food down here. Everything has jalapeños or hot sauce in it. It's almost a rite of passage."

"I've noticed. The last time I had wings with Kurt and Travis, it was a competition between them to see who could handle the hottest sauce." He shook his head. "I don't see how that doesn't fry away your taste buds."

"You get used to it," Liam replied. "And there's a difference between spicy food and burn-your-tongue-off food. From what Kate has told me, Travis and Kurt have had a dick-measuring contest going on for years."

"I wouldn't know," Erik said softly. Before he could say more, the waitress returned with their tea. Erik thanked her and lifted the frosted glass to tap against Liam's. "To friendship."

"To friendship," Liam agreed. He hoped Erik meant he wouldn't know anything about Travis's or Kurt's dicks rather than about the difference in spicy foods, but he didn't ask for clarification. He didn't want to know.

AT HALFTIME, Rice was ahead by seven, and Liam was high on the adrenaline of a close game. He nudged Erik with his shoulder. "Are you having fun?"

"I am," Erik said, though Liam thought he heard a hint of surprise in his voice. "I'm going to have to do some reading up so I know who the players are if I'm going to follow the team, though. The running back made a really great catch to score that last touchdown."

"Do you have a team of your own you follow?" Liam asked, already thinking about other things they could do together as friends. They'd discussed Peli Peli, but that was only one thing. They might not be able to go to the game in person, depending on what team it was, but they could definitely watch the game live on TV.

"I followed basketball more than football before I moved, not that the Lakers have done much lately. Even though LA has two NFL teams now, I never managed to get to a game. As much as I have a football team at all, I guess it would be the Vikings. Hometown loyalty, you know."

"If you like basketball, I bet we could get tickets to the Rockets-Lakers game," Liam said. "And there's always the Texans if NFL is more your speed than college ball."

"Liam! Good to see you here as always. And Erik, what a pleasant surprise." Liam looked up to see Eamon coming toward them, a knowing smile on his face. He barely refrained from groaning. Eamon would see the two of them together and make assumptions, and that would embarrass Erik and make things harder the next time Liam suggested something to do as friends. He just knew it.

"Hello, Eamon. Good game so far. The team is really shaping up this year," Liam said, hoping to divert him from any more personal observations.

"The players are certainly in excellent shape." He winked, and both Liam and Erik couldn't help but laugh. "I'm glad to see the two of you have worked out your differences." He clapped Erik on the back, and Liam wondered what Eamon might have said to him to make him blush.

"Liam had an extra ticket to the game, and since I hadn't seen Rice play before, he offered it to me." Erik met Eamon's eyes, though his cheeks stayed pink.

"I hope this means you'll be able to make the time for more Out and About events. Your presence was definitely missed." Eamon's gaze moved to Liam, who suddenly understood Erik's flush.

Damn Eamon for being a matchmaker when they were finally settling into friendship. "I was just telling Erik about the cruise we're hoping to announce at the next event," Liam said. "What do you think? Four or five days in the Caribbean?"

"Ah, Patrick loved cruises. Did I ever tell you about the Mediterranean cruise we took? The staff took most excellent care of us...." He shook his head. "Before your time, that was. In any case, in cruises as in most things, longer is definitely better."

Liam laughed as Eamon had clearly intended, although the shadow on Eamon's face whenever he talked about Patrick hurt Liam's heart. "Then I'll tell Kate to look into the five-day instead. Now we just have to convince enough people to attend that we make our minimum numbers. Unlike most of our events, this one will definitely have a quota we have to make to get the group pricing."

"Well, unless it conflicts with finals, which I am sure you will avoid, you can definitely count on me to attend. Now, I've taken up enough of your time. I hope to see you both again soon."

"I'm sorry about that," Erik said after Eamon walked away. "Eamon had something to say about my failure to attend several Out and About events. I'm afraid he may have read more into seeing us here together than it warrants."

"He had a few things to say to me too," Liam admitted. "He can read what he wants into things. We both know where we stand. Want a beer or something from the concession stand?"

Erik was quiet for a moment, his blue eyes downcast. Then he shook his head and smiled at Liam. "Maybe some popcorn or chips? Those wings were good but they didn't seem to stick with me."

"You should drink something too," Liam said. "It's too hot out here not to have something. I'll grab a couple of bottles of water to go along with the popcorn."

"Want me to go with you?"

"Nah, save our seats. I'll get this and you can get the next round, either today or the next time we get together," Liam replied.

"Okay, thanks." Erik's smile was warmer now, giving Liam hope that maybe they could make friendship between them work after all. The concession stand lines had died down somewhat now that halftime was almost over. Liam would miss the second-half kickoff, but that was okay. They needed something to drink, and he needed a break. He could tell himself all day that they were just friends and that he would be satisfied with that, but it did nothing to stop the simmering current of attraction he still felt.

Damn it all to hell and back, what was he supposed to think? Erik was an attractive man in the sort of understated way that Liam had always trusted more than the flashy gorgeousness that caught the eye of many of his friends. Men like that knew they were attractive and expected the world to worship at their feet because of it. Erik, on the other hand, was as humble as he was interesting, and that did more for Liam than anything else. Except he couldn't do anything about it this time, not without running the risk of driving Erik away completely.

He bought popcorn and two big bottles of water when he got to the concession stand and headed back to where Erik was saving their seats.

Friends.

They were friends, and he was going to be happy with that because the other option—nothing at all—was not an option he was willing to consider.

CHAPTER 20

ERIK STARED at the email notification he'd received from the Houston Symphony announcing that they were adding a second screening of the original *Star Wars* movie featuring the full orchestra performing the soundtrack live. The original performance had sold out in record time, which had pushed the symphony to add a second show, and Erik suspected tickets for it would sell out just as fast. Before he could overthink it, he filled out the online registration form to purchase two tickets.

Ever since the Rice football game, where he'd spent more time covertly enjoying Liam's excitement than following the play on the field, he'd been racking his brain to come up with something Liam might enjoy. The dinner at Peli Peli didn't count, since it had been Liam's suggestion in the first place, though that alone was enough for Erik to make sure it happened. The restaurant had turned out to be more romantic than he'd anticipated, but Liam hadn't commented on it, keeping their conversation on casual topics and ignoring the couple holding hands at the table next to theirs.

Aunt Marjorie had drilled into his head that when someone invited you to something, it was only polite to reciprocate. Unfortunately Liam knew Houston far better than Erik did, and everything Erik had considered was probably something Liam had already done before. And even though he knew he couldn't let it go anywhere, he wanted to give Liam something he wouldn't have done on his own.

A minute later, his email pinged with a confirmation that the tickets were his. Now he just had to dredge up the courage to call and invite Liam. Even though they'd shared several casual get-togethers by now, a part of him still worried Liam would turn him down. Not that he didn't deserve it after the way he'd reacted to Liam's first invitation.

He could wait until Friday, catch him after the next Out and About event, and make it seem casual, almost an afterthought, but that didn't seem fair to Liam, because this was anything but an afterthought. He couldn't go down the dating road with Liam, but he valued his friendship, and he didn't want Liam to doubt that.

He pulled out his cell phone, tempted to text but knowing that wasn't going to fly. With a sigh, he opened his Contacts list, his fingertips brushing over Liam's name with a caress he could never give the man himself. He'd have to wait until he got home, since he wouldn't want to distract Liam with a personal call at work. And manage not to talk himself out of the idea before then.

After he got home, warmed up his dinner, and went through the mail, he couldn't put it off any longer. The phone rang four times, and he was debating whether to hang up or ask Liam if he'd like to go to the concert in a voicemail message, when the call connected. Erik almost dropped the phone from suddenly nerveless fingers.

"Hi, Erik," Liam said on the other end of the line. "What's up?"

Of course, caller ID. "Liam. I was wondering if—I mean, do you think you'd be interested in—" He closed his eyes and took a deep breath. "I have tickets to the symphony playing the soundtrack to a screening of the first *Star Wars* movie on September 29th. Would you like to attend with me?"

"Seriously? You were able to get tickets? I tried when I got off work today and they were already sold out again. Yes, I would love to go with you," Liam gushed.

"I heard the LA Philharmonic play *The Lord of the Rings* symphony, and I always hoped they'd play to a screening of the films the way some other city orchestras have, but it never happened. John Williams wrote such incredible music for *Star Wars*, though, that I think this could be just as good." He was babbling, and he sounded like a geek, but he couldn't seem to stop himself.

"The Houston Symphony did *The Fellowship of the Ring* live. It was incredible. I never understood why they didn't do the others, because the show sold out, but maybe it was a question of copyright or something," Liam said. "And I agree about John Williams and *Star Wars*. I wonder which version of the film they'll show, since Lucas changes something every time he releases a new format."

"Han definitely shot first." When Liam laughed, Erik started to relax. He could do this. "Would you like to meet somewhere near Jones Hall for dinner before the concert? You'll have to suggest someplace. I could check on Yelp, but I trust your taste more than some random strangers."

"There's an Italian wine bar and restaurant called Little Napoli in Bayou Place, which is across the street from Jones Hall," Liam suggested. "It's fairly typical Italian fare, pastas, wood-burning grill, that sort of thing, but I enjoy eating there if I'm going to be in the Theater District."

"I love Italian." He'd have at least another hour or two of Liam's company. "How about if I pick you up around five? That will give us a couple of hours for dinner before the concert."

"Works for me. I'll text you my address. And since it's a Saturday concert, I won't be working, but we'll want reservations. Do you want me to make them?" Liam sounded so happy at the prospect that Erik couldn't help but smile.

"I'll take care of it." Erik wanted to keep Liam on the call, but he couldn't think of anything else to say that wouldn't make that painfully obvious. "I'll see you at Friday's event, then."

"I can't wait," Liam said.

Erik hadn't felt like this since high school, when he didn't want to hang up the phone on the guy he'd been crushing on. "Me too," he murmured, hoping Liam would attribute his eagerness to the concert. "Night, Liam."

He waited until Liam said "Good night" in return before disconnecting the call. He put the phone down on the table and moved a hand to the front of his slacks. He'd been hard since the moment Liam answered the phone, and his cock throbbed beneath his fingers.

He'd told himself he shouldn't do this again, but dammit, if he couldn't have Liam, he could at least give himself this. He slid down the zipper and eased his cock through the slit in his boxers. In his mind's eye, he pictured Liam at Schlitterbahn, his golden skin glistening with lotion, his lips swollen with Erik's kisses. Under his fingers, he wasn't stroking his own cock but Liam's. He could hear the needy sounds Liam would make, feel him thrusting into his grip. He caught the slick of fluid leaking from the tip and spread it down the shaft, biting his lip at the sensation. It was Liam nipping at his mouth, and he let his tongue slide out to taste him, salt and a hint of coconut. Liam's breath rasped unevenly, and a moan escaped when Erik sped up the strokes, bringing Liam closer and closer to the edge. His back arched, and hot fluid coated his palm. "Liam!" He kept stroking through the last trembling twitches, then dropped his head to his chest, panting.

Four nights before he'd see Liam again. Four nights of reliving the water park and the football game and the dinner at Peli Peli before finding new inspiration for his fantasies.

THE SECOND September event was dinner in a private room at a new hibachi restaurant in Memorial Park. It was a neighborhood Erik hadn't been to before—Liam had told him at the Rice game that Out and About was branching out into a larger area, hoping to grow their membership—and it took him longer than he'd expected to get there. By the time he'd found a spot to park and walked inside, several of the tables were already full. Travis waved to him from a cooktop near the back wall, and Erik made his way over. He knew three of the other people at the table and introduced himself to the two he didn't. That left one seat open, and Erik selfishly hoped that no one would notice it was free. Maybe he'd be able to get Liam to come sit with them once he and Kate had welcomed everyone.

"I'm looking forward to tonight," Travis said when Erik sat down. "I read some reviews, and everyone commented on the show being as good as the food. And you can't go wrong with hot Asian guys."

"I'll second that," one of the newcomers, a pixieish blonde woman, said with a grin.

"I thought you were going to drool over that server at the Korean restaurant we ate at last week," her companion, a curvaceous redhead, said with an answering smile.

That started a conversation about the best Asian restaurants in the city, though Erik wasn't sure whether the food or the hotness of the serving staff was the most important criteria. He made a mental note to check out several of the restaurants, since Liam had mentioned how much he was looking forward to the meal tonight. Before the group could reach a consensus, Kurt plopped down into the seat Erik had mentally been saving for Liam.

"No Martin tonight?" Travis asked.

"Another business trip," Kurt said with a frown. "He's going to burn out if they don't give him a break."

"Tell him we asked about him," Erik said, forcing himself not to show his disappointment that there was no longer a vacant seat for Liam at their table. "What about you? You look pretty strung out yourself. Did something happen?"

Kurt glanced from Erik to Travis and then back to Erik. "Nothing that some sake and good Japanese food won't cure."

Before Erik could decide what to say to that, Liam came up to the table. "Thanks for coming, everyone. We hope you'll have a great time tonight and that you'll take a look at the cruise that just went up on our website." He smiled at everyone, but Erik didn't think he was imagining it when Liam's smile warmed an extra degree when he looked at Erik.

He couldn't help but follow Liam's progress across the restaurant, where he joined a table of people Erik didn't recognize. He shouldn't have been surprised that Liam would sit with newcomers to the group, but he couldn't stop the fervent wish that he was sitting over there too.

When a chef approached the table, juggling a set of salt-and-pepper shakers, everyone at the table began to laugh and applaud. Even at that distance, Erik could see the delight and pleasure on Liam's face as he clapped along with everyone else before turning to say something to the man sitting next to him—the young, flamboyantly attractive black man.

A man who was closer to Liam's age and didn't have the hang-ups Erik did. A man who could offer Liam more than the friendship that was all Erik would allow himself to offer.

A young Japanese cook, his sleek black hair pulled into a tail at the back of his head, stepped up to their table and turned up the heat under the cooktop. "How is everyone tonight?" he asked. "Ready to have some great food?"

Erik forced himself to answer yes along with everyone else at the table. He managed to keep his gaze from straying to Liam's table, which became much easier when the chef painted a design on the cooktop with oil, lit a pair of wooden rods, and used them to set the oil aflame, then juggled the burning rods until the fire on the cooktop died down.

Erik clapped along with everyone else at the table as a cheer went up from another group behind them. Erik tried to relax and settle into the ambiance and the camaraderie of the group dining experience, but as the chef leaned to one side to begin chopping and tossing shrimp, it gave him the perfect view of the chef at Liam's table tossing a cooked shrimp right into Liam's open mouth. He shifted on his seat to make space for his suddenly awakening cock. Christ, he couldn't do this here, with Travis on one side of him and Kurt on the other. One of them was bound to notice, and he'd never hear the end of it.

The new guy sitting next to Liam reached up a hand to wipe the corner of Liam's mouth, and Erik had to clamp his hands to the sides of his chair to keep from getting up and yanking the man away. He had no right to be jealous when he couldn't promise Liam anything, had done his best to push him away, finally settling for friendship because he couldn't bear to cut Liam completely from his life. *Don't fuck up the only thing you've got.* Kurt nudged his side, and he turned his head just in time for a shrimp to bounce off his nose.

Kurt and Travis laughed like loons at that. Erik smiled wryly and picked up the errant shrimp with his chopsticks to pop it in his mouth. He paused for a moment to appreciate the crisp, slightly salty flavor of the morsel, not overcooked like shrimp too often was at places like this. That boded well for the rest of the meal, if he could just focus on his food and not on the guy flirting with Liam.

He resolutely kept his eyes on the show at his own table, applauding at all the right places and not glancing over when laughter or cheers broke out from the station across the room. He'd ordered a seafood sampler, and the combination of shrimp, lobster, silky diver scallops, and a surprisingly tender calamari steak was some of the best he'd ever tasted. Almost good enough for him to ignore the glimpse he caught from the corner of his eye of the stranger feeding Liam a morsel of something with his own chopsticks.

The chef at the station behind them finished up and bowed to the table, and then their own chef did the same, leaving Erik with only his food and Travis and Kurt's conversation as a distraction. "What do you think about the cruise Liam mentioned?" Erik asked for want of anything else to keep himself focused. "It sounds like it could be fun."

"Five days of unlimited food, drinks, and sunshine? Count me in," Travis said.

"There's no guarantee of sunshine," Kurt put in. "I was on a cruise once where it stormed the entire time. Half the passengers were seasick the whole week."

"Who pissed in your cornflakes?" Travis asked. "I suppose that means you won't be joining us?"

"No, I probably won't." Kurt dropped his napkin on his empty plate and stood. "Erik, I'll see you Wednesday." With a general wave to the table, Kurt walked away.

"Drama queen," Travis said with a roll of his eyes. "Since he's out for the cruise, do you want to share a cabin? You wouldn't have brought it up if you didn't plan on going."

"That would be great," Erik answered. Sharing with Travis would keep him from following Liam around like a lost puppy.

Liam chose that moment to stand up and clink his glass to get everyone's attention. "Thank you all for coming out tonight," he said when the conversation had dwindled to a minimum. "I hope you had a great time and enjoyed both the show and the food. We hope to see you back in two weeks at our next event, and don't forget to check the details of the Carnival cruise on our website. You can start signing up right away. The deadline is in a month, so don't take too long making up your mind."

Erik's mind was already made up. He just had to keep living with the decision.

ERIK KNOCKED on Liam's door at exactly five o'clock the day of the concert. Liam answered the door promptly, but his shirt was still partially unbuttoned and he wasn't wearing shoes. "I'm sorry, I'm running a little behind. Come on in. I just need five more minutes."

Erik stepped into the apartment and tried not to stare at the tawny skin on Liam's chest. He'd seen Liam with no shirt on at Schlitterbahn, but that didn't decrease the allure of partially hidden skin now. He made himself look away while Liam finished doing up the buttons. "This is a nice place."

"I like it," Liam replied. "Kate and I bought it together after college. I suppose at some point, one of us might want a place of our own, but we're both financially stable enough now that we could probably buy the other one out. Let me just grab my shoes and we can go."

Erik didn't stare at Liam's ass as he walked down the hallway and through a door into what was presumably his bedroom. *Nope, not going there.* He had it bad enough as it was. He didn't need images of Liam in his bedroom to make things worse.

Liam came back out a minute later, a huge smile on his face. "Okay, I'm ready now. Thanks for bearing with me."

"That's what friends do, right?" Erik didn't add that Liam had already put up with a lot worse from him. "Kate's not around?" From the cool looks she'd given him at the past few Out and About events, he got the feeling Kate wasn't his biggest fan, though he couldn't blame her for being protective of Liam. And it would be rude not to at least greet her before they left if she was home.

"No, she and Miri are out again tonight. Things are looking pretty serious between them from what I can tell. They're talking about sharing a cabin on the cruise, which will leave me in a room by myself." He grinned and winked at Erik. "Oh, the hardship."

At least he wouldn't have to watch Liam sharing a cabin with another man. Apparently the guy at the hibachi dinner hadn't made enough of an impression to be considered as a possible cabin mate. The thought made him smile. "I'm really looking forward to it. I signed up for the scuba-diving shore excursion. It's something I've always wanted to try."

"You're a swimmer, right?" Liam asked. When Erik nodded, he continued, "You should look into getting scuba certified. Then you'd be able to go diving on your own rather than just with the guided excursions. Probably not in time for this trip, but definitely for any future trips."

"There weren't a lot of places to scuba dive in Minnesota, and somehow when I moved to California, I never found time to take the classes. I'll have to look into dive shops that offer them here." Erik gestured toward the door. "Shall we? I put the restaurant's address into my phone, so I'll have the directions to get there."

"You'll love this place," Liam said as they walked out to Erik's car. "It's nice without being pretentious, and they have a great selection of wines if you want to try a few different things. They'll put together a wine flight for you based on what you're interested in."

"Maybe just a glass," Erik said. "I want to stay awake during the concert." He also remembered how the drinks at Schlitterbahn had weakened his resistance to Liam, and he wasn't about to make himself that vulnerable again. After they'd both climbed into his car and buckled up, he brought up the map function on his phone and pulled away from the curb. "Is there a particular dish you recommend?"

"Everything," Liam said with a laugh. "But the chicken marsala is my favorite. Kate swears by the eggplant parmigiana, but I'm not a big fan of eggplant."

"I'm partial to veal piccata myself." Erik patted his stomach. "Too much to work off at the gym if I go for one of those fried and cheese-heavy dishes." Not that Liam had to worry about that.

He parked the car in the underground lot that served the entire Theater District and followed Liam the short walk to the restaurant.

They checked in with the hostess, who seated them at a little corner table in the wine bar area and left them to look over the menus. "See anything that looks good?" Liam asked. "We could order two dishes and share if you're having trouble making up your mind. Kate and I do that anytime she doesn't order the eggplant."

Erik flashed back to the image of the cute guy at the hibachi restaurant feeding Liam a bite of steak. Probably not a good idea for his self-control. "I'll stick with the veal piccata, but you're welcome to eat off my plate anytime."

"You may regret offering," Liam said with a bright smile, "because I will definitely take you up on that."

The waiter arrived to take their orders. Liam ordered the chicken marsala and a glass of Chianti to go with it, leaving Erik to order his veal and wine when he was done.

"I'm so excited about the concert," Liam said when the waiter had left. "Do you suppose people will come in costume?"

"When I saw *The Lord of the Rings* symphony in LA, a fair number of people dressed up. There was one couple dressed as Legolas and Arwen whose costumes were phenomenal. You would have thought they'd stepped right out of the film."

"I don't remember seeing people dressed up at *The Fellowship of the Ring* here, but there's no one more obsessed than *Star Wars* fans, so hopefully we'll get some good cosplay tonight. I love seeing people following their passions."

Which left Erik out, since if he'd followed his passion, he'd have Liam naked in his bed. Instead all he had were his fantasies. Reminding himself why he couldn't have more, he took a sip of wine and concentrated on his really excellent meal. True to his word, Liam stole several bites of his veal, making an orgasmic face after the first bite that nearly sent Erik running to the restrooms to deal with his sudden flare of arousal. He could only hope that the concert hall would be too dark for Liam to notice if the same problem arose during the movie.

"You bought dinner at Peli Peli despite it being more expensive than Buffalo Wild Wings," Liam said when the waiter brought the check at the end of the meal. "That means it's my turn tonight."

"But I invited you tonight, so it's my treat," Erik answered, picking up the folder and reaching for his wallet.

Liam chuckled. "Listen to us, arguing over who's going to pay. How about we split it down the middle? I always feel ridiculous about trying to divide it out the last penny."

"What are a few pennies between friends?" Erik answered. "It will all even out over time." Because if he had anything to say about it, he'd be sharing many more dinners with Liam.

"I'm sure it will," Liam said with a grin. He pulled out his credit card and tossed it down beside Erik's.

After the waiter returned their receipts, they walked across Bayou Place to Jones Hall. As Liam had predicted, they were surrounded by numerous Hans, Leias, and Lukes, a few C-3POs, a collection of stormtroopers, and one very intimidating Darth Vader.

"Told you *Star Wars* fans were obsessed," Liam murmured just loud enough for Erik to hear as they turned in their tickets and headed toward their seats.

They were about to enter the auditorium itself when a loud voice called Erik's name. "I thought you only liked classical music," Travis said, walking up from behind them and patting Erik on the back.

"I didn't expect to see you at the symphony," Erik countered, since Travis had made his opinion of most classical music known when Erik had told him he played piano.

"Are you kidding? I wouldn't miss it. This is the best movie ever made." Travis's eyes widened when he spotted Liam. "Oh, I get it. Hi, Liam. Sorry to interrupt your date. Enjoy the show!" He was gone before Erik could explain to him that this wasn't a date, just a couple of friends getting together.

"Everyone is determined to match us up, aren't they?" Liam said, and Erik thought he heard a bit of wistfulness in Liam's voice. "They'll get it eventually."

Erik was sure he'd hear much more from Travis—he'd known him long enough by now to know he wouldn't let it go without some major razzing. At least he hadn't done it in front of Liam. He'd put up with enough from Erik already without having to deal with that too. Not sure what to say that wouldn't make his longing clear, Erik took Liam's elbow. "We should head inside. I can hear the orchestra warming up."

"WHEN AM I going to get to hear you play?" Erik asked when Liam applauded at the end of his weekly practice session. Liam had asked after the *Star Wars* concert if he could listen to Erik playing, and he'd managed to make it to Rice nearly every week since. Between that, the two Out and About events, and Liam's campaign to have him try every ethnic cuisine available in Houston—so far, they'd had Korean, Ethiopian, and Peruvian in addition to Peli Peli—they'd seen each other more than once a week all month. "You've been listening to my finger exercises for weeks now, and I've yet to hear you touch the keys. I'm beginning to think you don't play after all."

"Your 'finger exercises' are more intense than the full-length pieces most people play," Liam replied. "You'd laugh me right out of the practice room."

"I promise, not a snicker," Erik said, rising from the bench he'd been sitting at. "Here, it's all warmed up for you and everything."

"If you insist, but don't say I didn't warn you," Liam said as he took the spot Erik indicated. He ran through a couple of scales to warm up his fingers, nothing as complex as the Bach inventions Erik preferred, just simple harmonic scales. "Here goes nothing."

As Liam's fingers danced over the keys, the jaunty sounds of Scott Joplin's "The Entertainer" poured from the piano. "How's that?" Liam asked when he was done.

"*The Sting.*" Erik slid onto the bench beside Liam, careful to leave enough distance between them that they weren't touching. "This was always my favorite from that score." He spread his hands over the ivories, coaxing out the slow, bluesy notes of "Solace."

"I love that one too, but I don't know if I could still play it," Liam admitted. "But if we're doing music scores, we have to include this one." He started playing, his expression daring Erik to recognize it. It took him a couple of bars.

"'Music of the Night.' I'm not a huge fan of Andrew Lloyd Webber. But I know you know this one." Liam broke out laughing when Erik pounded out the bombastic opening notes of the *Star Wars* "Imperial March."

"We heard that with a full orchestra a month ago. Of course I know it," Liam said. "I bet you don't recognize this one." Before Liam could start playing, a knock on the door interrupted them, and Eamon poked his head in.

"Are you ready to go, Erik? Ah, Liam, I didn't know you were here tonight. Are you actually playing for once?"

"I am. I'm trying to play something Erik won't recognize." He tapped a note and then another, short little staccato pitches before setting his hands to the keys and expanding the melody into something more complete and recognizable.

Erik laughed. "You'll have to try harder than that to stump me. I told you I'd heard the LA Philharmonic play *The Lord of the Rings* symphony. Of course I recognize 'Concerning Hobbits.'"

"Yeah, but I have to go with things I can actually play on the piano well enough for you to have a chance of recognizing," Liam replied. "Your turn, if you have time."

"I didn't know this was a contest. What do you think, Eamon? Can he name this tune?" Erik cracked his knuckles and began to play a syncopated rhythm.

"He always did love the Broadway hits," Eamon said when Liam didn't immediately reply.

"'All That Jazz,'" Liam said after a moment. "I haven't listened to *Chicago* recently, so it took me a minute. Try this one." Liam's touch was light on the keys as he called up the first plaintive notes. When Erik frowned, Liam kept playing, the song getting darker as it went on.

"'I Dreamed a Dream,'" Erik said softly. That was a little too close to the truth for his comfort. He thought for a moment and then broke into a grin. "What about this?"

"'My Heart Will Go On'? Really, Erik? If you've descended into bad movie theme songs, we'll be here all night," Liam teased, bumping his shoulder against Erik's. "Let's see, what should I do next?"

"Personally I think you should be worried about Erik choosing *that* song just days before we all leave for the cruise," Eamon said archly. "Are you trying to tell us something, Erik?"

"Hey, I could have played this one," Erik retorted, picking out the theme from *The Love Boat*.

"And it's definitely better than this one," Liam agreed as he started the theme from *Jaws*.

"I can't argue with you on either of those," Eamon said. "Perhaps on that note we should consider dinner instead? Liam, you're welcome to join us."

"Yes, you should come too," Erik agreed. "I have a sudden taste for seafood."

Liam pulled out his phone. "I'm sure we can find something nearby… if I can get a signal in here." He stepped out of the room, leaving Erik alone with Eamon.

"I hope you don't mind Liam joining us," Erik said as he closed the keyboard. "I know he didn't have time to get anything to eat on his way from the Karat Patch."

"Of course I don't mind," Eamon replied. "I'm more concerned about the two of you having me along. And before you tell me you aren't dating, how many of your other friends come and listen to you practice piano?"

Liam stuck his head back inside before Erik could come up with an answer. "Goode Company Seafood? That's the closest."

"That sounds wonderful, my boy," Eamon said, sweeping out the door and taking Liam with him. "Erik is just packing up. He'll be right with us."

Liam's reply was lost to the closing of the soundproof door.

Erik picked up his jacket from where he'd hung it before he started playing and slung it over his shoulder before following. Eamon had given him some serious thinking to do.

CHAPTER 21

LIAM CARRIED his cocktail to the spot where he'd left his beach towel and stretched out on the lounge chair. November in Houston wasn't usually pool weather anymore, so he appreciated the warm sun on his skin. Across the pool Eamon was holding court—no surprise there. Maybe they should consider hiring Eamon, since he was doing an outstanding job of welcoming newcomers to the cruise. That they were all attractive and showing various degrees of bare skin was surely just coincidence. He didn't see any of the usual suspects in the group, though Kurt hadn't registered for the cruise, and he hadn't seen Erik and Travis since boarding.

He considered crossing the deck to join Eamon, but Liam needed a moment of solitude. He and Kate had gotten everyone checked in and settled for the cruise, and now he could sit back and enjoy himself until dinner. He'd have to put on his game face then to welcome everyone and explain the planned activities for the next five days—as opposed to the activities open to anyone on the ship. Of course everyone was free to choose which ones they wanted to do, but he or Kate or both had to show up at the planned activities to make sure everything went smoothly.

He took a sip of the fruity rum goodness in his hand and let the warmth of the sun soak into him. He'd been so busy getting things ready for the cruise that it felt like he hadn't sat still in months except for the time he spent with Erik. They saw each other at least once a week, and one week, they'd even gotten together three times, between Erik's practice, a play at the Alley Theater (Liam's idea), and a Texans game that weekend (Erik's suggestion).

He'd kept to his mantra of *friends, friends, friends*, and in some ways it was easier than ever. They *were* friends, close friends, even. He spent more time with Erik than with anyone other than Kate, and as much time as she now spent with Miri, that wasn't even always true. In other ways, though… he wasn't sure how much longer he could have everything he wanted so close at hand and so far out of reach. Each time they went out, Erik showed Liam some little facet of himself that increased Liam's attraction, from his caution with drinking to his wicked sense of humor when he challenged Liam to play "You Can Leave Your Hat On" during one of their weekly piano duels. He'd come to recognize Erik's caution as a piece of his inherent shyness, so each glimpse deeper was a jewel beyond price, giving him far more than his previous, shallow relationships had done. If this was all he could have, it would still be the best thing to ever happen to him, but it could be so much more if he could just convince Erik to give them a chance.

As if his thought had conjured him, Erik came into view on the opposite side of the pool, followed by—of course—Travis. Erik dropped the towel he'd been carrying onto a lounger and stripped off his T-shirt. His chest was coated with a thin dusting of hair that narrowed to a golden trail that disappeared beneath the waist of his deep blue swim trunks. The color brought out the blue in his eyes, not that Liam could see them from across the pool, and since Erik's head was currently turned toward Travis, who'd just whacked him on the butt with the hem of his towel. Laughing, Erik wrenched the towel away from Travis and shoved him into the water.

Travis surfaced a second later, spluttering and shaking the water from his hair like a wet dog. Erik wisely stayed out of range until he'd picked up Travis's towel and draped it across the lounger next to his. Then he walked to the edge of the pool and executed a perfect dive into the deep water.

Liam didn't stare. Really, he didn't, but he'd always had a thing for swimmers, and watching Erik cut through the water with strong, clean strokes was about to get embarrassing given the way he was reacting to the sight. He looked around for something to distract him, but nothing was close at hand. A moment later Erik surfaced on the near edge of the pool, right in front of Liam.

"Hi, Erik," Liam said, shifting to keep his reaction to seeing Erik wet and smiling from being too obvious. "Having fun?"

"The water feels fantastic." Erik slicked his hair back from his forehead. "I forget how much I enjoy swimming until I'm back in a pool again. I tell myself I need to find a place nearby where I can do laps, and then I forget until the next time I'm in the water."

Liam opened his mouth to offer to remind him, but before he could get the words out, Travis swam up behind Liam and pulled him under. The two tussled for a few minutes, until Erik escaped and held up his hands in surrender while treading water. "The lifeguard's going to throw us out for roughhousing if we don't stop."

"Carnival ships don't have lifeguards, but the staff might give you a warning if they think you're behaving recklessly." Liam was tempted to slip into the water with them, but he was pretty sure a wet suit would reveal what he was trying his best to hide.

"Then I don't have to stop," Travis said with a grin as he lunged for Erik again. Erik dove out of his way, leaving Liam torn between joining them in the water and looking anywhere but at them. Erik wouldn't think anything of it if Liam jumped into the middle of their play fight, but Liam wasn't sure his self-control could withstand the temptation to get his hands on all that bare skin under the guise of helping. In desperation, he grabbed the bottle of sunscreen and started reapplying it. He didn't really need it again yet, but Erik didn't know that.

When he looked back up, Travis had settled into lounging against the pool wall, his legs floating in the water while Erik treaded water in the deep end, his gaze fixed on Liam.

So not helping his resolve to respect Erik's "friends only" proviso a little while longer.

"Are we still on for the scuba-diving excursion tomorrow?" Erik asked. "I'm looking forward to that more than anything else. The sea life is supposed to be incredible."

"Definitely. The weather should be just like today, warm and sunny, perfect for diving," Liam said. He was a certified diver, but he couldn't dive alone, and going on the organized trip meant he could dive with Erik. "And then the day after, we can wander around the Yucatán, unless you changed your mind about signing up for the tour?"

"No, I'm not much for organized groups. I'd rather explore on our own and see how the people really live, not just the tourist attractions. Eat in a restaurant where the locals eat, not some overpriced chain."

"Yeah, me too. I know a couple of little places in Cancún I can't wait to show you," Liam replied, pushing down the thrill at Erik's choice of words. "On our own," not "on my own." "I found them on my first cruise, but it's more fun with two." And if Erik was wandering with him, he wasn't with Travis. Liam pushed that traitorous thought aside. Liam knew he'd been monopolizing Erik's time, not that Erik had complained. At least half the suggestions for things to do had come from him. Even so, Travis, Kurt, Eamon, his assistant Billy… they were all good for Erik in a variety of ways. The fact that Liam wanted to be special was irrelevant.

"I'm looking forward to it, but tell me if you need to cut out at some point. I know you have to make sure everything is running smoothly, and I wouldn't want to keep you from your responsibilities to the rest of the group."

Liam rolled his eyes at Erik, but he was smiling as he did. "We've talked about this. The only time I have to stick around is during an activity we're sponsoring, and we aren't doing any of those during shore time. When we're off ship, I'm all yours."

He regretted the words the minute they were out of his mouth, not because they weren't true, but because they were all too true—and not what Erik would want to hear.

"As long as I'm not taking you away from anything you have to do." Erik glanced over his shoulder, where Travis was chatting with a hot young thing in a skintight Speedo who was sitting on the edge of the pool. "Travis said something about dune buggy rides on Cozumel, but I'd rather learn some of the history of the Yucatán while we're here."

"From the looks of it, Travis's going to be too busy with Mr. Speedo over there to worry about what we're doing anyway," Liam commented. "One of these days, he's going to come on to the wrong person and get himself punched."

"It's a gift," Erik said with wonder in his voice. "Even when he gets turned down—which apparently isn't very often—he and the person he hit on both walk away with smiles on their faces. It must be his winning personality."

Liam snorted. Those weren't the words he'd choose, but Erik probably knew Travis better at this point, so he left it alone. "Makes my life easier if I don't have to worry about bad feelings at a later event." He glanced at his watch. "You're going to turn into a prune in there, and it's getting close to dinnertime. I need to get dressed so I can give the welcome speech tonight. I'll see you at dinner?"

"Any chance you're at table fifteen?" Erik asked.

"I don't think so," Liam said. "The cruise line assigns tables by cabin. They said they'd put us together as a group, but that's more than one table. We'll see who's sitting where and if I can switch with someone, but since it's just me, that might not work."

"That's okay, I don't want to disrupt anything. But I need to take a shower first to get rid of the chlorine." Erik glanced back at Travis, who was laughing at something Mr. Speedo had leaned down to say to him. He shook his head, then swam to the nearby ladder and hoisted himself out of the pool. "I'll look for you in the dining room." He started around the pool deck to retrieve his T-shirt, giving Liam an excellent view of the water trickling down his back and the globes of his ass flexing beneath the wet swimsuit.

Liam would be doing more than just getting rid of the sunscreen at this rate. He draped his towel over his arm so it would cover the bulge in his shorts and waved to Erik one last time before he headed back to his cabin for a quick wash and wank. He'd need it if he was going to survive dinner.

AFTER DINNER, Liam walked out to the bar on the main deck, although he'd stick with nonalcoholic beverages since he was diving in the morning. The one glass of wine he'd had with dinner wouldn't be a problem, but he knew better than to dive after drinking more than that.

He got a glass of tea and was looking around for a place to sit when Erik caught his eye, leaning against the railing and staring at the setting sun.

"What did you think of your first cruise ship dinner?" he asked, joining Erik at the rail.

"It was at least as good as I've had in some of my favorite restaurants. And between what I ordered and tasting dishes the other people at the table ordered, I ate more than I should. I thought a walk around the deck would help work it off, but the reflection of the sunset on the water is so beautiful, I had to stop to appreciate it."

"There's no time limit on that walk," Liam said with a smile. Erik's usually blond hair glinted red in the twilight, making Liam want to run his fingers through it to see if it was as soft as it looked. The only other time he'd touched it, it had been wet, and that didn't count.

So much for jerking off being a means of helping him keep things under control. He blamed the number of rom-coms that featured a sunset on a cruise ship as the backdrop for a passionate kiss.

"Want to walk with me?" he asked Erik, because if they stayed where they were, he'd do something stupid for sure.

When Erik didn't answer right away, Liam wondered if he'd pushed too hard, but he didn't want to go back to his empty cabin. If this had been a typical Out and About event, he could have kept busy mingling among the attendees to be sure everyone was having a good time, but they didn't have enough members to fill the whole ship, and they could be spread over ten decks. He'd taken a step back when Erik straightened from the railing. "I'd love to."

They walked in silence for a bit. Liam sipped at his tea until it was done, then fiddled with the glass to have something to do with his hands. The temperature dropped steadily as the wind picked up, making Liam shiver. "It's going to be time to head inside soon. Do you have plans for the evening? One of the shows, maybe? Or are you turning in early?"

"It would be a shame to sleep through my first cruise, wouldn't it? But I didn't have time to look at the itinerary for tonight's events. Is there anything interesting going on?"

"Depends on what you're in the mood for. They've got a Broadway medley show and a magic show in the two theaters, but there are other things too. I think I read something about a salsa class, and karaoke in one of the lounges."

"Does any of that interest you?" Erik asked. "To be honest, I was thinking about just enjoying the cool air on deck a little longer."

"We can certainly enjoy the deck as long as you want, but karaoke is always a blast." He shivered again. "I should have brought my jacket, though. I'm a true Texan, getting cold anytime the temperature drops below seventy-five."

Erik laughed. "This is a balmy spring day in Minnesota. Do you want to stop by your cabin to get a jacket? Then we could see whether you want to karaoke or just listen to other people."

"Do you mind? I'll have more fun if I'm not cold." In other circumstances he'd ask Erik to keep him warm, but he wouldn't cross that line, just wish he could.

"Of course not. You can't enjoy yourself if you're shivering." They walked in silence until they reached an elevator lobby. "What deck are you on?"

"Seven," Liam said. "They gave me a cabin upgrade as one of the group organizers. I'd feel guilty about it, but they gave everyone midrange cabins for the lowest price, so it's not like people are stuck in the tiny cabins while I have one with a balcony."

"You deserve some perks for all the work you and Kate put into running these events. Giving the two of you a larger cabin in exchange for all the bookings you brought their way seems reasonable to me." The elevator arrived, and Erik gestured Liam to precede him inside, then pressed the button for his deck.

Liam flushed a bit. "That's the worst part. They gave 'us' a larger cabin, but she's sharing with Miranda, so it's just me. Of course she had to go and tease me about finding someone to share it with in her absence, but...."

"It's still nothing to feel guilty about." The elevator stopped at deck seven, and Erik again paused to let Liam exit. "How are they doing? It must be a challenge to keep their relationship going, between Kate working two jobs and Miranda's residency."

"It's a challenge, for sure. It seems like half the time, Miranda can't make events or plan a date because she's on call or postcall, but I've never seen Kate as happy as she is when they're together." Liam led the way to his cabin and unlocked the door. Erik paused on the threshold while Liam went in to grab his jacket. "Out and About's first success story. Or at least the first one I've heard about."

Erik was silent until Liam shrugged into his jacket and closed the door behind him. "Do you want to walk a bit more first, or are you ready for karaoke?"

"You're the one who wanted to walk," Liam replied. "I'll keep you company either way."

"Let's enjoy the night sky for a while," Erik suggested. After taking the elevator back to the main deck, they strolled in silence until they reached a section relatively free of people. "Look at all those stars. Houston and LA have so much light pollution you can't see a fraction of them."

"When I was growing up, we'd go camping in the summer sometimes, usually at state parks, and the stars are the part I remember most," Liam replied, leaning on the rail and looking up at the sky. "We aren't far enough south for the stars here to be all that different from home, other than how many we can see."

"I'd love to visit Australia and New Zealand someday. The constellations would be totally different there." Erik glanced over at Liam. "Tell me if you start to get too cold."

"Getting there," Liam admitted, "but we can stay out a little longer. And a trip Down Under would be the ultimate Out and About experience. I think it'll be a few years before we're ready to handle something that large, though."

"If you're cold, we should go in." Erik straightened from the rail. "We have four more night to spend stargazing."

"True, and it should get warmer as we get closer to the equator," Liam said. "Karaoke is in the Alchemy lounge, if you're up for that. It's on deck four."

The lounge was crowded when they arrived, a number of Out and About members waving or calling out greetings as they threaded their way to the bar. "Would you like a drink?" Erik had to lean in to make himself heard, close enough for Liam to catch a whiff of some spicy scent.

"If we weren't diving tomorrow, I'd see if the bartender could make me a Blow Job," Liam replied with a smirk. "As it is, I should probably stick with tea."

"Two iced teas coming up," Erik said. His cheeks looked flushed, and Liam wondered if it was a reaction to the suggestive drink name, though it could just be the disco lighting in the lounge. The buff bartender Erik placed their order with gave him a speculative glance, then murmured something low enough for only Erik to hear that definitely made him blush, before turning away to pour their tea.

As Erik made his way back with their drinks, someone brushed by them to get to the bar, opening enough space to see across the lounge. "Erik, over here," Travis shouted, waving to capture their attention, Mr. Speedo still glued to his side.

Erik waved back and leaned down so Liam could hear him over the noise in the bar. "We should go say hi, or he'll never let us hear the end of it."

"Yeah, you're probably right." Liam took his glass from Erik and followed him across to where Travis and Mr. Speedo were sitting. "Who's your friend?" he asked Travis when they squeezed into the lounge chairs around Travis's table.

"This is Austin. He's here with his family, but his sister's dealing with her kids and his brother went to bed early, so he's hanging out with me tonight," Travis said with a wink and a leer. Erik chuckled and shook his head.

"Have you heard anyone good?" Erik asked after greeting Austin.

"A few so-bad-they're-good, but no one memorable." Travis nudged Erik. "You here to give it a try?"

"Not me," Erik answered emphatically. "What talent I have is on the keyboard, not vocals. How about the rest of you?"

Liam snorted. "I can't carry a tune in a bucket. I'd have to be falling-down drunk to consider it, which I'm not since we're diving tomorrow."

"I had a go earlier," Austin said, "but once a night is my limit. Besides, I have other things to do tonight." He snuggled closer to Travis's side, leaving no doubt in Liam's mind what—or rather who—he meant to do tonight.

Erik rolled his eyes.

"We need refills," Travis declared. "C'mon, Erik, help me carry them back."

Liam didn't really need more to drink—his iced tea was still half-full—but he took a larger sip since he obviously had another coming. Travis had his head against Erik's at the bar, and Liam turned away to gaze at Austin.

"Have you known Travis for long?" Austin asked, his gaze locked on the blonds at the bar.

"A couple of years, although not well," Liam said. "He dated my best friend at one point, but that didn't work out. Probably for the best. She's dating someone else now and is really happy. We met again a few months ago at a wine tasting."

"Ooh, he's adventurous, then," Austin said, his eyes lighting up. He glanced back at Liam speculatively, and for a panicked moment Liam was afraid he was going to ask Liam—or worse, Liam and Erik—to join them. "I hope he's as good in the sack as he is handsome."

Of all the complaints Kate had about Travis—and they had been legion—she'd never complained about his prowess as a lover, so Liam figured Austin wouldn't be disappointed, but there were some images he didn't need in his head. He and Kate had a strict policy of not getting involved with each other's exes—it would feel far too incestuous—so he'd never really given Travis a second look, even after he and Kate broke up, but Travis was handsome in a rough-hewn, wrong-side-of-the-tracks kind of way. If Liam preferred Erik's cleaner, more classically attractive face, that was his own problem, and one he'd just as soon Austin *not* share. "I'm sure you won't be disappointed."

Austin waggled his eyebrows. "I'll let you know tomorrow."

Liam almost asked him not to, but that seemed rude, so he settled for a nod and a shrug. "Up to you."

An arm reached around Liam to settle over Austin's shoulder. "Here you are," Travis announced, though Liam noticed Erik carried the tray holding their drinks and set them on the small tabletop. "Cheers, everyone." Travis clinked his glass against Austin's and drained it.

Erik sat back down next to Liam and took a sip of his drink, but it was the slightly disgruntled look on Erik's face that really caught his attention. He leaned in as close as he could without being obnoxious. "What's wrong?"

"Travis wants some privacy with Austin. They can't go back to his cabin because he's sharing with family, so he asked if I can find somewhere to kill some time for a while." He drained his glass and set it in the table, turning away from where Travis was nibbling on Austin's neck. "I feel like I'm back in college and there's a sock on the dorm room door."

"I have a private cabin," Liam reminded him. "You're welcome to hang out with me for a while, or even crash there tonight if you want. It's got two beds, so it's not like you'd even be putting me out."

"I'm... I don't want to impose on you. I'm sure I can find a quiet place somewhere to read or doze," Erik protested.

"This is a cruise ship. There's no such thing as a quiet place outside of your cabin," Liam said, trying to see Erik's refusal as being polite rather than not wanting to be with Liam. "Believe me, I've tried. But it's up to you. You know which cabin is mine if you decide to join me."

He stood up and nodded to Travis and Austin. "I'm going to turn in. Have a good night."

Travis's leer and Austin's simper assured him they had every intention of it, but they both wished him good night without further comment. He gave Erik one last questioning glance.

Erik looked at Travis and Austin, then back to Liam, clearly conflicted. Travis inclined his head away from the table and raised a beseeching eyebrow. Erik sighed and pasted on a smile. "Wait for me, Liam."

CHAPTER 22

AGREEING TO join Liam in his cabin was a bad idea, but the alternative was spending at least a few hours on the deck, and even to Erik the night was turning chilly. He'd just have to keep a tight rein on his self-control. He'd gotten lots of experience in that over the past few weeks.

Liam was waiting at the entrance to the lounge, and Erik tried not to focus on how good he looked leaning against the door, completely relaxed. He didn't seem to have any of the uncertainty or anxiety Erik felt. Of course, he was just offering a friend a place to crash for a few hours. It wasn't his fault Erik wanted so much more.

"I'm glad you changed your mind. I would have worried about you getting sick if you tried to sleep in one of the lounge chairs on deck," Liam said as they walked back to his cabin.

"I didn't pack anything warm enough to camp out," Eric answered. "I wasn't expecting anything like that until the Hill Country trip."

"Why would you? You have a bed in a cabin… except your cabin is occupied," Liam replied as they got to his door. He opened it and gestured for Eric to go in. "Make yourself at home. Who knows how long Travis will be. You could crash in the extra bed tonight if you want. That way you don't have to worry about walking in on something you'd rather not see."

The only thing Erik wanted to see was standing beside him, but that wasn't going to happen. There was no way he could pretend to sleep on Liam's spare bed, imagining what was going on in his cabin but replacing Travis and Austin with himself and Liam. He shook his head to erase the seductive vision before entering the cabin. "I'll give them an hour or so, but I won't impose on you longer than that."

"It's no imposition," Liam replied. "I enjoy spending time with you, no matter what the reason, but do you really think an hour will be enough?" He opened the drawer of the built-in chest and pulled out a T-shirt and some sweatpants. "Here. We're close enough to the same size that these should fit well enough to sleep in."

The image that inspired was even more vivid. "I—that's—no. I can't sleep here."

Liam shook his head. "Of course you can. I don't snore, and I don't bite." He waggled his eyebrows. "Unless you want me to. Seriously, though. You know Travis. He and Austin will be at it all night."

Something in Liam's voice made Erik turn to look at him. Did Liam think he and Travis…? "I don't know him. Not in, you know, the sense you mean. Or at least I think you mean." And now he was babbling like a fool. "This is a bad idea. I should go."

"Don't go," Liam said softly. "I'm sorry if I made you uncomfortable. I was trying to lighten the mood, not make it worse. And I know you and Travis aren't together, but I figured you were good enough friends that he'd bragged about his conquests. You really can stay here. Friends look out for each other, don't they?"

Friends. He'd known it wouldn't be enough, and spending more time with Liam had only made it harder to accept that he couldn't have more. The scruples he'd held on to for so long seemed pointless if, as Eamon contended, they'd been dating all along, even if they hadn't called it that. Where, then, was the line he couldn't cross? Having sex? Because if it didn't mean anything more than the offers he'd had from Jace and even Travis, he'd be able to resist just as easily. No, the problem was he'd lost his heart to Liam. And if Liam didn't feel the same, or broke him the way Mark had…. He couldn't take the risk. "I'm afraid," he admitted softly.

Liam frowned as he moved into Erik's space and drew him toward the chairs in front of the door to his balcony. When they were seated, he took a deep breath. "What are you afraid of?" His voice trembled a little as he spoke, as if perhaps he shared some of Erik's fears.

"You." Erik shook his head at Liam's expression. "And what you make me feel. It's easier to hide behind principles than to risk being hurt again. I know it wouldn't be intentional—you're not Mark—but that wouldn't make it any less painful."

"Believe it or not, I felt the same way, right up until I met you. When the last guy I dated broke up with me, he told me the only thing I was good for was sex and that I was lucky I had a nice ass, or he wouldn't have stayed as long as he did. I can deal with a lot of things in a relationship, but not being reduced to a sex toy. You're the only man I know who looks at me and sees me. Everyone else just sees an attractive body they'd like to get in bed, but with you, it's more than that. I mean, I like sex as much as the next guy, but I want more than just that. I want someone to go to football games or concerts or dinner with. Someone who will enjoy spending time with me outside the bedroom as much as inside. You've given me that," Liam said, reaching for Erik's hand. "If being friends with you means I get all that, I can live without the sex."

"Friends who enjoy spending time together without trying to get each other into bed. That's what I joined Out and About for." Liam's hand was warm in Erik's; he could feel the rapid pulse beneath his fingers.

"Friends is good," Liam agreed. "Friends is great, but friends doesn't help when I wake up lonely in the middle of the night. It's been so long since I had someone to chase away the dark."

"God, yes," Erik agreed before he could censor himself. "Someone to hold instead of waking up alone, to listen to things you can only admit in the dark. Someone who accepts you, loves you, for exactly who you are."

"I could be that person for you. If you'd let me." The hope in Liam's voice tore through Erik's defenses.

He stood up and moved to gaze out the window at the churning waves. "I'm a workaholic who's too boring to hold on to a man, at least according to my ex-lover. You have so many better options than me, Liam. Hell, you have guys coming on to you at every event. How long would you be satisfied with someone like me?"

"You aren't boring," Liam insisted as he joined Erik at the window. "I have spent I don't know how many hours with you now, and I have never been bored, whether we're watching a game or playing dueling pianos or sharing a cup of coffee or a meal. And maybe you are a workaholic, but at this point I have two jobs, so it's not like I'm sitting around twiddling my thumbs as I wait for you to come home. And if that isn't enough proof for you, what do you think all those guys coming on to me see when they look at me? They see an attractive body and a tight ass, and they make it more than clear that's what they're interested in. You don't treat me that way. You're the only one who doesn't."

"Oh, Liam." Erik turned and cradled Liam's face in his palms. "You're smart and ambitious and so damn positive you raise the spirits of everyone around you. Of course you're beautiful outside too, but anyone who can't see past that doesn't deserve you." When Liam looked up to meet his gaze, Erik lowered his head and touched his lips to Liam's.

Liam groaned into his mouth, returning the kiss with desperation, like he was afraid this would be his only chance. Erik soaked up every moment of it—the scent of Liam's cologne, the sound of every groan and whimper, the feel of his lips. He could go on kissing Liam like this forever. Far too soon, though, Liam pulled away. "Tell me you'll give us a chance. If you can't, I'll walk away now. It'll hurt like hell, but I'll do it, and we can still be friends. But if this keeps going, there won't be any turning back. It'll be all or nothing."

Erik closed his eyes, trying to imagine walking away from Liam again. He could see his insistence on not mixing business and pleasure for the rationalization it was, a way to keep from risking his heart after the pain of losing Mark.

But Liam wasn't Mark. He'd proven it in a dozen little ways, in their shared interests, in his undemanding acceptance, in his sunny disposition. Yes, it was a risk, but when the alternative was cutting Liam from his life completely, there was no choice at all.

"All or nothing." Erik claimed Liam's lips again with his own desperation this time at realizing how close he'd come to throwing this away.

Liam returned the kiss eagerly, meeting Erik breath for breath. He clung to Erik's shoulders and pressed his body the length of Erik's, leaving no doubt of his interest in the proceedings. Erik rocked against him, letting Liam feel his own erection in return.

Liam moaned into the kiss and wrapped a leg around Erik's thigh, trying to pull them even closer. It was enough to throw Erik off balance and he staggered, nearly falling into the chair. He broke the kiss with a chuckle. "Maybe I'm being presumptuous, but I'd just as soon not walk into any more furniture, and you have a bed right there. Two beds, though I don't think we'll need more than one."

"Not presumptuous," Liam murmured against Erik's jaw, where he was planting little nipping kisses. He pulled Erik with him until his knees hit the bed, and he fell backward, drawing Erik down with him. "Not at all."

Erik settled atop Liam, glorying in the feel of their bodies fitting together. "According to my ex, I was never very good at this," he admitted, though Mark had never aroused him the way the simple touch of Liam's body did.

"That's what you said about softball too, and look how that turned out." Liam cupped Erik's cheek tenderly.

Now that Erik had all of Liam beneath him, he didn't know where to begin. Liam's lips demanded to be kissed again, and he lingered there for a few moments, exploring their contour and texture the way he'd never allowed himself to before. Liam's tongue slipped out to meet his, and he followed it inside Liam's mouth, threading his fingers into Liam's hair to tilt his head to just the right angle.

Liam parted his lips more, giving Erik unimpeded access to his mouth even as he explored Erik's shoulders and back with his hands. Even through the fabric of his shirt, Erik could feel the heat of Liam's palms, making him yearn to feel that warmth on his bare skin.

And why not? They were doing this. All or nothing. They'd agreed. He sat up, smiling at Liam's whine of protest. "I'm not going anywhere," he promised. "Just let me—"

Liam caught on quickly, reaching for the hem of Erik's shirt while Erik started undoing the buttons down the front. "That'll take too long," Liam grumbled as he pulled the shirt up over Erik's head.

"You're better prepared than I was," Erik countered, pulling Liam's polo over his head and tossing it to the floor. He took a moment to admire the smooth torso he'd remembered in his dreams before leaning down to lap over one of Liam's furled nipples.

"Fuck, do that again," Liam demanded, and Erik obliged, moving to the other side of Liam's chest, licking and nibbling until both nipples stood in moist reddened peaks.

Liam dropped back against the bed, undulating beneath Erik as he continued to tantalize the nubs of flesh. Liam dug his fingers into Erik's back. "Don't stop," he begged. "Do—oh!" Erik smiled against his skin at Liam's reaction to the hint of teeth. He couldn't help but wonder what else would make Liam react like that.

Eventually the rest of Liam's chest became too tantalizing to resist, and Erik let his lips roam over the tanned skin, pausing at especially sensitive spots to suck or nip gently. The uninhibited sounds Liam made went to his head more than all the drinks he'd skipped since their kiss in the waterpark. Slowly he made his way down until he could dip his tongue into the hollow of Liam's navel, but the waist of his khakis barred him from moving any lower.

Liam raised his head when Erik paused. "Take them off," he urged, but Erik slid upward first, letting his chest rub against Liam's and wringing a hiss from his own throat at the brush of his nipples over damp flesh. He let his weight settle against Liam and kissed him again, slowly. This wasn't just about sex. He'd take all the time he needed to prove that to Liam.

Liam rolled his hips against Erik's, but beyond that small urging, he seemed perfectly content to kiss and be kissed, driving home to Erik once more how lucky he was to have found someone whose own desires matched up with his. Liam dropped one hand from Erik's shoulder to his side, stroking the lines of his ribs and worming between them until Liam could tweak Erik's nipple. Erik bowed his back to make enough room between their chests for Liam to explore as he wished.

What he wished seemed to be threading his fingers through the light dusting of hair and tugging gently at Erik's nipples, a part of his anatomy Mark had never shown much interest in. He mentally kicked Mark out of the bed and nipped at Liam's lips until his eyes fluttered open. Erik eased a hand behind Liam's head and urged him upward, pushing up with his other palm to widen the space between them. "I'd love to feel your mouth on them."

"Hell yes," Liam murmured before latching onto Erik's nipple with his mouth. He licked and sucked avidly at one side before switching to the other and giving it the same lavish attention. When he finally released Erik, he met Erik's eyes and winked. "Anything else you want to get my mouth on?"

"I'm sure I'll think of something eventually." Erik shifted until he was straddling Liam's hips. "In the meantime, there's more of *you* I want to get *my* mouth on." He unbuckled Liam's belt and unfastened his khakis but didn't push them down yet. Instead he nibbled at the strip of skin he'd revealed, ignoring the hard cock tenting Liam's boxers.

"Tease," Liam muttered. He caressed Erik's cheek with one finger but made no move to push Erik closer to his erection. Good. Erik wanted to linger, to draw things out until they were both desperate for it, until there could be no doubt this was more than just getting off.

"Only if I don't deliver." Erik turned his head to capture the finger between his lips and sucked it inside, giving Liam a foretaste of what they both wanted before releasing it. "We'll get there... eventually."

"Fuck, you're going to kill me," Liam groaned. "Do you know how long it's been since anyone touched me? I'm not gonna last."

Erik grinned. When had he ever played with a lover like this? It felt so damn good. "Then you'll last longer the second time, won't you?" He rubbed his cheek over Liam's cloth-covered cock, breathing in the musky scent of arousal and smiling when it twitched against his face. He worked a finger into the flap of Liam's boxers and followed it with his tongue, barely flicking it against the heated flesh. Liam nearly shrieked.

"Again," he gasped, bucking up against Erik's mouth. "More."

"Let's get rid of these first." Erik slid his fingers under the elastic waist of Liam's boxers and pushed pants and briefs both down his legs. He had to kneel to work them over Liam's feet—he'd kicked off his shoes at some point and hadn't been wearing socks, so Erik let the pile of fabric drop to the floor and sat back on his heels, drinking in his first sight of Liam fully nude. Damn, he'd been an idiot. Beautiful and responsive and loving—Liam was everything he'd ever dreamed of.

"You too," Liam said, crunching up to sitting. "Let me see what I've been fantasizing about."

Erik hesitated, hoping he'd live up to Liam's expectations, but delaying wouldn't change anything. He toed off his shoes and shucked the rest before straightening to let Liam look.

"Christ, you're perfect," Liam said in a breathy whisper. "How the hell did I get so lucky?"

"Hardly perfect," Erik protested, "as I've more than proven. One of the reasons I love you is that you haven't held that against me."

"Perfect for me, then," Liam said as he pulled Erik toward him, tilting his face up for a kiss. "I love you too, in case you hadn't figured that out yet."

The simple admission nearly brought tears to Erik's eyes. He couldn't find the right words, even if he could get them past his tight throat, so he settled for pouring his emotions into his kiss, cradling Liam's head and feeling the truth of Liam's love in every touch.

Liam patted the bed beside him. "Lie down with me?" Erik hastened to do as Liam asked, stretching out on the bedspread next to Liam so they lay on their sides facing each other. Liam was a feast spread out before him, and he didn't know where to start. To judge by Liam's expression, the feeling was mutual.

Finally Erik couldn't resist the need to touch, gliding his fingertips across Liam's cheek, down the cord of his neck, circling the hollow of his throat. He could feel the pulse beating in Liam's chest as he coasted along his rib cage and followed the swell of his hip to the crease where it met his thigh. Liam caught his breath when Erik slid one finger upward into the tangle of hair at the base of his cock.

Liam rolled to his back, giving Erik uninhibited access to his body. "Turn around," he urged. "That way I can reach you too."

Erik wasn't sure how long he'd be able to hold out himself once Liam got his hands on him, but this wasn't a one-off. They could do this again and again. That gave him the control to twist around on the bed until he faced Liam's feet and he could feel the heat of Liam's breath ghosting against his cock.

Given Liam's earlier impatience, Erik wouldn't have been surprised if he went straight for Erik's cock, but instead, Liam nuzzled the patch of hair at the base, breathing deeply and tantalizing Erik's shaft with the hint of stubble from the day. Liam had accused him of being a tease, and he was certainly returning the favor now.

"You smell so good," Liam said softly.

The same was true of Liam, and despite his plans to take his time, Erik couldn't resist the enticing muskiness that was so close and still too far. He bent to lap at the rosy head of Liam's cock, whetting his tongue with the salty taste.

Liam moaned, and Erik needed to hear more. He circled the base with one hand to better control his ministrations and traced the vein that beat on the underside, then slid lower to lave at the sac below.

"Oh fuck," Liam gasped reverently, his breath hot against Erik's erection. "Do that again." He turned his head and closed his mouth around the head of Erik's cock, sucking it lightly while he tongued at the slit.

Erik pulled one of the globes into his mouth and rolled it with his tongue, which made Liam hum with pleasure. He repeated the attention to the second while gliding his palm up and down the shaft and could feel it tighten. He let the globe slide free and shifted forward just enough to tongue the smooth skin behind Liam's balls.

"Yes," Liam moaned as he spread his legs wider. Erik mourned the loss of the heat around his cock, but it only took a moment for Liam to return to what he'd been doing, drawing Erik in deeper this time so that his cock bumped the back of Liam's throat. Liam tapped his hip, urging him up onto his knees straddling Liam's head. "Perfect," he purred and swallowed Erik down to the root.

With that kind of incentive, there was no way this would last much longer, and Erik was determined to give Liam as much pleasure as he could first. His new position made it easier to reach Liam's crease, and he dragged his tongue down the length of it before focusing on the furled entrance. He circled it several times before spearing into it, trying to press as far in as he could, but it wasn't far enough. Letting his elbows hold his weight, he brought a hand to his mouth and wet a finger, then worked it in alongside his tongue, stroking Liam's cock with his other hand to the same rhythm Liam was sucking him.

Liam thrashed wildly beneath him, so much that Erik might have been worried if it weren't for the way Liam gripped his hips, first holding him in place and then urging him to move, rocking down into Liam's mouth and throat. Need sparked along his nerves, driving him closer and closer to the brink. It wouldn't take much to snap his control, but he held on as long as he could, determined to take Liam over the edge with him.

Erik wiggled his finger a little deeper, until he found the knot of nerve that made Liam cry out around his cock. Stroking his fingertip over that spot, he knelt up until he could take the head of Liam's cock into his mouth. The wet suction was enough to tip Liam into orgasm, and he stiffened and then shuddered beneath Erik, who swallowed his release hungrily, only lifting his head when his own climax racked him, stealing all control as lightning raced along his nerves. His limbs gave out and he collapsed onto Liam, his breath rasping unevenly.

Liam peppered kisses along the inside of Erik's thighs where they lay on either side of his head, prolonging the zings of pleasure. After a few minutes, though, the kisses turned into little nips and finally a bite on the lower curve of his ass. "Off," Liam demanded. "You're heavy."

"You can top next time, then," Erik countered, but he rolled over and then scooted around until he was facing Liam again. "That is, if you want to?"

"I'm good either way," Liam replied, "although we might have to raid the ship's pharmacy. I didn't expect to get lucky, so I didn't bring supplies. Or maybe you could snag some from Travis. He owes you for kicking you out of the cabin."

"I think I owe him." Erik spooned around Liam and kissed the side of his throat. "We might not be here if he hadn't."

"At least not tonight," Liam allowed. "I'd like to think we'd have gotten here eventually even without his help."

"Maybe, but not this quickly. I can be pretty obtuse, as you've seen."

"We'll work on that," Liam said, snuggling closer into Erik's embrace. "And on moving my investments to another firm."

"You don't have to leave the firm, just switch to a different advisor. I can highly recommend Richard Walters."

"Tomorrow. Or when we get back to Houston," Liam murmured. "Tonight I just want to enjoy the fact that you're really here. And for the record, your ex was an idiot."

"I'm not planning on going anywhere." Erik closed his eyes with a prayer of thanks that despite himself, he'd found the connection he'd longed for.

Epilogue

Three months later

LIAM LOOKED up from the tandoori chicken he and Erik were cooking at the sound of the door to the townhouse opening. A moment later, Kate came into the kitchen. "Well, look what the cat dragged in," Liam teased. "I was beginning to think you'd forgotten you lived here."

Kate rolled her eyes at him and set her purse down on the counter. "Be nice or I won't tell you my news."

"All I have to do is wait you out. You can't keep a secret," Liam retorted.

"Fine. I gave notice today. In two weeks, I will officially work full-time for Out and About." Kate paused dramatically until Liam caved.

"And?" he prompted.

"And Miri asked me to move in with her," Kate said in a rush. "I know that leaves you in a lurch. She can cover the rent at her place without me paying anything, if I pick up the groceries, so I can keep paying the mortgage here until we can sell it or you can find a roommate."

"Kate, that's wonderful." Liam pulled her into a hug and spun her around. "We were actually going to talk to you about that soon anyway."

"About the job or about the townhouse?" Kate asked.

"About the townhouse. Erik's lease is up in a couple of months, and we've been talking about moving in together," Liam said. "Either here or somewhere else, depending on what you wanted to do. If you're moving out, we could maybe buy you out instead of having to move somewhere new."

"Congratulations on the job," Erik added. "It's great to know that Out and About is doing so well."

It had taken a while for Kate to come around when Liam assured her he and Erik were serious about a relationship, but when she'd seen how happy he made Liam, she hadn't been able to hold on to her irritation. She gave Erik a hug in return.

"I wanted to wait until Liam could quit too, but this will make it so much easier for us to only have to work around Miri's work schedule and not my mine too. Or at least only one of mine."

"It won't be long," Liam said. "I'm training Sam to take my place, and we interviewed someone today who I think will make a good assistant manager. Another couple of months and I'll be down to one job too. Are you staying for dinner? There's plenty if you want to hang around."

"No, Miri is off tonight, so I'm going to have dinner with her and celebrate all my good news. Enjoy yourselves, boys, but don't do anything I wouldn't do."

"Like that rules anything out," Erik observed with a smirk.

Kate whacked his shoulder the way she would have bopped Liam if he'd made the same comment and waltzed out grinning.

"So do you want to buy out Kate, or would you rather look for something else?" Erik asked. "It wouldn't take me any longer to get to the office from here than from my place." They'd proven the truth of that over many mornings after the nights Erik had stayed.

"I don't know. What do you think? The advantages are that it's a nice place in a convenient neighborhood, we wouldn't both have to move, and we've already paid off a good chunk of the mortgage, but I don't want you to feel like you're moving into my space. I want it to be our place," Liam said, wrapping his arms around Erik's waist.

"It will be our space," Erik assured him and dropped a kiss on his lips. "Anywhere we're together is our place. In fact, depending on what your interest rate is and how much you have left to pay off, maybe I could buy out Kate's portion of it. Then it really would be our place."

"I kept all the payment records. I can tell you how much it would be if you give me an hour," Liam said, "but only if you want to. We can convert Kate's room into a guest room for your aunt or into an office for Out and About. We'd get a larger tax deduction that way. And I've been saying it's time to repaint and update the look a bit, so we could do that together. That way you'd feel like you had a hand in decorating it as well. We could even find the space for a piano after Kate moves some of her furniture out. What do you say, Erik? You want to move in with me?"

"Just try to kick me out," Erik answered, and the chicken was forgotten as he demonstrated to Liam just how much he wanted to stay.

Growing up in Chicago, NICKI BENNETT spent every Saturday at the central library, losing herself in the world of books. A voracious reader, she eventually found it difficult to find enough of the kind of stories she liked to read and decided to start writing them herself.

Facebook: www.facebook.com/100011754789784

When ARIEL TACHNA was twelve years old, she discovered two things: the French language and romance novels. Those two loves have defined her ever since. By the time she finished high school, she'd written four novels, none of which anyone would want to read now, featuring a young woman who was—you guessed it—bilingual. That girl was everything Ariel wanted to be at age twelve and wasn't.

She now lives on the outskirts of Houston with her husband (who also speaks French), her kids (who understand French even when they're too lazy to speak it back), and their two dogs (who steadfastly refuse to answer any French commands). The cat pretends they're all beneath her, no matter what language they're speaking.

Visit Ariel:
Website: www.arieltachna.com
Facebook: www.facebook.com/ArielTachna
Email: arieltachna@gmail.com

UNDER
THE
SKIN

NICKI BENNETT
AND ARIEL TACHNA

Police detective Patrick Flaherty has no illusions about Russian mobster Alexei Boczar, but that doesn't stop his fascination with the bodyguard to one of the most ruthless families in Chicago's growing Eastern European crime community. From the moment Patrick meets Alexei's eyes over the body of another Russian mobster, Alexei is a thorn in Patrick's side, refusing to cooperate with the police and turning all of Patrick's questions back on him. Alexei's hard-as-nails persona whets Patrick's professional determination to get the information he's sure the gangster is hiding, while personally Patrick just wants to get his hands on Alexei's hard body.

The tattoos marking Alexei's skin tell the story of his criminal past, but the more Patrick learns about Alexei, the more he wants to know, until he finds himself over his head in a relationship that might cost him his job and could well cost Alexei his life. Alexei is equally fascinated by Patrick's willingness to overlook his past and even his present associations, but he has secrets of his own that could drive a wedge between them forever.

www.dreamspinnerpress.com

CHECKMATE

Nicki Bennett
and
Ariel Tachna

All for Love: Book One

When sword-for-hire Teodoro Ciéza de Vivar accepts a commission to "rescue" Lord Christian Blackwood from unsuitable influences, he has no idea he's landed himself in the middle of a plot to assassinate King Philip IV of Spain and blame the English ambassador for the deed. Nor does he expect the spoiled child he's sent to retrieve to be a handsome, engaging young man.

As Teodoro and Christian face down enemies at every turn, they fall more and more in love, an emotion they can't safely indulge with the threat of the Inquisition looming over them. It will take all their combined guile and influence to outmaneuver the powerful men who would see them separated… or even killed.

www.dreamspinnerpress.com

ALL FOR ONE

Nicki Bennett
and
Ariel Tachna

All for Love: Book Two

Aristide, Léandre, and Perrin pledge only three loyalties in life: their king, their captain, and their passion for each other. So when the musketeers discover a plan to accuse M. de Tréville of treason, the initial impulse to kill the messenger, Benoît, is tempered by their need to unmask the plotter. But their first two suspects, the English ambassador and Cardinal Richelieu, prove to be innocent, forcing the musketeers to delve deeper into the inner machinations of the French court.

Meanwhile, Aristide finds himself falling in love with the ill-fated messenger, a blacksmith without a home who rouses all of his protective, possessive instincts. Benoît, however, has no interest in any man. Torn between desire and duty, Aristide must find a way to protect the king and clear his captain's name—all while heeding the demands of his heart.

www.dreamspinnerpress.com

STRONGHOLD

Nicki Bennett
and
Ariel Tachna

All for Love: Book Three

"Are you surprised that strength is drawn to strength?"

For the last six years, the gypsy healer Raúl has lived a life he never dreamed possible. Gerrard Hawkins has stood at his side, his love a source of silent strength like nothing Raúl has ever known.

When a letter from Gerrard's estranged father forces them in separate directions—Gerrard back to England to make peace with his family and Raúl to Saintes-Maries-de-la-Mer for his annual pilgrimage— Raúl expects to suffer for their parting, but he holds on to their plans to meet again in France when Gerrard has satisfied his father's demands.

Gerrard left England never expecting to return, especially after he pledged his life and love to Raúl. Yet he cannot dismiss his father's offer of peace without some acknowledgment. When he arrives in England to find tragedy, his sense of duty toward his family's tenants wars with his promises to Raúl.

As tensions mount and illness spreads in France, Raúl stands as a bastion of hope, but his strength is not limitless. Gerrard is the rock he leans on, and without that strength, Gerrard's arrival in France may come too late.

www.dreamspinnerpress.com